The new Zebra Regency Romance logo that you see on the cover is a photograph of an actual regency "tuzzy-muzzy." The fashionable regency lady often wore a tuzzy-muzzy tied with a satin or velvet riband around her wrist to carry a fragrant nosegay. Usually made of gold or silver, tuzzy-muzzies varied in design from the elegantly simple to the exquisitely ornate. The Zebra Regency Romance tuzzy-muzzy is made of alabaster with a silver filigree edging.

An Improper Proposition

"My dear Mary, do you know that I have often been considered a connoisseur of women?" Ravenstoke's tone was as casual as if they were discussing the weather. "Therefore you can believe me when I say that your body is perfectly formed and one to be appreciated."

Mary gasped, and her astonished eyes met his. His were mischievous, and she shook her head ruefully.

Ravenstoke did not move from her bedside. His eyes remained fixed on her. "You do not believe me?" he asked, his voice like raw silk. "Shall I make love to you to prove my statement? I assure you it would be my pleasure."

Mary stared at him, spellbound, her heart racing. She drew in a quick breath and tore her gaze away. "That won't be necessary, my lord. I believe you."

"Somehow I thought you would, little coward," Ravenstoke said provocatively. "Now get your rest. If you are a good girl, I will return and entertain you this evening."

"Entertain me?" Mary said sweetly, pouting her lips as she had seen other girls do. "I am almost afraid to ask how, my lord. . . ."

THE BEST OF REGENCY ROMANCES

AN IMPROPER COMPANION   (2691, $3.95)
by Karla Hocker

At the closing of Miss Venable's Seminary for Young
Ladies school, mistress Kate Elliott welcomed the invita-
tion to be Liza Ashcroft's chaperone for the Season at
Bath. Little did she know that Miss Ashcroft's father, the
handsome widower Damien Ashcroft would also enter her
life. And not as a passive bystander or dutiful dad.

WAGER ON LOVE   (2693, $2.95)
by Prudence Martin

Only a rogue like Nicholas Ruxart would choose a bride on
the basis of a careless wager. And only a rakehell like Nicholas would then fall in love with his betrothed's grey-eyed
sister! The cynical viscount had always thought one blushing miss would suit as well as another, but the unattainable
Jane Sommers soon proved him wrong.

LOVE AND FOLLY   (2715, $3.95)
by Sheila Simonson

To the dismay of her more sensible twin Margaret, Lady
Jean proceeded to fall hopelessly in love with the silver-
tongued, seditious poet, Owen Davies—and catapult her
entire family into social ruin . . . Margaret was used to
gentlemen falling in love with vivacious Jean rather than
with her—even the handsome Johnny Dyott whom she se-
cretly adored. And when Jean's foolishness led her into the
arms of the notorious Owen Davies, Margaret knew she
could count on Dyott to avert scandal. What she didn't
know, however was that her sweet sensibility was exerting a
charm all its own.

*Available wherever paperbacks are sold, or order direct from the
Publisher. Send cover price plus 50¢ per copy for mailing and
handling to Zebra Books, Dept. 2931, 475 Park Avenue South,
New York, N.Y. 10016. Residents of New York, New Jersey and
Pennsylvania must include sales tax. DO NOT SEND CASH.*

A Suitable Connection

Cindy Holbrook

ZEBRA BOOKS
KENSINGTON PUBLISHING CORP.

ZEBRA BOOKS

are published by

Kensington Publishing Corp.
475 Park Avenue South
New York, NY 10016

First printing: March, 1990

Printed in the United States of America

With love to my very special family: my parents Don and Lorraine Holbrook, and my sisters Kathrine and Deborah

Chapter One

URCHIN AND LORD

A dishevelled urchin, dressed in baggy clothes that looked to be hand-me-downs three times removed, munched with unabashed relish upon an apple core. He took his rest under a grand old oak that stood, majestically alone, in the middle of a grassy field. An ill-cut crop of burnished curls framed his oddly composed little face, but a spate of miniscule freckles playing across his straight nose, and a tender, mobile mouth, saved him from a look of gravity.

The urchin suddenly ceased his munching, raised one gritty hand to his puckered brow, and squinted into the distance. His slight body stiffened as blue, blue eyes ascertained that a horse and rider were advancing from across the field.

"Confound it," the urchin said in a distinctly female voice. She swiftly grabbed a brown bundle and shinned up the old tree, successfully blending in with the foliage. Thus hidden, she sat, patiently.

The equestrian appeared to check in the distance, but proceeded to ride aimlessly across the field. "Ahh, I'm in luck," the watcher thought as the rider made to pass her elevated refuge. Unfortunately, at

7

this juncture, the rider appeared to notice the value of the large tree, for he directed his horse into its shade and alighted from his mount, a truly superb black with the sleekest of heads. The stranger then stretched with all the involvement of a well-satisfied cat.

The urchin peered through the branches, her blue eyes rapidly assessing both man and horse. They were, without a doubt, fine representatives of their respective species. The blue eyes fixed on the man, however, as that impressive specimen stretched once again with powerful grace.

He was tall and though his height was formidable, his movements belied it. They held a loose-limbed quality that sat oddly, but not unpleasantly, upon his well-muscled frame. His hair was of the darkest black, his brows heavily marked.

Now evidently relaxed, the man ambled over into the shade of the old oak. Without warning, he peered straight up and pinned the urchin with a stunning emerald gaze.

"Mind telling me what you are doing up there, boy?" he asked cordially. The "boy," shocked and dismayed, teetered on her perch for one breath-snatching moment. As the bundle she clutched plummetted to the ground with an ominous thunk, the girl, harbouring no desire to follow her unfortunate bundle, gritted her teeth and righted herself with superhuman effort.

She regained her errant breath. "I . . . I'm looking for birds' nests. I have a veritable fondness for . . . birds," she said gruffly, as the man raised one sable brow in amusement.

"Do you, halfling?" he said in a deep, mellow voice that sent unaccountable chills up her spine. "I, too, enjoy certain types of . . . birds."

8

The urchin bit back a smile and feigned ignorance. Whereupon the man suddenly frowned, stunned intensity flickering through his eyes. The girl tensed and sighed quietly in relief as he turned his disconcerting gaze towards the field. Nothing could be read in his eyes when he finally turned back.

"Why not come down here?" the man asked congenially.

"Why should I do that? It is extremely comfortable up here." The urchin plucked a verdant leaf and held it up as proof of her pleasure.

"Because, stripling," the man said patiently, "I am in need of directions and I doubt not that any information you render from such exalted heights will prove exceedingly jumbled."

"You are looking for directions?"

"Is that not what I just said?"

"Oh. . . . In that case, I'll come down. One moment, please."

The urchin inched across the branch and began her descent. She came to the last branch and lowered herself down, preparatory to dropping the last few yards. The stranger walked over and raised his arms expectantly.

"Sir, I can do it myself."

"I have no doubt, but I fully intend to catch you," the man replied with irritating good humor.

"I do not wish your help," the girl said rudely, a flush rising on her face.

"But I wish to give it. Now you can either hang there like a stubborn monkey or you can allow me to catch you. Those are your choices."

The urchin, feeling not at all like a stubborn monkey but rather like a foolish trout about to be snagged, muttered an expletive and tried desperately to pull herself back up onto the branch. She wriggled and tugged and kicked, earning an infuriating chuckle from below. Straining, she redoubled her efforts. She slipped and, with a muffled yelp, sailed into the man's waiting arms. A frisson of shock, chased closely by sheer indignation, coursed through the youth as the stranger caught her with cavalier ease. Why, the infernal man wasn't even rocked by the impact!

"Ah, yes." The man smiled that well-satisfied-cat smile and hugged her close. "I did not think I was going mad, as yet."

"Sir, please set me down!" She refused to meet the green eyes.

"Certainly, infant." The stranger smiled and lowered the now-stiff figure to the ground. "You see me, your obliging servant. Faith, I admire such enterprising youths as you."

"Now, sir," the urchin said firmly, after securing a few comforting steps away from the towering stranger, "if you will but tell me your address, I will strive to help."

"You will, will you? What a positively generous . . . lad . . . you are."

The girl's lips quivered slightly, and she bowed. "I but endeavour."

"Yes, I can see that you try," the man said. "Alas, you seem quite eager to speed me on my way."

"Sir, I only wish to aid you to your destination," the girl said dulcetly.

"Ah, yes, my destination." The man appeared deep in consideration. "You know, it is quite bacon-brained of me but all of a sudden, I remember the directions to Grantham Hall."

"Grantham Hall?" Wariness flooded the urchin's eyes. If this man was a friend—nay, even an acquaintance—of the infamous Ravenstoke, duke of

Denfield, all caution must be applied.

"In fact," the man said in an angelic tone, "now that I think on it, it is my home."

"Your home!" the youth gasped. She stepped back a quick one-and-a-half paces.

"Yes, my home," the man agreed, flames of devilish delight springing into his eyes. "It appears you have heard of me if that quaint little gavotte of yours meant anything."

"Only by reputation." *Faith, who hadn't heard of the man's reputation.* All the naughty children whose mothers wished to frighten them into submission knew of the dangerous duke. His was a reputation to incite doting fathers to grab their sabres, loving husbands their duelling pistols and anxious mothers their fair female offspring. Though the men, of late, had stayed their hands from their weapons, for the duke had wounded his man thrice in the duel. Only wounded, true, but since he had told his misfortunate challengers the exact mark he would hit, ere he shot upon that very point, he was considered a man best left alone.

In fact, many went so far as to whisper that the duke was in league with the devil. If his unholy skill with the duel and his wicked successes with the ladies did not prove it, his infernal luck with the cards did. He should have been ruined ages ago by his high-stakes gambling, yet he remained famously — or rather, infamously — wealthy. Still others viewed the mere fact that the man yet lived at the ripe age of five and thirty proof, in itself, that he had a pact with the Lord of Darkness. Gracious, the urchin thought with an unhappy humor, the man must be out of his mind to ask such a question. Her eyes focussed once again upon the fearsome prospect before her.

"Yes, you are right. You're in the devil's own fix now." The man nodded as if reading her mind. "And it would behoove you not to trifle with me."

"Trifle with you? I'd never, Lord — Why that is the last thing I would ever wish to do!"

"So, you are one of those," the duke said, seemingly nettled.

"One of who?"

"One of those virtuous females that do not desire to be trifled with," he said, as if to a slow wit.

"F-f-female?" Her blue eyes widened. Then she sighed. "I feared you knew."

"From the very start."

"From the very start? How?"

"My dear innocent, anyone but a paperskull could tell within a trice."

"You'd be surprised, my lord," the lady replied coolly.

"I am never surprised, my dear."

"Which means you lured me out of the tree on purpose." Full knowledge dawned on her.

"I really did want to make sure, you see," Ravenstoke said, apologetically. "Now, why don't you tell me why you are dressed in those absurd clothes and why you bolted up the tree when you spied me."

"I bolted up the tree specifically so you wouldn't stop and talk to me. I'd never have thought you could see me from so far off — you must have very fine eyes."

"So I have been told." He bowed, grinning wickedly. "But not exactly for that reason. Now why the clothes?"

"I thought it best to travel as a boy, since unaccompanied females are so often . . . importuned," she said pointedly.

"Only too true. But, pray enlighten me, would it

12

not have been just as simple to have travelled in the conventional mode? With a companion?"

"Not when one is running away."

"Oh, God! Not a runaway? I suppose you took your governess in dislike?"

"Indeed, no. I held her in the greatest affection, but I have not seen her for these past three years."

"Gammon." Ravenstoke surveyed the girl's slight figure, unfashionably tanned face, and sheared brown curls.

"Oh, no. It may help you to know that I am fully twenty years of age."

"What?" He grasped her chin with strong, tapered fingers, and dragged her close for a merciless inspection. Though her face was smooth, the sapphire eyes that gazed back held calm reserve and an unflinching composure. "Why so you are. Then why this runaway?"

"I know full well what you are thinking." The lady grimaced and gently drew her face from his grasp. "That this sort of thing should be left to the infantry and young misses. Under most circumstances, I would agree, but, as mortifying as it is to admit, I find it necessary."

"Why?"

"Now promise not to laugh, and I will tell you."

"Only because you know you must," Ravenstoke said, gently taunting.

"Well . . . yes."

The duke laughed.

"The truth is, I am running away from an unwanted marriage."

"Oh, no!"

"Oh, yes."

"From a true villain, I have no doubt."

"I consider him so."

13

"And there must be a wicked stepmother, yes?"

"No, a wicked stepfather."

"Yes, certainly," the duke said mildly. "Everything as it should be—the Minerva Press would applaud. Now, might I know your name?"

"That I would rather not say."

"Quite understandable. I sympathize. Nevertheless, I will have your name."

The lady studied him intently for a moment, obviously weighing the matter. Then she came to a quick decision. She spun on her heel and sprinted across the grassy field.

"Damn!" Ravenstoke thundered after her and reached her in several long-legged bounds. They thudded to the ground and a muffled groan tore from the young woman. Ravenstoke eased his weight off her, only to roll her over and pinion her firmly again. "That was a silly start," he rasped.

"So it would seem," she gasped through a pained chest, trying to win back her breath. She lay dazed for an instant, her brain rejecting the pain coursing through her back.

Finally she looked up into the blazing green eyes above her, and knew she might have committed a grave mistake in running from this man. "I thought," she said shakily, "that you might not care to exert yourself in chasing after an unknown woman."

The anger evaporated from the duke's face, and he laughed. " 'Gads, and here I thought you said you knew my reputation. Chasing after unknown women is my raison d'être. You've only piqued my interest all the more—now you really must tell me your name."

A silence fell as the lady ran through her nonexistent options.

"Don't bother to create an alias." The duke

grinned heartlessly. "I am far better at recognizing a lie than you would ever be in telling one."

"Are you sure? I am generally considered quite good at hiding my thoughts."

"Are you? How strange. You seem easily readable to me. Now—your name."

She sighed. "It is Mary."

"Mary? Excellent And your surname?"

Mary groaned inwardly; she would lose all anonymity if she told this dissolute duke that. She steeled herself, refusing to let the growing panic overcome her, for despite the duke's taunting, she knew she had the discipline to contain her emotions. She'd never show fear, for fear often brought out the baser instincts in men; this man hardly seemed the type to react in such a way, but she would not chance it.

Mary marshalled her thoughts, for she knew only her wits could help her; it was painfully obvious she was helpless when it came to strength.

"Your last name, Mary." His words pulled her back from her revery.

". . . Castleton," she said finally.

"Damn!"

"Yes." Mary smiled, despite her fear. "I thought you might say that."

"So he's the wicked stepfather," Ravenstoke said. "Somehow, I'd never have cast him in such a role. A buffoon perhaps, even a knave, but not a villain."

"True . . . but he is set upon marrying me to a man I have no desire to wed." A glimmer of fear did appear in her eyes.

"Why? Is he unhandsome?"

"Oh, no, he is handsome enough—in a brutish sort of way. But he beats his dogs."

"Ah, does he?"

15

"Yes, and he is inordinately proud of his pack. If he beats that which he cherishes, I doubt I can fare any better."

"A point to consider," Ravenstoke agreed, the slightest of smiles tugging at his lips. "And who is this dog beater—or must we wrestle over that?"

Mary flushed; indeed, that was the last thing she wished. She already regretted precipitating this scene. The weight of his body was playing havoc with her breath, and she felt she was about to faint. "It is Squire Jameson," she told him quickly.

"Squire Jameson," the duke repeated, a frown descending. His emerald gaze studied her with renewed intensity. Mary returned the look steadily, though her every nerve and muscle tingled. Fear, she realized, did strange things to one.

"No," he said after a moment. "You would not fare any better." He seemed to be lost in thought as he shifted her into a more comfortable position, pulling her against his body. Suddenly, Mary knew why he was so dangerous to the fair sex; with that one, unconscious move, he had somehow disarmed her. Totally against her will, her muscles relaxed and she felt foolishly, absurdly safe. The man was dangerous indeed.

Yet, knowing there was nothing to be done, Mary patiently waited for this unusual man to speak. And she knew she would never forget the smell of the grass and earth of this particular day.

"No." His green eyes focused on her once more. "He would try to break your spirit. A sad mistake, I should think. You would need a much gentler hand upon the bridle."

Mary couldn't restrain a gurgle of laughter. "You are a horseman, I see."

"I beg your pardon?"

"I mean, you must like horses. One can always tell the animal a man most cherishes from the terms he applies to women. Squire Jameson intends me to come to heel like his favorite hound, and you would use a gentler hand on the bridle, very much the way you would treat your best hunter, I should wager."

"Which clearly makes me a horseman," Ravenstoke said wryly. "Though I assure you, madam, I do treat my women differently from any horses of my acquaintance."

"Yet for all that, I would still like to know which receives the better treatment—the horses or the women?"

He chuckled. "A home thrust, little wasp. You do not think much of us poor males, do you?"

"Surely as much as you men think of us poor females," Mary assured him kindly.

"Touché, child. But pull back, pull back. I have no intention of brangling over man's iniquities—or woman's, for that matter."

"I am glad to hear it. Then will you release me to go on my way?" Relief slipped through her control and threaded her voice.

"Oh no, not yet. I find this all too intriguing by far. Whither are you bound?"

"That is no concern of yours."

"Tsk, Mary, how uncivil. It is foolish of me, I own, but I am making it my concern. So where are you going? And don't dig in your heels over the matter or we will simply lie here until you tell me." He smiled devilishly at Mary's instant flush. "It could be all day for all I care—but considering my reputation, it might be advisable for you to tell me. After all, there is only so much a man of my stamp can bear." He brushed a stray curl from her forehead with easy familiarity.

17

The man is a demon, Mary thought hazily, as warning bells shrilled in her head. First he could cozen one into feeling absurdly safe and the next moment let one know she was a foolish lamb wrapped in the paws of a wolf. "I . . . I am going to London," she said swiftly, as he ran a caressing finger along her jawline.

"Little coward." His voice, too, felt like a warm caress. He chuckled and flicked her nose. "So this little innocent is off to London town. Of course. It could only be so. And what do you intend to do, once there?"

"Become a governess or a companion," Mary replied, her chin lifting slightly.

"Oh, God! What romantic tripe have you been dipping into?"

"None, sir! I am perfectly capable of teaching children. Indeed, I have an extremely fine education."

"Perfect! With the single exception that you will be mistaken for the very charges you plan to instruct."

"That is only for the present," Mary retorted, stung. "With my hair properly dressed, and the correct attire, I will look every inch my age, if not more. And you cannot say that twenty is too young."

"No, indeed. It is shockingly long in the tooth," Ravenstoke agreed affably.

"People are easily led into seeing what they expect to see," Mary persisted, though it made no sense, she knew, to argue with this man. "I have merely to act like a governess to be accepted as one. Fortunately, I have no great beauty, which I own would be a severe setback."

"No beauty? No . . . perhaps not . . . of the classical sort . . . but you'd best reassess the matter, I think. Your eyes alone will have the younger sons

18

pinching you on the back . . . stairs."

"I can wear spectacles for that."

Ravenstoke peered at her. If she skimmed back and restrained her unruly sun-tipped curls, and hid those striking eyes behind tinted spectacles, and disguised the supple body he held—as she had as an urchin—she could possibly pass as a governess. Somehow, the thought of this self-possessed woman willfully turning herself into such a creature enraged him.

"Don't be a little fool," he said testily. "I have a good mind to take you back to your stepfather."

"No!" Mary cried, alarm running through her at his determined look. She erupted into motion, struggling violently without thinking. When pain shot through her, she froze, stunned.

"What is it?" he demanded, as agony washed her eyes and she paled.

" 'Tis . . . nothing," she said slowly, averting her gaze from his searching one.

"Tell me." He shook her slightly.

Mary flinched and bit her lip. An ironic smile crossed her strained face. "My stepfather—in the face of my obstinacy, you must realize—has taken the squire's oft-repeated advice and tried to beat some sense into me. As you can see, he failed."

"My God!" Ravenstoke's face was thunderous. He rolled away from her and sprung up, pulling her from the ground in a fluid movement. "Dammit woman, why didn't you tell me!"

"It has not . . . pained me before," Mary said quietly, unable to admit to her pride. "Truly, it is healed—I would not be travelling otherwise."

"Faith, you need a caretaker!"

"That is the last thing I need from what I have seen." Her frame was stiff, her voice bitter. "I fare much better left to my own devices, thank you. I did not ask you to accost me."

"You do cut to the point," Ravenstoke said, his jaw tightening. "I wish to God now I hadn't, but that is water under the bridge. I have, unfortunately, discovered your circumstances, and I cannot find it in me to let you go on your foolish way."

"Not even if you try very hard?"

"Not even then, you little wretch." He smiled at her pugnaciousness. "And don't think I like it any better than you. Only think how shocking it is for me to discover that I still possess a jot of chivalry. I thought myself well rid of the niggling thing. Quite tiresome, really. I don't have the slightest idea what to do with you."

"Nothing, my lord, positively nothing," Mary said firmly. "Believe me, sir, I did not mean to ignite this distressing chivalry in you. It is a mere aberration that will surely pass. I will be only too glad to forget it."

"I have no doubt." Ravenstoke smiled, complaining to the world at large, "All other females cry for chivalry, but not this one."

"Indeed," Mary smiled, for the man did have a charm. "I relieve you of the onerous task. I am sure such unaccustomed behaviour could be very dangerous, even fatal, to your health. So for the sake of your well-being, I will bid you goodbye." Mary smoothly turned away and walked off as naturally as possible; she did not get far.

Ravenstoke's voice rang out. "Woman, don't push me! You will come with me if I have to throw you over the saddle myself."

Mary turned back with an imperious air that sat oddly with the urchin's clothes and blowing curls. "That would be abduction," she said in a tight voice.

"Call it what you will, but don't dare make me come after you again. I swear I won't play the noble the next time I take you to the ground. My restraint only goes so far—I am no saint."

"No one would mistake you for one." A shiver ran through Mary at the unleashed power blazing from the man. She stood riveted to the spot as he stalked over and grasped his horse's reins, then walked it straight up to her. "Madam," he bit out, bowing deeply, "we await your pleasure."

A strong urge to flail at him welled up within Mary. Evidently the stallion sensed it, for he sidled away, whinnying. Mary pulled in her anger as she saw his eyes roll. "Hello, you handsome creature," she said softly, erasing the tension from her voice. "Your master claims you await my pleasure—do you?"

The big horse cocked his ears and, after regarding her with liquid brown eyes, nudged her playfully. At that moment, despite all the fears of the day, Mary felt she had found a friend. "Sir," she chided him gently, as she regained her footing, "you are much too big to be flirting with me like that." The horse nickered and stood studiously still as she swung herself into the saddle.

"Satana likes you," Ravenstoke said, an odd expression on his face. Throughout their entire meeting, the slight woman had been uniquely controlled, yet, in the presence of the large horse, she had opened up with an amazing warmth that had Satana nuzzling her like a puppy. "That is uncommon. You must have a way with horses."

"I like them."

He swung himself into the saddle behind her and took the reins. Suddenly, he chuckled. "It is clear you do not treat men as you do horses. A pity."

21

They rode in leaden silence. Mary leaned forward, as far away from Ravenstoke as was humanly possible upon a horse. The duke kept only the slightest restraining hold upon her, a knowing, but gentle smile playing upon his lips.

"Where are we going?" Mary finally asked.

"We take our rest at the Merryweather. Do you know of it?"

"I have heard of it." She nodded, unbending a margin. Her muscles ached from the tension, and it felt unnatural to ride a horse so stiffly.

"And you, madam, will then change out of that scandalous garb and into a proper dress, which I assume is in that bundle." There was a minatory note in his voice; such strict words, from a man Mary knew to be one of London's reigning libertines, tickled her reviving sense of the ridiculous, and she bit back a smile.

"This is not scandalous garb if one believed me a boy, my lord. Indeed, it is quite proper, if a little unfashionable."

"But it is patently obvious that you are a girl."

"Not so, my Lord. You are the only one to have seen through my disguise."

"You have done this before?"

"You mean run away?" Mary asked, willfully obtuse.

"No, dress as a boy!"

"Certainly—though not for the past few years. It—"

"Hell and damnation. There is Judson ahead, and he has spied us. The devil's in it now."

A brawny farmer hailed them from the field and all but flung his hoe down in his eagerness to stand before Lord Ravenstoke. "Good day to you, my lord." Judson panted, touching his forelock as he

22

approached them.

"Good day to you," Ravenstoke said coolly, his arm tightening around Mary. She merely smiled impishly.

"It is right fine to see you again, my lord. Do you be planning to stay long?"

"I have not decided as yet." Ravenstoke's voice dropped icily as Judson's eyes strayed with lively interest to the figure before him. A moment passed while Judson waited in the hope of an introduction; the duke maintained a stiff-lipped silence.

"Well, welcome home, my lord." Judson sighed as he realized no introduction would be forthcoming. "Hope you and the lad have a pleasant stay."

"Thank you, Judson." Ravenstoke nodded quickly and prodded Satana forward. He left Judson staring after them, frustrated curiosity rampant upon the farmer's broad face.

Ravenstoke and Mary once again rode in silence. "Well," he said finally, "aren't you going to point out that he mistook you for a boy?"

"No, my lord," Mary said serenely. "That was self-evident."

"Piqued, repiqued, and capoted." Ravenstoke laughed—and then groaned. "Lord, and Judson the greatest gossipmonger this side of the Channel."

"Just think, my lord, you have created yet another scandal, and without a woman involved this time." Mary chuckled, uncharitably enchanted with the idea. "The whole village will know within the hour that you rode in with a grimy urchin set up before you. Speculation will run rife on what you plan to do to me."

"Let them wonder," Ravenstoke said lazily. "Serves them right if they are so blind—"

"Oh, no, it is merely that they do not possess

your"—Mary sought the right word—"perspicacity where the feminine sex is concerned."

"You mean my experience, little vixen. Ah, here we are." They turned down a curve and came upon a neat-enough building, boasting an ostentatious sign far outstripping the accommodations, and proclaiming the building the Merryweather. "Luck is with us," Ravenstoke said. "It seems a quiet day. A common occurrence, it would appear," he added, as the absence of an ostler became self-evident. He alighted from his horse. "Stay here with Satana and I will procure rooms."

Mary watched Ravenstoke's back with coiled concentration as he strode towards the inn. This was her chance; she bit her lip and steeled her nerves. Just let him pass through the portal, dear Lord, and she could be off.

His foot hit the threshold, and Mary's heart jumped in anticipation. Then he halted, his body stiffening. He swung around with lightning speed, his eyes pinning her in accusation. She lidded hers swiftly, seeking to veil her thoughts—not fast enough, it seemed.

"For shame, Mary." The disappointment in his voice affected her strangely. "I would not have thought it of you." He crossed and pulled the reins from her clenched fists. "Did you plan to take Satana as well?"

"Not far," she said softly. "I would have made sure to return him."

"Ah, then I must be grateful."

"Don't say that," Mary protested. "Do but think on it, my lord. I cannot travel with you. I appreciate your kindness, but I wish to make it on my own."

"Why? Do you fear for your reputation?"

"No, I have never worried about reputation. Liv-

24

ing with my stepfather has seen to that."

"What, then? Do you think I'll ravish you? Would it help if I assure you that you are not to my taste."

"I did not think it," Mary returned quietly. "That was not my fear."

"Then why?"

Mary sat a moment, confusion showing in her eyes. "Because I have my own life to arrange . . . it is my responsibility and no one else's. I need to start taking care of myself as soon as possible."

The tightness around the duke's eyes seemed to ease, but he still held the reins. "Mary, you must postpone your independence a while longer, for I will not let you go. I have said I will see you safe; despite my reputation, I will."

"That is sheer arrogance, my lord," Mary shot back, the blue of her eyes deepening with sudden anger. "I am sorry, but I will go no further with you."

"Why persist in thinking you have a choice? Now get down from the damn horse."

Mary shook her head slowly; an inexplicable sadness turned her eyes dark. "This is absolute folly, my lord, for both you and me."

Ravenstoke's jaw tensed; a hooded expression descended. Then he laughed sharply. "Let the folly come, Mary, for I will not release you. I refuse to let you escape into a world that is just waiting to rend a tasty morsel like you apart. I would very much mislike meeting you in a bawdy house six months from now, because you were snatched up by an abbess your first day in London. Now this discussion is finished." He reached up and hauled her unceremoniously into his arms. He held her there, his grasp tightening, reminding her of his strength.

"Set me down, my lord. There is no need for this

Herculean display of power."

Ravenstoke looked startled, then began to chuckle, his laughter shaking her. "Ah, Mary, you are a rare treasure."

"I will be a hysterical rare treasure if you don't set me down soon," she warned sternly, though admittedly his humor was contagious.

He quirked a challenging brow at her and, with a wicked grin spun her around in dizzying circles until she clung involuntarily to his shoulders. He came to a stop, an irrepressible look upon his face, very similar to the one a little boy would wear when offering his governess a frog. "You haven't fainted yet, Mary." He smiled slowly. "That is what I admire in you." He set her down as she began to flush, evidently deciding not to chance it further. "Now my dear, we will enter the inn together. Allow me to do the talking. I believe we must play it by ear."

Chapter Two

MINE HOST'S UNFORTUNATE EXPERIENCE
WITH THE NOBILITY

"Innkeeper," Ravenstoke called as he strode into the dimness of the inn. Mary lagged behind, leery of what this large, unpredictable man might do.

"My Lord Ravenstoke," a voice gasped. An unusually short, round little man with a shiny face and balding head rushed toward them, every few steps jerkily interrupting his progress to make a hasty bow. "It is so good to see you again. Was it not just last year you gave us the privilege of your patronage?"

"Patronage? Ah, yes, I stopped over for ale. It is . . . Jonas, isn't it?" Ravenstoke asked after only the slightest of pauses. The little innkeeper beamed with pride and bobbed up and down. Mary was impressed. She certainly could not fault Ravenstoke's memory or his courtesy. "Jonas, we will be spending the night. My cousin and I." Mary jumped in surprise at the connection, but then gurgled slightly. She was nudged covertly by her "relation," who cast her a mischievous glance.

"Very good, my lord. It will be an honor." Jonas rubbed his hands together in high expectation. "I will have the best room in the house prepared immediately."

"Make that two rooms, Jonas, and the private parlor."

"Two rooms?" Jonas repeated, his face falling like a deflated soufflé.

"Yes, two rooms. Will there be any difficulty in that?"

"N-no, my lord," Jonas stammered. "Only my second-best room is under repairs. I . . . I do not have another room befitting the young master."

"I do not care where you put the boy," Ravenstoke said with offhand negligence, "Just as long as it is not with me. I refuse to tolerate his . . . peculiarity."

"Peculiarity?" Jonas asked, rising to the bait like a well-stuffed trout. The 'young master,' too, looked at Ravenstoke, curious as to what his peculiarity might be.

"Yes," sighed Ravenstoke. "He has a distressing tendency to wander in his sleep."

"He wanders in his sleep?" Jonas eyed Mary as he would a three-legged duck. Mary tried to look suitably apologetic, though her mind raced ahead. What was Ravenstoke doing?

"Yes," the duke affirmed, a dark hint in his voice. "I own it is not totally uncommon, but the boy suffers from such a vivid imagination, you see."

"Ah, yes . . . and this is bad?" asked Jonas, bewildered.

"Very bad," Ravenstoke informed him. "His dreams are generally most violent and audacious."

Violent? Mary suddenly decided she didn't want to know what Ravenstoke was doing.

Not so Jonas. "Violent?" His now-widened eyes surveyed Mary in shock. Mary attempted another penitent look.

"Yes, terribly violent," Ravenstoke confirmed solemnly. "One night, he dreamed he was leading a charge in battle. Gad, you should have seen the mayhem that broke loose."

"Wh-what happened, my lord?" Jonas unconsciously tangled his hands in his apron as he spoke.

"What didn't? The household was awakened to the most bloodcurdling war cries. When I arrived, the scamp had already trussed up his nursemaid and was just then chasing his lady mother about the room with a candlestick, intent upon skewering her. I know you will say there was no real danger, for the candle was unlit, but he really should not have called his own mother a bloody, heathen infidel—or sworn that he would spit her like a pig and feed her guts to the birds, for that matter. The dear lady swooned dead away."

Mary tried desperately, but a chuckle escaped. Jonas's dilated eyes flew to hers in horror.

"But do not let that trouble you," Ravenstoke soothed. Jonas, his skin turning a peaked green, looked at him as if beholding a ghost. "I have taken the precaution, while travelling, of locking him in the room at night, so if you would please give me the key, I'd be much obliged. And mind you, if he bangs on the door or calls out, do not heed it."

Mary's enjoyment of the story died a swift death. She looked at Ravenstoke with blossoming irritation mingled with grudging respect.

"Thank God!" Jonas bleated the words like a man handed a reprieve from the noose. Beads of sweat dappled his shiny head. "Is there anything else that I can do?" he whispered to Ravenstoke, while casting Mary a furtive look.

"Do you have a room without a window?"

"My lord! Never say that—"

"Oh, plenty of times," Ravenstoke said with an airy flick of his hand. "Knots the sheets, ties them off, tosses them out the window, and he's gone, vanished into the night. Can't count how many times I've had to chase him down. The most unfortunate occurrence was when he thought he was escaping marauding pirates and mistook a stable boy for a brigand. Coshed the poor devil over the head with a shovel.

"Never say, my lord!"

"Most unfortunate. Left the poor soul quite daft for a twelvemonth."

"But he was much better after that," Mary piped up. She was worried that the little man was soon to fall into an apoplexy.

"Yes. Indeed, they say he even remembered his dear mother's name, just this month past," Ravenstoke said in hearty tones. "Well, I, for one, am ready to rid myself of this travel dirt. We will be wanting supper in two hours, Jonas."

"Y-y-yes, my lord," Jonas stuttered, realizing that hosting an aristocrat was not nearly what he had imagined it to be. He bowed quickly and bustled away hastily. He could have sworn as he left that he had heard the lad laugh outright, but surely one so young could not be so devoid of sensibilities as all that—could he?

Two well-sated figures leaned back in their chairs, a finished repast before them. Ravenstoke sipped from a brandy, while Mary nibbled on the last piece of cheese from the tray.

"That was excellent." She sighed. "I'd forgotten I'd not had anything but an apple since yesterday evening."

"Is that when you escaped?"

"Yes, escaping can be a famishing affair," Mary said pleasantly. She reached for the last pear.

"At least you needn't worry about that anymore," Ravenstoke said suavely. Mary looked at him inquiringly. "There won't be another escape—not from me."

"No, I can well imagine," Mary grimaced. "Lord, such a Banbury tale you told poor Jonas. It was utterly fiendish."

Ravenstoke shrugged. "I did not want you trying the door tonight, or engaging someone's help with your own sad tale. I'd just as well have my sleep."

"Well, there is no fear of missing that. Do you know the maid actually made the sign of the cross when she came to my room."

"Excellent."

"And my room!" Mary protested in mock horror. "It is totally barren. And the blankets have been tacked to the foot of the bed!"

"So our Jonas is a cautious man," Ravenstoke remarked. "An admirable trait. Just let that be a lesson to you. I can, and will, outmaneuver you at any time."

Mary cocked her head to one side. "Yes, I do not put it past you anymore."

"Remember that," he said quietly. The banter of a moment before was gone.

Mary slowly put down the pear she ate and looked away, silent. "Poor Mary," Ravenstoke said with gentle mockery. "To have jumped out of the frying pan, only to land in the fire."

"No, my lord," she replied calmly. She didn't like the cynicism in his voice. "No matter our disagreement, I am not such an innocent as not to know I could have met with a worse fate."

31

"You believe so?" His self-derision was evident.

"I know so. I have played hostess to too many of my father's friends not to know the different types of men there can be in this world."

"Your father's friends? Good Lord, they are nothing but coxcombs, roués, and loose screws. 'Tis no wonder you have no difficulty eating with such a libertine as I."

"Why, no, my lord, your table manners seem excellent."

He laughed then, all seriousness forgotten. He wagged an admonishing finger at her. "Best beware your tongue, my girl, or I will banish you to your barren room."

"Oh, yes, my barren room." Mary reached for her water glass. "You will allow me to repay you at a later date for these expenses, won't you?"

"No, Mary. Abductions do not work that way."

She set her glass down with determination. "Then I simply cannot stay here tonight. It wouldn't be proper."

"Proper! You sit there dressed as a boy and instruct me in what is proper? Lord, woman, not a blasted minute of this day has been proper! Why choose such a rubbishy thing to become missish over?"

Blue eyes clashed with green. Ravenstoke sighed as the blue eyes failed to flinch. "Very well. Jot it up, and you can owe it to me. To be paid in the future when you are an established governess."

Mary's face lit with real pleasure. "Thank you, my lord."

"Don't thank me. I plan to charge an exorbitant interest."

Mary trilled her delight; he smiled back at her, an enigmatic expression on his face. He swirled his brandy within the glass and asked lazily, "Why is your stepfather bent upon marrying you to Squire Jameson?"

"I'm not sure. . . . I presume it is for the settlement he thinks he is to get. And also, he would have me safely off his hands before I'm at my last prayer."

"Has Jameson been a suitor of yours for a long time?"

Mary smiled, but her eyes became strained. "Suitor? No, not if you mean is he in the way of sending flowers and such nonsense. But he seems to always signal me out. Though Lord knows, I have done everything to avoid him, even becoming rude sometimes."

"Has he ever made improper advances toward you?" Ravenstoke asked quietly.

"No, he has always been very polite—which only confuses me more."

"Why?"

"Because the man unsettles me. I always have a feeling of . . . I know it's silly, but I have a feeling of danger when he is about. And the more polite he is, the more I feel it." Her eyes had taken on a haunted look; then she realized Ravenstoke was watching her intently and attempted a quick smile. "There, isn't that truly an example of dramatic imaginings? And how utterly rag-mannered of me to say that of him to you. But . . . you have a way of making me feel I am talking to a very old friend."

"Of course. It's the secret to my success. Surely you have other suitors than Jameson?"

This made Mary smile, quite mischievously. "Oh, yes. The curate, for one."

"Not old Smidgely!" Ravenstoke objected, shocked.

"The very same."

33

"Faith, never say that scrawny old proser went down upon bended knee."

"No, of course not—but Mr. Handleford did."

"The widower with five of the spottiest children ever spawned? Mary, you little liar! He never did!"

"Yes, indeed he did. After he put down a dainty pillow, of course. But alas, I let him slip through my fingers just as I did Mr. Smidgely. Imagine Stepfather's bafflement."

"Castleton is always baffled. Why didn't he give you a proper season like he should have?"

"What?" There was an edge to Mary's voice at this. "And spend my mother's money in such a wasteful manner?"

"Your mother's money?"

"Forgive me. I quite forget which gossip you would know and which you wouldn't, due to your infrequent visits to the hall, all of which I assure you the villagers have cherished. Why, we feast upon those stories for months afterwards."

"Termagant! What story have I missed?"

Mary sat quietly for a moment. "My mother was Julia Summerville. She married my true father, Lieutenant Robert Johnston."

"Johnston!" Ravenstoke echoed, surprised. "I'm sorry, Mary, I did not know. They say he was an excellent soldier—his name was forever in the dispatches."

"He was rather wonderful," Mary said wistfully. "It came as such a shock when he died in a carriage accident, after surviving all those battles."

"Is that when your mother married Castleton?"

A distant reserve descended upon Mary's face. "Yes, after Father died, the life drained from Mother as well. She had been such a lively, beautiful woman, you know. But after Father's death, she just didn't seem to care about anything. Within a year and a half, she married Castleton."

"Why? Surely she did not love him?"

"No, she loved only my father." Mary shook her head, her eyes solemn. "Perhaps too much. I don't know why she married Castleton; I suppose she thought I needed another father, and she, a protector. Protector! He ran through Mother's fortune within the first few years, and Father's in these past. I thank God Mother died within a year after she married him. I would never have wanted her to realize what she had done."

"How old were you then?"

"Twelve."

"Lord, what a life!"

"Oh, no, it wasn't so bad," Mary protested. "I had my governess, Manny, to take care of me—she was a dear. And most of the time Stepfather was away gaming in London. And when he was home, he rarely interfered with me, as long as the household was well run and I played the proper hostess to his friends."

"But now he wants you to marry Jameson?"

"Yes. I suppose it had not occurred to him before that I could be of use in that direction. I cannot be said to possess overpowering beauty or feminine graces," she added wryly. "And then again, Stepfather and I do not rub along together very well. He claims I am much too uncomfortable."

"Why is that?" Watching the serious, composed face before him, Ravenstoke could well guess.

"Because I am," Mary said, her eyes lighting as if she'd read his mind. "I'm a shocking bluestocking, you see.

"Castleton blames Manny for it, but he shouldn't. Left to our own devices, she and I studied pretty much anything we wished. She was the only child of a scholar, and neither of us cared overmuch for the feminine accomplishments, so we spent a great deal more time studying the arts and literature, as well as Latin." Mary's look dared Ravenstoke to comment.

"And that is why you believe you will make a suitable governess?"

"I know what you are thinking," Mary replied, a glint in her eyes, "but I would not be such a ninny-hammer as to admit to that kind of unfeminine knowledge. I do know the required accomplishments, though not to any superior degree."

"An honest woman! I never thought I'd see the likes."

"I told you I am uncomfortable."

"No, Mary." He shook his head. "Not uncomfortable. Just out of the ordinary. I would—"

She was never to hear what he would do, for their conversation was suddenly fractured by a loud, wrangling voice from outside the room.

"I tell you, I will search this room, fiend seize you! I don't give a rap what mighty lord is in the parlor!"

Mary's eyes flew to Ravenstoke's in consternation. "My stepfather."

"So it would seem. Be pleased to tend the fire."

Mary opened her mouth to inquire, thought better of it, and obediently went to the fire. It appeared she would once again be playing things "by ear," an occupation his lordship seemed to excel in. It would stand to reason, of course, what with the necessity of escaping jealous husbands and such. Pray God he could deal with one additional, enraged stepfather.

The door burst open and a stocky individual, resplendent in a purple waistcoat and canary yellow pantaloons, stood puffing and snorting in the doorway. Little Jonas clung limply to the man's arm and his voice squeaked in entreaty for "sir" not to "disturb his lordship." The man only growled and flung him off, sending the unfortunate innkeeper reeling into the doorframe.

Castleton looked wildly about him. Ravenstoke snoozed before a crackling fire, tended by a slight boy. The intruder snorted once again. Ravenstoke, upon this sound, seemed to awaken slowly.

"That you, Ravenstoke?" Castleton blasted, as the duke opened one lazy eye.

"I believe so," Ravenstoke replied, opening the other. He yawned, wide and long. "Your servant, Castleton. Jonas, old man, you look to be in a pelter," he went on in mild surprise as the little man wrung his hands and gibbered incoherently. "It is all right, Jonas. You may leave us."

"My lord, I'm sorry, this man simply barged his way in here!" Jonas cast a venomous look towards Castleton. "I told him he could not disturb you and the young—"

"Yes, yes, Jonas. I said that would be all."

"My lord, if you wish I will call the stable hands and have this intruder thrown out," Jonas said with the noblest of gestures.

"So you do employ such beings after all?" Ravenstoke queried, diverted. Jonas looked sheepish, for in truth he had only one stable hand, and that a boy who didn't even shave yet. Ravenstoke smiled in understanding. "Do not put yourself about, Jonas. I do know this man. I assure you, I will not hold you responsible for a lunatic like this."

"Lunatic!" Castleton's face turned scarlet. "Blister it, Ravenstoke, that ain't nice."

"Jonas, do leave us," Ravenstoke said, waving the innkeeper away. Jonas's face purpled alarmingly, and he bowed stiffly and fled. If his lordship wanted to entertain bedlamites, then let him. He was fed up with aristocrats and their strange ways. Lord, just give him back his common but customary clientele and he would never aspire to a noble establishment again!

"To what do I owe this interruption, Castleton?" Ravenstoke inquired as soon as Jonas had exited. "You look positively wretched."

Castleton stopped dead in his tracks, rearing as if he'd been slapped. "Well, if that ain't the outside of enough. I can't help it—I've lost my demn girl, you see."

A fire iron clattered to the hearth. Castleton's reddened eyes swung suspiciously to the boy by the fire. "Who's that?"

"I really don't know," Ravenstoke yawned. "I do not make it a habit to be on first-name basis with the hired help. I will ask him, of course, if you desire it."

"No, uh . . . guess not," Castleton said, disgruntled. His eye turned to Ravenstoke, lounging in his chair, athletic legs crossed out before him. His gaze glued itself to Ravenstoke's boots in instant desire. "I say, Ravenstoke, those are demn fine boots! Hoby, I'd wager. B'gad, they're dusty! Shouldn't treat them like that, son. Here—you, boy. Leave the blasted fire alone and attend to his lordship's boots. See to it that they are properly cared for."

"No need for that, Castelton," Ravenstoke said with a negligent wave.

"No need to? Of course there is! Demn, it hurts my eyes just to see them! Here, boy! You deaf or something?" Castleton crossed and plunged himself into the chair opposite Ravenstoke.

Mary quivered and made a desperate play at putting the irons away. Knowing she dare not delay longer, she sidled over to Ravenstoke, her back firmly to Castleton. Bending down with a bewildered look, she lifted Ravenstoke's well-shod foot. Ravenstoke, his devilish nature surfacing, merely smiled at her with bland unacknowledgement. She glared and tugged. The boot stubbornly refused to part from his foot. Ravenstoke's smile widened wolfishly.

"Hey, no!" Castleton bellowed at the back end of the boot boy. "What the blazes do you think you're doing? You can't pull it off thataway, you country noddy! Those boots are Hoby's, burn it! Turn round and pull, caperwit; turn round and pull!"

Mary straightened, catching her breath and her temper. Her eyes shot Ravenstoke a frustrated appeal.

"Castleton," Ravenstoke reproved, "do stop harassing the boy." He pulled his boot from Mary's clutch and swung his legs to the far left. "I'll lay you odds that the lad is new here, isn't that so, boy?" Mary nodded her head vehemently. "Well, then, we must have a lesson, boy. Pulling at the boots as you were is useless. You lack leverage. But there is another way. If you will be so good as to go and stand in front of me, turn your back to me, and take hold of my boot, I will do my poor best to aid you."

Mary once again sidled over to do his bidding. Dutifully, she turned her back to Ravenstoke and lifted his boot, wondering what purpose it could serve. Then she flushed; Ravenstoke had just put his other booted foot to her backside.

"Now pull," he said. She had just enough presence of mind to grip the boot as Ravenstoke applied a healthy boost. She and the boot went flying.

"I'll be hanged if I have ever seen such a green boy in all my days." Castleton shook his head as the small figure scrambled off the floor. "Why, the boy's a complete looby."

"Yes, he does seem rather . . . unknowing. But never fear, he shall learn." Ravenstoke said it with an enjoyment that set Mary's blood boiling.

She straightened her slight shoulders and returned to him, a stubborn expression upon her face. She clinched the second boot and clenched her teeth as she felt Ravenstoke's foot again land upon her posterior. Determined, she maintained her balance this time. The minute the foot was free, however, she dropped Ravenstoke's leg with a resounding thwack. She grabbed the boots and stalked off, ignoring her stepfather's call to use champagne in the blacking. She never wanted to see either man again.

"My dear Castleton," Ravenstoke said, watching the stiff retreat of the little figure, "I had no idea that you were such a . . . knowing one."

"Won't find no flies on me," Castleton said with blatant pride. "No, sir, I'm nobody's pigeon for the plucking."

"Indeed, it is apparent that one need not even try to tax themselves to fool you. Now, perhaps you would be so kind as to tell me to what I owe this visit. You know I refuse to play cards with you. I won too much last time."

"Hang it, you always seem to have the most infernal luck. Can't understand it. Someday, it's got to change. And demn, won't I like to see that," Castleton crowed, as if that day had already dawned.

"I sincerely hope not. If you're not here for cards, what are you here for?"

"Huh? No, no, didn't come to see you. It's my girl I'm looking for."

"You've misplaced a girl?"

"No, not misplaced. The confounded chit has run off."

"Oh, I see. Well, I'd advise you to let it be. If a ladybird wishes to leave, there's generally nothing you can do about it." There was a commiserating look on Ravenstoke's face, a truly noble performance since no ladybird under his patronage had ever desired to take flight.

"No, no, it ain't that!" Castleton said quickly. "It's my curst stepdaughter! She's taken French leave."

"Ahh, things are clearer. Whyever did she do that?"

Castleton ran a hand through what was to have been a fashionable coif. "Blister it! Stumps me. Queer sort of girl, you know."

"No, I don't know," Ravenstoke said pleasantly.

"Well, she is! A difficult bit, very difficult. Doesn't know what's good for her. Ungrateful chit."

"Dear me, never say she ran off with an undesirable party—even a libertine, perhaps?

"Ha! Not a chance. She's only a dab; she'd never catch the eye of a discerning man."

"Indeed?" Humor lightened Ravenstoke's eyes.

"Of course not! Only wish it was a man she had. No, come to think of it, can't be just any man. Got to be the one I've picked out for her. Trouble is, she's got no use for men. Can't understand it."

"No?" The faintest sarcasm traced the word. "Well, it all sounds very confusing, but I can safely say I haven't seen a female fitting your description."

"Didn't think you had." Castleton sighed. "I can't find the chit anywhere. It's as if she disappeared off the face of the earth. It's demn confusing and demn tiring as well. Chasing here and there to no good purpose. But I got to. Things could get ugly if I don't find the girl, let me tell you."

Ravenstoke, unfortunately, was not to hear Castleton's next words, for there was a rap on the door, then Jonas stuck his ashen face inward. "My Lord Ravenstoke . . . m-may I please have words with you?"

"Certainly, Jonas. Come in."

"Ah, no, my lord." Jonas cast an inexplicably frightened eye at Castleton. "I'd rather talk to you in private, my lord. . . ." His words trailed into a whisper.

Ravenstoke nodded negligently, but there was a sharp look in his eyes. "You will excuse me, Castleton," he said pleasantly, and rose.

"Hmm? Oh, go ahead, dear boy, go ahead." Castleton waved absently, his brow furrowed in abstraction. "Don't mind if I set a spell and catch my wind. I'm getting too old for these shenanigans."

Ravenstoke closed the door and turned to the fidgeting innkeeper. "Now what is it, Jonas?" The man stood like an errant schoolboy, his hands tucked behind him. He attempted one untranslatable gurgle, failed, shook his head miserably, and pulled two gleaming Hoby boots from behind his back. He lifted them up and hung his head in shame.

"My boots, I presume?" Ravenstoke's tone sent Jonas cowering further. "What of them?"

"I . . . I found them in the stables, my lord."

"In the stables . . . What, pray, were they doing in the stables, Jonas?"

"They were there in . . . in—in place of Mr. Castleton's h-horse."

"I'll kill the little devil," Ravenstoke said lowly.

"We . . . we did not know he had gone to bed, my lord, or else we would have been much more—"

"Confound it!" Ravenstoke swore. He trained a deadly eye upon the quivering Jonas. "I need not tell you that you face a very delicate situation, Jonas. If Mr. Castleton finds you have misplaced his horse—"

"Oh, my lord, please—oh, please no." Jonas's white face flushed beet red. "I could never hold my head up again—think of my business."

"Then I advise you to offer your best wine to Mr. Castleton. Make it on the house, of course, and offer to play him at cards."

"But I don't play cards!" Jonas wailed.

"Neither does he. I will go after my little fool of a . . . cousin . . . and attempt to return him and the horse, with Castleton none the wiser. You may tell Mr. Castleton that I will wish to play cards with him shortly."

"Oh, my Lord, thank you—only do hurry! I would never be able to tell that . . . that man that I've lost his horse."

"Then act quickly," Ravenstoke ordered. Snatching his boots from Jonas's frenzied grip, he strode from the inn.

The little vixen! To steal her own stepfather's horse and leave him with the buffoon was the outside of enough, Ravenstoke thought, as Satana's hooves pounded along the road. If he ever caught up with her, he'd rake her over the coals so that she never dared to stray from him again!

He had to find her. Travel at night was dangerous for anyone, let alone an innocent-looking boy who was, in fact, a female. His jaw tightened, and he spurred Satana onward. Suddenly, from out of the darkness, he heard voices.

"Please, sir, you are tangling the reins all the more." It was Mary. "Thank God," Ravenstoke murmured. He pulled on his own reins as he turned a bend. There, dead center of the road, the moonlight illuminated two sidling, entangled horses, a battered cart, a wizened old man, and Mary, all standing and stomping amidst vegetables of various and sundry sorts.

At any other time, Ravenstoke would have delighted in such a scene, especially since the farmer's horse wore a concoction of cabbage leaves between its ears, but now, unaccountably, the muddled scene filled him with rage.

In truth, Mary's predicament was not to her liking either. She pulled in her frayed temper as the farmer before her continued to rant and rave.

"Don't tell me what to do, you young cockerel," the old man wheezed. He shoved a rheumatic fist, full of reins, under her nose. His vigorous movements only succeeded in causing the horses to whinny and caracole amongst the carrots and cauliflowers.

"Sir, Champion is a very high-strung animal," Mary said patiently. "Please do not continue to upset him."

"Upset him!" the little man sputtered, straightening his stoop. "Why that horse is a sway-backed, fretsome animal of no account! It is my poor, sweet Jocelyn who needs tending."

"I fully agree with you, and Champion is short in the wind as well," Mary said sincerely. "My father has dreadful taste in animals, but to help your Jocelyn we must help Champion."

"Yes, I would say that that is the gist of the matter."

Mary knew the voice, and sensed its anger. She twirled around. Ravenstoke, his approach silent, now stood behind her. Involuntarily, her eyes fell to his feet. She should not have left the boots, she thought regretfully.

"Excellent idea, you say?" The farmer glared at Ravenstoke cantankerously. "And who might you be, gov?"

"I am this young scamp's . . . uncle." Ravenstoke trod through the cabbage and took the reins from the awed, unresisting farmer.

"You're . . . this young jackanapes's uncle?" The farmer paid no attention to the loss of Jocelyn's reins, so busy was he, studying the obviously well-heeled man. "Well, look at what your nephew has gone and done! He came tearin' round that bend like a demon out of hell, and ran me and poor Jocelyn right down. Why, he's gone and ruined a whole cartload of my finest vegetables—I was just cartin' them to market to sell in the morning."

"To sell in the morning?" Mary echoed in disbelief. For the farmer to be out at this time of night meant he must have been returning late from the market, and, from the smell of it, late from the alehouse as well. She bent and picked up a rubbery, aged carrot. "I see you didn't succeed in sell—"

She yelped as Ravenstoke pinched her. "What my charge means to say," Ravenstoke interrupted, clamping a rough hand on Mary's shoulders, "is that we see you can't possibly sell your produce now. I will be only too glad to make restitution for the cartload."

"I knew you was a right 'un," the old man said. A craggy smile split his features, and he quoted an exorbitant price without the blink of a lash.

Mary gasped. She was about to object when Ravenstoke squeezed her shoulder tightly. She snapped her mouth shut instead.

"That sounds reasonable." Ravenstoke pulled out his coin purse. "I do apologize for the young hellion's misdeeds. He is a difficult lad, nearly the death of his poor mother. Indeed, she waits anxiously at home for his safe return. If you will forgive me, we really must be on our way."

The old codger, gleefully counting his hoard, nodded absently as Ravenstoke freed the entangled reins and briskly wrapped poor Jocelyn's about her master's arm. When the man remained intent on his coins, Ravenstoke grabbed up Champion's reins. "Come . . . nephew. We have much to discuss."

Mary flushed, but refrained from comment as he dragged her aside and threw her up into the saddle. Ravenstoke mounted Satana and prodded him forward.

The ride back was a strained, silent one. Mary surreptitiously peeked at the grim man riding beside her. Her heart sank with each step that brought her closer to the inn—and her stepfather.

They rode silently into the stables. The stable boy, a scrubby individual with a black gap where two front teeth had once resided, jumped up at their arrival. He gasped, gibbered, and cut out, running towards the inn.

Ravenstoke dismounted from Satana and stalked over to Mary, who remained mute and still in her saddle. She sat ramrod straight, her blue eyes all-consuming in her white face.

"Madam," Ravenstoke said curtly. He raised his hands and lifted her from the saddle. He had made a decision to be patient, but when he felt the slim body tremble in his hands, his anger and fear came raging back and he shook her sharply. "You little idiot! What the devil did you think you were doing? It was sheer luck you met up with that old man instead of some highwayman who would have taken everything you had, including your damn, cherished virtue. How dare you think you could escape me? I could beat you for this!"

Mary's eyes seemed to shimmer, and she swiftly lowered her head.

"Oh, damn, Mary." Ravenstoke pulled his hands from her as if he had been burned. "I didn't mean that. Any man that would dare to beat a woman is no man at all."

"What do you plan to do?" Mary asked with quiet dignity, her head averted. "Are you going to give me back to Stepfather?"

"No . . . I don't think so. It is evident he can't control you—faith, even I am taxed to control you! That was a truly horrible thing you did, you know? Stealing your own stepfather's horse and leaving me stuck with the man."

Mary nodded, a small nod. Ravenstoke smiled and raised her chin, forcing her to look at him. "I have a proposition for you."

A wary expression crossed her face. "Yes, my lord?"

"No, not that, you goose," he laughed. "I propose that since we have both had a fatiguing day and it is apparent that you will continue to run me ragged with these escape attempts—"

"Run you ragged!"

"Which only stirs us both up," Ravenstoke continued smoothly, "I propose we cry a truce for, let us say, two weeks."

"A truce?"

"A truce," he affirmed. "For two weeks only, in which time we will repair to Grantham Hall, recuperate from our shocks and escapades, and decide what is to be done. During this time I promise not to turn you over to your stepfather, or anyone else. In return, you will promise to desist from running away. If, at the end of two weeks, we cannot agree upon what you should do, we will then resume hostilities."

"That is it?" Mary asked finally.

"That is it." He watched her pause, indecision on

her face. "You will be perfectly safe from me. I do not ravage ragamuffin urchins."

Mary's eyes flew to his. Then she smiled slightly. As weary as she was, she believed him, perhaps because she was so weary. She felt the exhaustion of the hunted and knew that she needed refuge; if it was to be with a self-professed rake, so be it. "Sir . . . I accept."

"Then it is settled. You may have made a pact with the devil," he said, echoing her very thoughts, "but I will try to be a good guardian angel for two weeks. After that, you cannot count on anything."

"I will strive to accept that guardianship," Mary said wryly. "And after that you cannot count on anything."

He offered her his hand. She took it. They smiled, slow smiles of understanding.

"Oh, my lord!" Jonas's shrill voice interrupted their brief moment of peace. "Thank God you are returned! And the horse and boy with you! You must hurry. Mr. Castleton has put away two bottles of my finest claret, but that is neither here nor there; I have won twenty guineas from him, but he has shot the cat. He has fallen under the table, and I cannot get him out—he keeps hugging the table leg—"

"Calm yourself, Jonas," Ravenstoke said. "You have done an excellent job. I will go to him immediately."

"My lord, he is not an easy man when foxed," Mary said hesitantly.

"Do not worry—though I had hoped to talk to him." Ravenstoke bowed with a reassuring smile and headed towards the door. Jonas, a fretsome spaniel, padded after him. The duke turned at the threshold. "By the way, I know I run the risk of sounding as if I am treating you like a horse, but there is a jar of excellent liniment oil in my left saddlebag. It should aid and comfort your back tonight."

"Thank you, my lord." Mary bowed like a proper lad. "If it is used upon Satana, I know I can depend upon its excellence."

"Imp." Ravenstoke's look grew oddly serious, and he added, softly, "I may be a dark angel, infant, but I mean you no harm." Mary, unable to speak, nodded with a wavering smile.

Jonas looked from the duke to the strange boy whose head was now bowed. Well, in his opinion the only devil there was that innocent-looking, horse-thieving, sleepwalking stripling. Now there was a regular limb of Satan! He shook his head and hurried after his lordship, only too glad to leave the changeling child's presence.

Chapter Three

RAKE RAVENSTOKE RESCUED

"You might as well take one, my lord," Mary suggested with a twitch of her lips. Her eyes remained fixed upon the chessboard. The two sat in quiet comfort within the Grantham Hall library. Mary had only been there a week, but she knew that the library was a room she would dearly miss when she left.

"One what, Mar—Marcus?" Ravenstoke asked.

"Why, a cheroot from the box on the table that you have eyed rather longingly these past few minutes."

"You are far too observant, my dear—you will not mind?"

"Not in the least. I quite like the scent, in fact."

Ravenstoke smiled, a warm smile that sent Mary's eyes back to the board. "You are a woman of exceptional taste, Mary. However could your stepfather call you uncomfortable when you play chess so well and allow a man the enjoyment of a cigar in his own house. Faith, I have not met another woman like that. Not even my grandmother, whom I highly esteem."

Mary smiled at this. "Father always disappeared into the garden to blow a cloud, since Mother was much like your grandmother. It was the time I always waited for, because I could catch him alone and have him all to myself."

"You must have been a precocious brat," Ravenstoke remarked as he lit the cheroot.

"So I have been told. Manny said she wished I had been a boy from birth so that she could have had some shred of an excuse for my abominable lack of feminine decorum."

"Ahh, but then you would be nothing out of the ordinary. Is that why you dressed as a boy when young?"

"Oh, no! That started on a wager. My friend Thomas forbade me to go to the horse auction—he said a young girl would draw attention."

"A mild way of putting it."

"I said I would go as a boy, then. Thomas swore I would get caught."

"But you didn't, of course."

"I didn't. After that, I'd always go as a boy if it added to my convenience."

"It appears you were allowed a great deal of license," Ravenstoke remarked lazily.

"Not as much as when Mother and Father were alive, but yes."

Ravenstoke only nodded, but Mary could not like the understanding in his eyes. "And how about your youth?" she said quickly, to divert the subject. "I remember that you went to boarding school. Thomas and I thought that must have been the most adventuresome and exciting place imaginable. Was it?"

"No. Do you intend to make a move at some point?"

Mary dutifully returned her eyes to the chessboard. She said, nonchalantly, "I would think you must have been a precocious child yourself, my lord."

"You do not give up, do you?" Ravenstoke sighed. "Yes, Mary, you can safely say that I was a precocious child. And no, boarding school is no place for precocious young boys. I advise you never to send your children there."

Mary's eyes flew to his in hurt surprise and then dropped. "I think that highly unlikely, my lord." She bit her lip and then continued. "You never came home for the holidays. That's why Thomas and I were sure you were enjoying yourself far too much."

"I went to my grandparents," Ravenstoke said, his voice gentling. "How did you know all of this?"

Mary's eyes grew mischievous. "Why, you are the only living duke in the vicinity. It is only natural that the neighbourhood hangs onto every little word and every little deed their duke does."

"I see." Ravenstoke frowned. "Thank God I am rarely here, then."

"Oh, no, my lord! You do the neighbourhood a great disservice, for then we must look to the letters from London and the papers for the news. It keeps the post inordinately busy."

"Impertinent brat. You do not seem properly impressed."

"No, my lord," Mary grinned. "You forget, Father knew the top military men and Mama hosted grand society. Why, I've been dandled on the knee by dukes, I'll have you know."

"And you will soon be over one's knee if you do not make a move," Ravenstoke threatened.

"I am thinking, my lord," Mary said serenely. She surveyed the chess pieces. "You think you have me cornered don't you, my lord?"

An appreciative smile played about Ravenstoke's eyes. "I would never presume, my dear."

"May I ask you a question, my lord?" Mary inquired, staring fixedly at the board.

"Certainly."

"It has often bothered me. Whatever happened to your lady friend, the one that took it upon herself to ride through the town as Lady Godiva one midnight. As I remember, it was terribly cold that evening — did she catch pneumonia?"

"My God!" Ravenstoke exclaimed, his cheroot frozen in midair.

"I am sorry," Mary apologized quickly as she saw his bemused expression. "I did not mean to shock you. I quite forgot myself."

Ravenstoke gave a sudden shout of laughter. "My word, Mary, you do ask the most stunning questions. I certainly hope these are not the general inquiries you make of gentlemen?"

"No, I do try to curb all my impulses of conversation. But with you I quite forget to watch my tongue."

" 'Gads, I should think you needn't. It would be a strange thing indeed to have to watch the proprieties around me. But wherever did you hear about that peccadillo?"

"Oh, the servants will whisper and — I should not admit it — that is when I listen the hardest."

"Eavesdropping can be a dangerous thing, little one."

"I know." Mary sighed. "I do try to curb that habit as well."

"Poor Mary, hedged in by such restrictions all around . . . and that 'lady' you asked about was not my friend. She was . . . er . . . a friend of a visiting friend. And yes, she did catch a frightful cold."

"She did not catch it to her death, I hope?" Mary said, quite serious.

"Is that what has bothered you?" Ravenstoke's brow quirked in amusement. "No, it was not fatal. The lady had an excellent . . . set of lungs, you see."

"I see." Mary picked up her king's bishop and moved it across the board. "Checkmate."

"What?" Ravenstoke stared. "Mary, you little devil . . . so that was what all this was about."

Mary grinned, but shook her head. "No, the conversation was by far the more interesting game. You must understand, there is very little to do at home but play chess."

"I concede defeat." Ravenstoke knocked over his king in surrender. "And since you are champion, I have a prize for you. You will find a satchel in your room with a change of clothing."

Mary froze, her hand tightly grasping one of the pawns. "I do not remember ordering clothes," she said slowly.

"Of course not. You could hardly risk it. Therefore, I did."

"Why?"

"My dear," he said patiently, "you yourself admitted your costume is quite unfashionable, and I do not wish to look at it one day longer. Faith, no one would take you for a cousin of mine, no matter how distant."

"I will not take the clothes from you," Mary said tightly. She knew she was behaving ungraciously; but she felt beholden to this man already, and she was getting deeper in his power every day.

"Then put it on the tab with all the rest," Ravenstoke said, calmly enough, though Mary could see the vein twitch at his temple.

"No," she objected. "I will never be able to repay

you at this rate. Send the clothes back."

"I will not," he said firmly. "You will wear them and that is that. Consider it a service by your host."

"I do not feel like your guest at the moment."

"Well, you are," the duke snapped. "You forget your promise to me quite swiftly, it seems. Indeed, perhaps you were planning to run away this very evening. Then I would agree that the clothes are unnecessary."

"I keep my word." Mary flushed. "But I did not promise to let you buy me things. Can't you see, we are acquaintances, met by chance, and yet, suddenly, you are running my life. What game do you play?"

"What game do I play?" Ravenstoke replied whimsically, reaching to tamp out his cheroot. "Why, that of the shining knight in armor. Only mine, alas, is quite tarnished, and the fair damsel quite unwilling to be rescued."

"Don't! I appreciate what you have done for me, but what you think I need and what I want are two different things. It is my life, and I do not want any man, no matter his noble aims, to rule it!"

"Is that why the clothes rankle? Lord, woman, they are but rags, not blood money."

"Yes, but you buy more and more things and spend more and more money. Soon I will never be able to repay you—I will be beholden to you forever."

"Even when it has been forced upon you?" Ravenstoke asked, an unreadable expression in his eyes.

"Yes. Even then."

"You are a strange woman, Mary." The duke sighed. "The clothes were meant to please you, not to insult your honour. Most women of my acquaintance would be in heaven if I gave them new clothes." He caught her quick look before she lowered her eyes. "Ah, yes. Then again, I do keep company with a different sort of female. But dammit, Mary, why must you let your pride and mistrust of men drive you to destruction — for that is surely where you are bound."

"I hardly think a life as a governess is destruction," Mary said coolly.

"For a woman of your spirit, it is. And what if you don't gain a post? You'll be left at the mercy of London. You have courage, but sometimes courage cannot help."

"Then what would you have me do?" Mary asked, stung. "Return to my stepfather and marry Squire Jameson?"

"No, I wouldn't have that. But return to Castleton and look about you. Marry someone else. You are a woman — you should have children and a loving husband to protect you."

"Protect me?" Derision twisted the corners of her lips. "No, I think not." She rose, feeling betrayed. Over the week, she had grown to respect this man, no matter his reputation, yet he would send her back to her stepfather. A defeated weariness descended upon her. "I thank you for your concern, my lord. I . . . I believe I would like to rest before dinner."

His green eyes searched hers, and then he sighed. "Yes, very well. And, Mary, wear the blue outfit tonight."

"The blue outfit?" she repeated numbly, turning uneasily. "How many outfits are there, my lord?"

"Oh . . . only three or four," he replied blandly.

Mary entered the front hall with a light step. She had just returned from an afternoon ride and had not yet donned any of her new clothing for dinner.

Spotting the duke's housekeeper, Mrs. Trafford, she slowed; the woman stood before the parlor door, abstraction marring her motherly face. "Excuse me, Mrs. Trafford."

"What?" The housekeeper jumped as if startled out of a trance. "Oh . . . Marcus."

"I'm sorry to startle you, but we should be having company soon. I saw a carriage approaching from the south drive."

"Company?" Mrs. Trafford echoed, aghast. "Land's sakes!"

"Is anything wrong?"

"Marcus, Lady Jane has been closeted with his lordship for over half an hour."

"Indeed, that is a long time," Mary said slowly, "but what of it?"

"She is unchaperoned."

"Unchaperoned?" A sick feeling gripped Mary. "Then she could be considered compromised if word leaked out."

"And that is what has me in such a pucker." Mrs. Trafford was so anxious, she never wondered how a boy would know the niceties of etiquette. "That Lady Jane has had her cap set for his lordship nigh unto two years now."

"Does . . . does he love her?" Mary couldn't understand why her chest constricted so.

"I don't think so," the housekeeper replied. "I hope not. She'd be no good for him if he did."

Mary looked at her, then studied the door speculatively. "He said he was not to be disturbed," Mrs. Trafford murmured, as if reading her mind.

"Did he?" Mary's face was set. "I believe that will be unavoidable in any case. And then he will be considered to have properly compromised her." After only the slightest hesitation, Mary bent down by the door and expertly put her eye to the keyhole.

Ravenstoke stood with his broad shoulders propped against the fireplace mantel. Of the lady, Mary could only see her back, for she faced the duke. Yet even at that angle, Lady Jane Pelham displayed a trim, elegant figure. Mary pulled back and placed her ear close to the keyhole.

"Really, Ravenstoke," the lady chided, her voice cultured, "here I offer you my hand and fortune, and you have nothing to say."

"My dear, what can I say? I am overwhelmed and flattered, but I fear I must decline your enchanting offer."

"You refuse? Why?" Her voice cracked with irritation.

"Rather, why do you, my dear, wish to align yourself with such a poor fellow as I?"

"Because I want you, and I fully intend to have you. And not in the way you think. You are a handsome man, and we know how you've broken the hearts of half the ladies in town. I don't mind— that's what makes you such a prize. You would not have to worry that your intrigues and infatuations would upset me. I am not some silly miss to fall into a decline over your peccadillos."

"My dear, you must love me very much."

"Love? You jest!" Lady Jane said scornfully. "What is love to people like you and me, Alastair? We do not have it in us to love or be faithful—that is why we are so admirably suited. And don't deny it, we both must marry."

Mary's body shook at these words. What kind of coldhearted woman would say this to a man? True, Ravenstoke was autocratic, and probably the libertine he said he was, but he'd shown her kindness such as no other man had since her father. Mary decided then and there to put a spoke in the woman's wheel, whether the duke approved or not. She placed her ear all the closer.

"What a charming notion you have of me," Ravenstoke was saying. "It causes me to wonder why you wish to marry me."

"I told you—you are handsome, rich, and have a reputation," Lady Jane said as if reading from a household list. "I rather fancy capturing the elusive Rake Ravenstoke where others have failed."

"Alas, I fear you do not have this fish on the hook yet."

"Oh, yes I do," Lady Jane replied with a purr.

Mary had heard enough. She sprang from her knees and turned to Mrs. Trafford, who stood anxiously by, evidently awaiting developments. "I believe Lady Jane is expecting the company we hear in the drive. Do admit them."

"But Marcus . . ." Mrs. Trafford objected.

"Only let them in," Mary soothed quietly, "and I will see to the rest. I fear Lady Jane must face a disappointment."

Mrs. Trafford stared; then her motherly face lit up with a rather malicious grin. "Very well, Marcus, very well."

Mary smiled impishly in return and flitted to the door. She cracked it open cautiously. Lady Jane had entwined her arms about Ravenstoke and clung to him; Mary seized the moment to slip into the room undetected. She closed the door silently and looked around her. Her eyes lit with triumph when she spotted a vase of fresh-cut flowers upon a side table. She looked at the couple, her heart queerly pained, and she sidled over to the table with resolution.

"Lady Jane," the duke said, his eye upon the blonde pressing against him, "you, of all people, should know you cannot seduce a seducer. We have been through all this before."

"But this time I am wiser."

Lady Jane's smugness made Mary grit her teeth.

Loud voices suddenly rumbled from outside the room. Ravenstoke looked to the door swiftly. Lady Jane laughed and, stepping back, screamed. Her hand flew to her bodice, and, with cool purpose, she ripped it, then screamed again.

Mary grabbed the vase and pulled out the flowers just as the door burst open. "What the devil's going on in here?"

"My Lady Jane," Mary shouted over the booming voice. The lady spun around, her bodice gaping wide; Mary, her face set, stepped forward and pitched the vase's contents over the dishevelled lady. Rivulets ran down her while twigs and leaves caught in the open cleavage of her breasts. Lady Jane screamed in unfeigned shock.

"Here, you young fiend!" a deep voice rasped. "What the hell are you doing?"

Mary, clutching the empty vase, whipped the satisfied smile from her face and turned to look at the frozen couple that stood within the doorway. Both were undeniably stout, with little to distinguish them. Lord Pelham had greying hair, and Lady Pelham, mousy brown. Though Lady Pelham did have two chins to her credits. Lord, Mary thought, amazed, how did these two sire such a stunning child?

"Sir," Mary said, widening her eyes in awe, "she was falling into an apoplexy I've never seen the like of before."

"Why, you little toad," Lady Jane hissed, her eyes slitted in rage. "Look what you have done!"

"But . . . but I thought you couldn't breathe,"

Mary objected in hurt innocence. "You screamed so loudly all of a sudden and clutched your chest so that—"

"Shut up!" Lady Jane's fingers curled into unsightly claws. "Shut up! Mama, Papa, Ravenstoke attacked me!" She was attempting to ignore the staring child and the chuckle coming from Ravenstoke who was behind her.

"Oh, merciful heavens. Then he must pay." Lady Pelham's voice had the stilted, halting tone that hinted at overrehearsal. She raised one pudgy hand to her brow in a gesture best left to the great Siddons.

Mary had to stifle a giggle, so poorly did Lady Pelham declaim her lines. Lord Pelham coughed and tried to glare Mary down. She levelled a knowing look at him, and he averted his eyes. "Er, well now, puss," he harrumphed, "let's not go off half-cocked. Better tell me what happened, first."

"Papa," Lady Jane said, her voice low, her eyes boring into him, "I told you. Lord Ravenstoke attacked me."

Mary shook her head vigorously. "Oh, no, my lady. I am sure you are confused—perhaps you have a fever. For, remember, my Lord Ravenstoke did not touch you. You walked toward him and then, suddenly, you screamed. I saw it," she added righteously. Then she turned to Lord Pelham. "Sir, does she often succumb to delirium?"

"Why, you little brat!" Lady Jane screeched, loudly enough to outdo a costermonger in Covent Gardens. "Mama," she demanded, wild-eyed, "do something!"

"Pelham, do something," her mother repeated frigidly. "How can you stand there listening to some pernicious snip rather than your poor, dishonored

61

daughter, just now attacked—ravished!"

"Oh, no, my lady, how can you say so?" Mary, wide-eyed, spoke in a shocked tone. "I didn't see anything like that. I know I shouldn't have sneaked in here and listened to everything—everything—my lady said to my lord, but when she arrived, she was so beautiful, I could not help but follow."

"Papa!" Lady Jane's voice rang with frustration. She looked at Mary as if she'd like to have her drawn and quartered.

"Just a moment, puss," Pelham said, reddening. A confused expression was in his eyes; evidently, this was not how things were to have proceeded. He raised his hand as Lady Jane made to speak again, and then he turned to Ravenstoke. "Ravenstoke, who is this boy, some servant?"

"Oh, no, he is a distant cousin of mine. And he is far older than he looks—far too old, in truth, to be playing these pranks anymore. He has been taken to task innumerable times at home for secreting himself where he oughtn't. Why, his parents check under their beds and in their wardrobes before they go to sleep." The duke turned a supposedly stern eye on Mary. "And I'll have your mouth for washing, young man, if you so much as breathe a word of Lady Jane's indisposition to your mama."

Mary hung her head and scuffed her toe upon the Aubusson carpet. Faith, she was getting good at this. "No, sir," she said in a recalcitrant voice. "I won't say nothing."

"Now apologize to the young lady for throwing water upon her. That was uncalled for." There was a thread of amusement running through Ravenstoke's voice. Mary looked up at him swiftly, objection in her eyes, to see his shine mischievously. Indeed, it was an unnecessary, but satisfying touch. "I did take the flowers out," she muttered to herself.

She made a face at Ravenstoke under cover of her arm, and then said, "I'm sorry Lady Jane for throwing water on you. I was just trying to help—I thought you were mortal sick."

"Pelham, do something!" Lady Pelham whispered shrilly enough for the whole room to hear.

"Like what, dammit?" her husband returned just as indiscreetly. "The little bas—ah, boy—was in the room all the time. Ravenstoke's cousin. Can't argue that one."

Mary's eyes met the duke's briefly in shared amusement.

Lord Pelham coughed. "Harrumph. I . . . think we'd best be on our way. Er, forgive the intrusion, Ravenstoke, but you know how the womenfolk are. Always getting some tottyheaded notion or other."

"Yes, I fully understand." Ravenstoke bit back a smile.

"Come along, Jane," her papa said. "You'll only catch your death of cold that way."

"But, Papa —we're not just going to leave?" The lady's face was that of a woman who'd had the carpet pulled out from under her.

"Yes, my dear, that's exactly what we are going to do," Pelham replied gruffly. "There ain't no use flogging a dead horse. Now cover yourself, for God's sake."

Lady Jane spun on Mary, eyes blazing with impotent fury. "You little fool, you've ruined everything!" Her hand snaked out to box Mary's ear with ringing viciousness.

"Jane." Ravenstoke's voice sliced the air. "Do not dare to strike Marcus again. I have borne with much, but *that* I will not tolerate."

Lady Jane snatched her hand back, her eyes

shooting venom. "You will pay for this, you little monster, don't think you won't!" She turned to Ravenstoke. "Goodbye, my lord. Despite everything, my offer still stands—I advise you to reconsider it. I hope to see you in London.

"And if I were you, I would whip that pestilent brat within an inch of his skin."

Ravenstoke bowed low. "Yes . . . but as you see, you are not me. Goodbye, Lady Jane."

The young woman stiffened, then, with an imperious sniff, swept from the room. Her mother followed, piercing Pelham, Ravenstoke, and Mary with a scathing look before she stormed out.

"Ah well, Ravenstoke," Pelhamn puffed, red-faced, "glad to see you're an understanding man. Sorry for the fuss, but when my puss gets the bit between her teeth, there's no stopping her."

"I can very well see that. Think nothing of it."

"Thank you." Pelham left hastily.

Ravenstoke walked to the door and closed it solemnly. He turned and eyed Mary; she looked back cautiously, wondering if he was displeased. "You do have a tendency to jump into trouble," he said in a low voice. He strode over to her and raised a warming hand to Mary's reddened ear. "Are you all right, child?"

"Perfectly, my lord," Mary mumbled—true words, now that she knew he was not upset. She flushed and took his hand from her heated face.

He grasped her hands in his large ones. "You are an absolute minx, and I thank you from the bottom of my heart." With a smile he raised her hands and turned them upward to kiss their palms warmly.

Mary trembled slightly and jerked her hands away. Living with a rake is a hazard, Mary thought, for they seemed much more tactile than ordinary men.

Idiot, her brain whispered, that's what makes them rakes. She cleared her throat and said, as lightly as possible, "Then we are even, my lord. For you saved me from Stepfather."

"Ah, but this was an even greater service. I am in your debt now."

"I would not say that," Mary smiled.

"Lord, woman, I don't take it lightly. Imagine if I had been forced to marry Jane—and I own, she almost had me. I must be growing old and lax," he said, shaking his head.

"Yes." Mary went swiftly to sit on a chair, for, all of a sudden, her knees didn't want to support her. "I wouldn't say it was wise of you to entertain Lady Jane alone."

"No, it wasn't," the duke agreed ruefully. "In truth, I had hoped to talk some sense into her."

"You had poor Mrs. Trafford all a-twitter."

"Is that how you knew? I must increase the good lady's wages." He laughed suddenly. "I will never reprimand you again for eavesdropping. In fact, you have my blessing to do it anytime you wish."

"A dangerous blessing, my lord," Mary said, a twinkle in her eyes. "Only think of the education I will receive."

"I count upon your discretion." Ravenstoke grinned wickedly. He settled himself in the chair across from her. "Lady Jane certainly caught me unawares this afternoon."

"She has the tactics of a general," Mary observed, "though she lacks a certain finesse." Then she added, in an offhand manner, "I do not think she is the lady you should marry."

"An understatement," Ravenstoke remarked. Amusement lurked in his eyes.

"And I would not take the lady's words too much

to heart," Mary said, hiding her own, still-seething anger over what Jane Pelham had said.

Ravenstoke raised his brows. He studied Mary a moment, his eyes suddenly lidded and enigmatic. "Do you truly think I was hurt by her? My dear, what are we to do with you? Do you think to protect the wolf? Understand this, sweet Mary — Lady Jane's reading of my character was on the mark. I have fully earned my reputation."

"You mean you have fully lived up to your reputation," Mary countered.

"Have it what you will," Ravenstoke said, as if he were suddenly weary. "It makes no odds — it is too late to change my life. But Lady Jane erred in one thing. I will never marry. I would not wish that upon any woman — I have too much of my mother in me for that."

Mary sat silently, as she watched a shadow cross his face. She did not speak. Then she frowned as a new thought entered her head. "Does this sort of thing happen to you often, my lord?"

"What?"

"Women chasing after you and throwing themselves at you?"

"Ever since I came into the title," he said sardonically. "Before that, not as often — there was always a chance that my father would finally become tired of my escapades and disinherit me. That dampened the ladies' ardor somewhat."

"It could not be good for one's character, such attention," Mary said, rather disapprovingly.

Ravenstoke laughed. "No. Thank heaven I had none before that to ruin."

"You must have had some — how else to explain your treatment of me now?"

"Lord, child, I was never one to leave a drenched

66

puppy in the rain." His lips curled. "I have told you, I do not know why I wish to help you. Perhaps the role of knight errant was so novel, I could not resist."

"That would explain it." Mary nodded, humor glinting in her blue eyes.

He laughed, as she'd known he would. "Ah, Mary, you are an enchanting child. Now, what can I do for you after your salvation of me today. . . ? I know, I will buy you more new clothes!"

"Don't you dare, my lord," she said severely. "Indeed, it was my pleasure."

"Yes, it evens things out a bit for when you escape into the dead of night, doesn't it, infant?" There was a knowing look in Ravenstoke's eyes.

Mary's widened, so unexpected were his words. Her chin lifted. "That is no way to keep the truce, my lord."

"No . . . it isn't. How remiss of me. Now, what would you like to do?"

"If you have time, I would very much like to see your lands. I see you have used some new methods; I have tried to convince Stepfather to make those changes."

"But that would require an outlay of money and would benefit your people," Ravenstoke said caustically. "So Castleton would never do it. Come along—I could use the exercise."

Chapter Four

MARY PLAYS A GAME OF MISCHANCE

Satana screamed and reared on his haunches as a sharp stone pelted off his hindquarters. Mary clung to the great horse as he bucked, her soothing words a steady murmur beneath his snorts of fury. The stablehands who had been watching Mary exercise the stallion started running and yelling, only feeding Satana's fear.

"Get back!" Mary shouted to Thomas as he ran forward. Satana scraped the air with his hooves. Yet another stone ricocheted off the black and the frothing horse rose, screeching his outrage. Thomas stood, paralyzed with fear, directly in Satana's descending path. Mary pulled on the reins, forcing the great horse to twist and turn, avoiding the man by a whisper.

As the crazed horse performed a frightening pirouette, the reins were torn from Mary's hands. She flew from his back, her body hitting the ground with a sickening thud.

Two dirty youths suddenly sprinted from behind a bush, slingshots in hand. "Get those boys!" Ned, the head groom shouted. A frozen moment ticked by before two stable boys shook themselves from their trance and raced after the disappearing forms.

"Oh, God! He ain't moving," Thomas choked out, walking, dazed, toward the sprawled body.

"Don't touch him," Ned warned him as he knelt down. "It might be wrong. Get the master."

Another stable boy tore off towards the house, leaving a silent, anxious group encircling the still figure. "Cor, the master's going to kill us," John said, his young voice cracking.

"What could we do. There ain't no keeping that boy and Satana away from each other," Ned replied.

"I ain't never seen a lad ride like that. He saved my life," Thomas rasped.

"Tell that to his lordship," John said. "He's going to be in a fury—gawd, here he comes!"

The boys drew back as Ravenstoke stalked up. He stopped sharply when he saw Mary on the ground, like a rag doll thrown down by a child in a tantrum. His eyes raked the hands. Not one among them could meet his gaze. The duke swore long and lowly, sending a quiver through the group as he knelt beside Mary, his face a controlled mask. He ran gently, questing hands over her body.

"Is . . . is he all right, my lord?" Thomas trembled as he spoke. "We didn't know what to do."

"You did rightly," Ravenstoke said quietly. "I don't think there is anything broken, though his ankle seems to be swollen. . . . You are all fortunate it is not worse. Fetch me some water."

Ravenstoke rolled Mary over and gently cradled her head in his lap. His tapered fingers stroked the contours of her skull, searching. "There it is." He pulled his hand back, and a concerted gasp ran through the crowd—his hand was smeared with blood. "No, it is light," Ravenstoke said, and, taking his lawn handkerchief, he wiped the dirt from Mary's lips and face. John ran up, panting. With earnest eyes, he proffered a tin of water. The duke dipped the handkerchief in it and wiped Mary's bruised forehead.

Her eyes flickered open at the cooling touch. Sunlight shattered in her mind, and she closed her eyes again with a groan.

"No, Mar—Marcus," Ravenstoke commanded. "I want you to open your eyes for me. Open them for me, infant."

Why does his voice sound so far away? And why does it sound so urgent? That is not like him, Mary thought numbly. She focused her will and lifted her lids. Familiar emerald eyes burned down into hers; she gazed back, bemused.

"Yes . . . very fine eyes," she murmured, before she knew what she said. Then memory rushed back at her. "Ravenstoke?"

"Yes, child?"

"It wasn't Satana's fault. Something spooked him."

The grimness in Ravenstoke's eyes lightened. "Peter told me . . . but, faith, isn't he a bit large for you to try to protect?"

"He's a good horse . . . is he all right?"

"Yes, he's standing over there, looking penitent. Now stop worrying. He's in far better condition than you."

Mary chuckled. Her body retaliated at such an unguarded movement, and she groaned.

"Where does it hurt, my dear?"

She tried to think, her brow furrowing. "Oh . . . I think . . . everywhere."

"You were unconscious for a while."

"Umm . . . that would explain . . . the pounding."

70

"I would imagine," Ravenstoke remarked drily. He slid his arms under her legs.

"What . . . what are you doing?" Mary asked quickly, bewildered. She felt terribly foolish.

"Carrying you to the house," Ravenstoke said calmly, and lifted her up. Mary winced and bit her tongue.

The duke looked to the head groom. "Ned, find those boys."

"Yes, my lord. James and Dan went after them."

"Good!" The duke's face hardened.

"What boys?" Mary asked. She could feel Ravenstoke tensing.

"Added help," he replied. "Now be quiet and rest."

Mary smiled faintly at this, having learned better than to chuckle. "Yes . . . bully," she murmured, and sighed. Her head hurt so viciously that she let it fall to Ravenstoke's shoulder for support. Strange, she could hear his heartbeat, a steady, reassuring rhythm. She unconsciously raised her hand to his chest to feel that pulsing. Feeling it beat steadily beneath her palm, she sighed and drifted off.

Mrs. Trafford greeted Ravenstoke at the front door, and she almost crumbled in concern when she beheld Mary, limp in the duke's arms. "Is the poor child hurt badly, my lord?"

"I'm not sure. A cut on the head, but no broken bones from what I can tell."

"Oh, thanks be to God."

"Please bring me some water, bandages, and laudanum," Ravenstoke said, carrying Mary up the stairs.

He took her to her room and carefully laid her upon the bed. He then sat down on it himself, gazing at her. With a feather-light touch, he brushed the damp curls from her dirty forehead, sighed, and lifted her tiny hand in his. His fingers ran gently over the lines in her palm, like a Gypsy's searching out her fortune.

"Is the boy still not awake?" a concerned voice asked from behind. Ravenstoke stiffened and looked up to discover Mrs. Trafford standing in the doorway.

"Yes, but don't worry. It is more shock than anything else that I can see. He should enjoy a good rest — he'll probably wake up devilishly uncomfortable, but I will give him laudanum for that."

"Yes, my lord," his housekeeper said. She shook her head sadly. "Boys do seem to fall into trouble so fast. Do you wish me to help you?"

"No, Mrs. Trafford. I will be able to manage, but please be so kind as to prepare that excellent tisane of yours for when he awakens."

"Certainly, my lord. It will be a pleasure." She handed Ravenstoke the supplies he had requested, and left the room.

Ravenstoke looked to the sleeping Mary and sighed. "I doubt any mere child could cause as much trouble as you do, Mary." He measured out a dose of laudanum in a glass and sat down, then lifted her to a sitting position. "My dear, I want you to drink this." He raised the glass to her lips.

Mary swallowed the liquid, making a dreadful face in her sleep; the duke chuckled softly and eased her back. He rose and looked about her room until he found the jar of liniment he had given her, upon the dresser. Rummaging through the drawers, he uncovered a nightshirt he had ordered for her with the new clothes. He held it up critically. " 'Gads, the child must drown in this."

He walked solemnly over to the bed and smiled wryly as he stared down at Mary. "You will try a man's control, woman." He shook his head ruefully, then set about undressing and bathing her. His hands were steady and efficient, but there was a set tilt to his jaw. He pulled back a moment. "Lord, Mary," he said to the silent figure, "how ever did you manage to hide such a body?" He turned her over to apply the healing liniment to her back, and swore softly when he saw the heavy welts that striped it.

A half-hour later, there was a scratch at the door. Mrs. Trafford entered with a mug to discover his lordship ensconced in a chair at the foot of Mary's bed, reading a book. She clucked under her breath; the duke looked as weary as the child. There were some that would talk about his nasty reputation, and indeed, when he had visited in the past, there had been cause to tremble; but his gentle treatment of this lad must redeem him, at least a little. She cleared her throat hesitantly, and Ravenstoke looked up.

"Ah, your excellent tisane," he said. "Please set it down. Marcus hasn't awakened yet, but I have no doubt he will presently."

"Yes, my lord. Would you like anything for yourself perhaps?"

"No. I will be fine."

Mrs. Trafford refrained from comment. She took one last look at the pale little figure in the bed, and murmured, "Poor boy."

"Yes," Ravenstoke said, a sudden stress in his voice. "He is lucky it was not worse. Thank you, Mrs. Trafford."

As Mrs. Trafford closed the door, Mary stirred and let out a stifled moan. She opened dilated eyes and blinked, as does a kitten when set in unfamiliar territory. She blinked again, her eyes focusing, as best they could, upon Ravenstoke.

The duke rose and pulled his chair to her side. He sat down and poured a glass of water from the table by her bed. As dreadful as Mary felt, she couldn't help smiling. Lord Ravenstoke made an odd nurse-maid, to be sure.

"Welcome back to the world." He smiled and lifted her with strong arms so that she might drink from the glass.

Mary had rarely experienced such conflicting emotions. Whereas she felt fidgety and nervous with Ravenstoke's arms around her, she also felt comforted and protected being in those same arms. For her, they seemed to sum up the contradictions of the man.

She murmured a thank you, and Ravenstoke laid her back against the pillows. "There, that should help you. Mrs. Trafford has also prepared a tisane for you."

"Thank you." She forced the words through a dry throat, and ran her tongue over her numb lips in bewilderment. "My mouth feels fuzzy."

"It is from the laudanum."

"Oh," Mary replied, relieved to understand the loss of sensation.

"Your reaction to the fall makes it clear that you have not been sleeping as well as you should," the duke said reprovingly. "You have not been applying the liniment as thickly as necessary."

"I know," Mary said, still terribly foggy. "I had difficulty reaching . . ." She stopped midsentence and wriggled slightly. There was a notable absence of the customary pain. She lay confused for a moment; then a horrible idea crossed her mind. Her eyes flew to Ravenstoke. "What . . . who?"

"Does your back feel better?"

"You—who changed my clothes?" Her voice had

74

sunk to a whisper.

"Your most obedient servant." He was watching her closely.

"I see," Mary said, after a choked moment. She flushed deeply. "How unfortunate."

"I did not consider it so," Ravenstoke said with teasing humor. Then he grew serious. "There was no other way. You would have been discovered. Only imagine Mrs. Trafford's shock if she had helped, as she offered."

Mary nodded in hopeless acknowledgement. "I understand."

"You wouldn't have wanted her to fall into a dead faint, would you?"

"No," Mary said tightly, just wishing he would cease.

"That is, if she ever managed to get through all the yards of material binding you about. How did you ever expect your back to heal when it was so suffocated?"

"I'd rather not talk about it, my lord."

"Well, I would. You had best become a girl soon, for such restrictions cannot be healthy." Mary averted her eyes and bit her lip, flags of color on her cheeks. "Oh, good Lord, Mary, don't blush so! It is not as if I am unaccustomed to the female form — you did not shock me."

"I must be grateful, then." She still refused to meet his eyes.

"Yes, I rather think so." Her eyes flew to his at this, full of uncertainty and misery. "What is it, Mary? Why this embarrassment? Oh, I know I should be merely happy that you are not throwing things at me, or indulging in fits of hysteria, but you've always shown yourself to be a lady of reason on most occasions. What is it?"

"I am sorry, but you are wrong. This is one time I wish to be missish."

Ravenstoke frowned, puzzled. Then his face grew thunderous. "My god, you're ashamed of your body!"

Mary started, pulled in a breath, and said, as evenly as possible, "My lord, I do not feel up to fencing with you right now, and I ask you to cease this talk."

"My dear Mary, do you know that I have often been considered a connoisseur of women?" Ravenstoke's tone was as mundane as if they discussed the weather. "Well, I do not mean to puff off my own consequence, but it is true. I can safely say that my judgement can be respected. Therefore, you can believe me when I say that your body is perfectly formed and one to be appreciated. Indeed, considering my approval, you were quite fortunate that you were so completely unconscious."

Mary gasped, and her astonished eyes sprang to his. His were mischievous. Leave it to Ravenstoke to say such things, she thought. She shook her head ruefully. "I don't know why I am surprised over this conversation. Well, sir, I thank you for attempting to cheer me up in your own inimitable, if decidedly improper, way."

Ravenstoke did not move from his chair, and his eyes remained fixed on her. "You do not believe me?" he asked, his voice raw silk. "Shall I make love to you to prove my statement? I assure you, it would be my pleasure."

Mary stared at him, spellbound, her heart racing. She drew in a quick breath and tore her gaze away. "That won't be necessary, my lord. I believe you."

"Somehow I thought you would, little coward," Ravenstoke said, provocatively. "Strange . . . for in all other respects, you are such a courageous woman. No, no, don't fly out at me, I know I've behaved badly. But I will not apologize. And I assure you, it will prove much worse if I ever catch you falling into embarrassment over your body again. Is that clear?"

"Perfectly clear," Mary said stiffly.

Ravenstoke laughed. "Lord, my dear, you sound like Joan of Arc standing at the stake. That certainly puts me in my place. A cut direct—my sensibilities are in shambles."

"Then we are even, my lord."

"Oh, a hit, a palpable hit!" He smiled at her. "Only promise?" he added gently.

She looked at him, once again mesmerized by his eyes. She shook herself mentally. "I promise."

"Wonderful." He stood up. "Now get your rest. If you are a good girl, I will return and entertain you this evening."

"Entertain me?" Mary quizzed with an unexpected humor. "I am . . . almost afraid to ask how, my lord."

The duke grinned at that. "Merely a game of chess, my dear. Unless you wish otherwise."

"I do wish otherwise, my lord," Mary said sweetly, pouting her lips as she had seen other girls do. It surprised her to realize she was enjoying flirting, for it was usually not in her style.

Ravenstoke's brows rose appreciatively, though his eyes were suspicious. "Yes, my dear?"

"I would like to play"—Mary hesitated for the proper effect—"cards, my lord."

Ravenstoke shouted his delight. "You are a minx, Mary. Cards it will be, then." He walked to the door, then turned. "And Mary?" he said, as sweetly as she had spoken.

"Yes, my lord?"

"Play that game with me once our truce is over

and you will certainly bear the consequences." He bowed with courtly grace. "Au revoir, my dear."

"Very well, Ned," Ravenstoke said to his head groom the following morning, as the man stood before his desk. "I need not tell you that this must not go beyond these walls."

"No, my lord," Ned said quietly. "Have no fear."

"I also suggest that once the child is recovered, he is not to be left unattended."

Ned did not blink an eyelid. "It will be arranged, my lord."

"Excellent. I knew I could count on you." Ravenstoke smiled. "And I see no reason Marcus must know of this protection, do you, Ned?"

"None at all, my lord."

"Youths — you know how they are. They do like to feel independent."

"Yes, my lord, they do. It is their way."

"Especially this one," Ravenstoke said, his eyes humorous. "That will be all." There was a scratch at the door. "Come in."

Mrs. Trafford entered.

"What is it?"

"My lord, Squire Jameson awaits you in the hall and wishes to have words with you."

"Squire Jameson?" Ravenstoke's brows rose. "Things grow more interesting. . . . Send him in by all means. And Mrs. Trafford, please see to it that Marcus has complete bed rest. I do not wish to see him below stairs, no matter what the circumstances. Is that clear?"

"Yes, my lord." Mrs. Trafford recognized that tone of voice. It was the one not to be disobeyed. She exchanged a silent look with Ned, and both made their swift exits.

In but a moment, Jameson stood before Lord Ravenstoke. He was a man of forty, with handsome features cut from a coarse mold. Of a bullish frame, he looked best in country clothes. His eyes were a rusty brown, very similar to the color of the foxes he so loved to hunt down.

"Hello, Jameson." Ravenstoke greeted the older man as he rose from behind his desk. "I have not seen you in years. Have a seat, and I'll ring for brandy."

"No need to do that," Jameson said, with a smile that failed to reach his eyes. He sat down on the winged chair that Ravenstoke proffered. "Heard you had quite a day yesterday."

"Word travels fast," Ravenstoke remarked as he sat in the opposite chair.

Jameson shrugged. "You're in the country now. Folks care about what others are doing."

"Yes, I'm beginning to find that out."

"So your cousin took a spill yesterday?" Jameson asked politely, while his eyes wandered in inattention over the room's fine furniture.

"Yes. Satana became spooked and threw him."

"It's a marvel you let the boy ride the horse at all."

"I forbade him to, but it seems the lad can't stay away from Satana. He's a rather headstrong youth."

Jameson's eyes narrowed. "There's a way to remedy that. It doesn't pay to allow insubordination."

Ravenstoke shrugged his shoulders. "His mother would make my life miserable if I so much as touched a hair on his head."

"What's a woman to know about those things?" Jameson's mouth curled with utter contempt.

"Ah, but relations can be the very devil," Ravenstoke sighed. "I'll be quite happy when I have the child safely delivered to his doting mother in London. Perhaps you would care to meet the boy?"

"No, perhaps another time." Jameson's eyes sharpened. "You know, you could have knocked me over with a feather when Castleton told me you were visiting."

"Yes . . . I admit I would prefer to be elsewhere, but you know how family duty is. Even I, unfortunately, cannot escape it on occasion. Strange you should mention Castleton—the man seemed all to pieces the last time I met him. It appears he lost his daughter."

"Yes." Jameson's face took on an ugly look. "She is my fiancée."

"Your fiancée? Why, I do hope you have found her, then."

"No, not yet." A vein twitched at Jameson's temple. "But I will, never fear that."

"But this is amazing. I would have thought you would have retrieved her by now."

"No, not Mary Castleton." A primitive excitement leapt into the man's face. "Her fool father has let her run untamed for years. She's a cunning sort, not easily caught. But I'll take care of that, don't you worry. She'll learn to come to heel when I'm through with her."

"Ah, yes. . . . They say you are one of the finest sportsmen in the country."

Jameson looked startled at this, but then he smiled slowly. "You appear to be a man after my own heart."

"So it would appear." Ravenstoke's smile was faint. "What I can't understand is how you let your filly escape in the beginning."

"I didn't. Her bumbling stepfather did. I told him he didn't hold her leashed tight enough, but he's a

80

simpleton. Mary can run rings around the old ass. But that's what I like. She's got a spirit that needs disciplining, and I'm the one to do it! Damn, she's already given me the best chase I've ever had."

"It would appear so."

"It only makes the kill all the sweeter." His eyes stared off into space, and a hard smile crossed his thick lips.

"I had no idea country life held such pleasures."

Jameson's eyes swung back to him. "Simple pleasures, my lord, simple pleasures. But you wouldn't know about that, now, would you my lord? You'll be leaving soon to take the child back to his mama, isn't that so?"

"Yes. How unfortunate." Ravenstoke sighed. "I was beginning to wish to meet your delightful bride — once you run her to earth, of course."

"Oh, I'll find the vixen," Jameson said with confidence. "And she'll be my wife before you ever clap eyes upon her."

"Indeed?" Enjoyment lurked at the very back of the duke's eyes.

"Yes. I know your reputation. Don't think I'd let you meet her before I tie the knot. I won't have you sniffing about her with her unriveted."

"Such faith you have in the lady."

"You and I both know there ain't a woman you can trust." Jameson laughed harshly. "They'll always be twitchin' their skirts at another man, unless you let them know who's master right off. Then they won't be playing off their tricks."

"You must be a devil with the ladies," Ravenstoke said smoothly. "Well, I have enjoyed becoming better acquainted with you this visit — is there anything I can do for you while I'm still here? Would you like me to find this Mary for you, perhaps?"

"No, she's mine to hunt, all mine." His eyes sharpened into a threat. "Remember that, Ravenstoke."

"My dear man, who am I to interfere with your hunt," Ravenstoke replied, raising protesting hands. "I only thought perhaps that is why you came to visit today."

James smiled in pleasure. "I did. One must check all possible holes where they can hide."

"I am sure I do not like being compared to a hole," Ravenstoke complained. "But I can appreciate your thoroughness."

"I am certainly thorough." Jameson rose. "I must be on my way. I have enjoyed this, Ravenstoke."

"And so have I. Oh, so have I."

Ravenstoke saw him to the door, and returned to sit in his chair. A grimness was about his mouth and eyes, a grimness that would have warned anyone who knew him to employ the utmost caution. A scratch at the door directed his eyes toward that portal. Mrs. Trafford appeared.

"Will you be wanting luncheon soon, my lord?"

"No, I seem to have lost my appetite. I had forgotten how tiresome Jameson can be. . . . It seems our little Marcus has a tendency to attract the most unhealthy of attentions. I fear he must recover faster than I had thought."

"My lord?"

"Hmmm . . . yes, I do believe a change of scenery will definitely benefit him. But how do you get a recalcitrant child to do what you want?"

This, Mrs. Trafford did know. "Why, simple, my lord. You merely inform the child."

"No, that will not work with this one. So how?" He mused on the question for a few moments. "The child has a strong sense of honor, it seems—that should be the key. Yes, please hold luncheon for an hour or more; I believe I would like to engage Marcus in a game of chance. It's a pity he plays so well, but I still hold the better luck, I trust."

"You have excellent luck, my dear." Ravenstoke smiled as Mary laid down her hand with a triumphant crow.

"I needs must with you, my lord. Your fame with the cards is well justified."

"I'm overcome by such praise. You are not too tired to play another game, are you?"

"Oh no, not at all," Mary said, her blue eyes sparkling. "What shall we wager on this time, my lord?"

"That depends," he said slowly shuffling the cards.

"Let's see, we played for provinces and countries already," Mary said, ticking them off on her fingers. "And for palaces. I can't believe I lost Versailles to you." She shrugged. "You have me at a stand; suggest something."

Ravenstoke looked up from the cards with a contented smile. "I fully intended to. Let us gamble on something real this time."

"Real?" Mary echoed. "Why, that would be a crashing bore for you, I'm sure. I don't possess enough to even make a worthwhile stake."

"Oh, I don't know," Ravenstoke drawled as he flipped a card. "It could be interesting."

Mary stilled. She unaccountably sensed danger. "What would you have me wager?"

"Your freedom."

"My freedom? What do you mean?"

"Why, I mean your freedom from my control." He smiled kindly. "If you win, you will gain that at the end of the week. Come now, Mary," he said as he saw her startled face, "surely you did not think I would let you walk blithely out of here come the time."

"I don't know what I thought," Mary said, trying to mask her hurt. He'd been such a companion over the past few days, she'd thought he just might. "But I doubt you could hold me against my will for very long."

"I could. You did come close to escaping before, but I have your measure now. Of course, I could always settle the issue quickly by returning you to your stepfather. I doubt you'd escape him again."

"You would not do that!" Mary said, her chin jutting out.

"Would I not?" Mary's eyes fell before his, and she paled. A muscle tensed in his jaw as he watched her. "Ah, so you are not too sure. Such trust."

Mary stiffened, and her eyes blazed at his jibe. "You, yourself, said the role of knight is interesting for its novelty. I cannot be novel forever. That would be a foolish hope when so many ladies before me have proved that an impossibility with you."

Ravenstoke's eyes flamed. "Just so, my dear. Now, are we agreed upon your freedom as my stake?"

"And what is to be my forfeit if I lose?"

"You will come to London with me and allow my grandmother to present you for the season, at my expense."

Mary stared at him. Of all the possible things he might have offered, this was not one she had expected. "But why?"

"To make an eligible connection, of course. You are to strive to find a suitable match by the end of the season. If you fail, and only if you fail, will I consider finding you a governess's post."

"Why, that is preposterous!"

"Preposterous or not, that is the game I offer. Or else I truss you up and cart you back to Castleton with instructions on how to control you."

"Oh, no, my lord, Stepfather does not have your wiliness."

"Do you choose to chance it?"

Mary stared at him. "You are mad, my lord."

"Highly possible. Well?"

"So we play for my freedom, and either way you control the future of my life. . . . Very neat, my lord, very neat."

"But that's only if you lose."

Mary stared at him. Yes, only if she lost. If she won, she could go free, but if she lost, he'd drag her to London to make a suitable match. What of his grandmother? Surely she wouldn't commit to such a scheme for an unknown girl. And he depended upon her attracting a suitable match; Mary knew full well her lack of attraction for the male sex. Ah, yes, even if she lost, she would win in the end—and at the heavy-handed duke's expense. But she would not refuse to play and have him return her to her stepfather in a fit of rage.

She lifted her chin at this and looked Ravenstoke in the eye steadily, an angry smile on her face. "Very well, my lord. You think you hold all the cards, don't you? Well, deal them—for I intend to win and never to have to set eyes upon you again."

His brows quirked, and a gleam entered his eyes. "My lady rises to the occasion," he said, an undefinable note in his voice. "You are sure you are rested?"

"Why such concern, my lord?"

"I would not have you say the game was not fair or honestly played." He dealt her the first card.

"For then you could not hold me to it, is that it?"

Mary picked the card up.

"Yes." He continued to deal. "And I would not have that."

"No, you would much prefer to have a chance-met girl forced into marriage for God knows what reason." Mary surveyed her cards. "Or perhaps I should say the devil's own reason."

"Say whatever you wish, my dear," Ravenstoke said with amusement as he, too, looked at his cards. "Only do play."

"That I will, my lord," Mary said with a tight smile.

And they played. A silence settled upon the room as each bent will to luck and skill. Blue eyes and green eyes became equally blank as they considered their discards. The hand fell evenly, but Mary picked up the saving card to win her the round. "Very nice, my dear." Ravenstoke nodded.

"I'm so glad you approve, my lord," Mary said curtly, refusing to fidget as her body cried out to do. Ravenstoke had shown a deadly skill that she had only suspected before. It was surely the luck of the cards that had rescued her. She picked up her second hand, believing that surely justice — and therefore luck — would remain on her side.

The minutes ticked by, and the second hand was played out, much more slowly. Ravenstoke's discards were as speedily performed as in the first, but Mary refused to be intimidated and took her time. It was to no avail; Ravenstoke took the hand.

"You still did not do badly in that one," he said. "Do you wish to rest a moment before we deal again?"

"No, my lord," Mary snapped, knowing he must see her strain. "Why would I wish to do such a thing as that? After all, the remainder of my life may rest upon this hand, and all because your . . . your . . ."

"My caprice, perhaps?"

"No. Rather, your arrogance, I would say. You are a man who simply does not like to be overruled." She accepted her cards once again; a quiver ran through her as she picked them up. Dear God, do not let this man win, she prayed. Certainly a benevolent God would not let such a man win for such a purpose!

But when the duke turned over the king of hearts, God did just that. Mary stared down at the card in stupefaction. She sighed and wearily laid her head down upon the pillow, refusing to meet Ravenstoke's eyes. He didn't speak so she looked up; he was gazing at her with an oddly regretful look.

"Well, my lord, you win," she said, her lips twisting with bitterness. "When do we leave for London?"

He reached for the cards and reshuffled them. "On the morrow."

"So soon?"

"You will find I always collect swiftly upon my winnings."

"But what of your grandmother? Surely you must contact her first."

"She is not your concern." Ravenstoke rose. "You'd best get your rest. Tomorrow should prove a long day for you."

"I have no doubt," Mary said with an edge to her voice. Watching him walk to the door, she could not help herself. "My lord, have you but considered that I may still win in this game of yours? It is highly unlikely that I will take, as you did say, a suitable match."

Ravenstoke shook his head. "No, Mary. I knew that was what you would think, and in truth that you thought it the ace up your sleeve—but you will take, Mary. With my backing and support, as well as that of the Dowager Duchess of Denfield, you cannot possibly fail."

Mary was stricken. Her eyes fell from his and she nodded, a quick, defeated gesture.

Chapter Five

THE ACQUAINTANCE OF THE DUCHESS OF DENFIELD IS MADE

Adams, long-time butler to the Dowager Duchess of Denfield was prompt to answer the rap of the door-knocker at her town residence. Years of training, and only that, saved him from the indignity of exclamation when he beheld Lord Ravenstoke before him, cradling a tousled, slumbrous woman within his arms.

"Good day, Adams. Is her ladyship at home?"

"Yes, my lord," Adams replied, thankful to discover that his voice did not quiver. "May I tell her that you are calling?"

"No, not yet." Ravenstoke walked past him, carrying his sleeping burden. "First let me take the child upstairs and see her comfortable."

"Yes, my lord."

"Am I in time for tea?"

"Why, yes, my lord—it will be served shortly. Will the"—Adams looked with uncertainty towards the sleeping woman—"the . . . er . . . child, be wishing tea as well?"

"No, she just fell asleep, quite against her will, of

course, and I do not intend to wake her. She will have my head for it, no doubt."

Adams blinked in disbelief before he could catch himself. Rarely anyone dared to take the duke to task, and he thought it highly unlikely that such a small female waif would do so. "Certainly, my lord."

The drawing-room door swung open and both men stopped.

"Adams," an imperious voice said, "did I hear someone at the door?" A diminutive lady appeared, leaning upon a cane. Though slight, Lady Sophia, dowager duchess of Denfield, held her body as if tall. The use of the cane did not subtract from her presence, but rather lent her distinction. Her hair was silver, beautifully coiled about an exceptionally unlined face.

"What excellent hearing you have, dear grandmama," Ravenstoke said.

"Alastair! So good to see you. I thought you were rusticating with that fool Ferdy." Her cane tapped upon the marble floor as her bright brown eyes located him. They narrowed at the sight of Mary. "What are you doing with that girl?"

"Carrying her upstairs. She is burnt to the socket."

"I'm so glad to hear it; I feared she was dead. And who might this burnt-to-the-socket girl be?"

"Castleton's stepdaughter."

"Good God—that toad! What in heaven's name are you doing with his stepdaughter?" The duchess peered more critically at the slumbering girl.

"Why, I found her in a tree."

"And so you brought her here to me." The duchess clapped her hands together in feigned delight. "Why, how kind of you, Alastair. You know how I wish for girls found in trees."

"Yes, I thought you would enjoy it. Shall it be the

gold room?"

"Mm? No, the blue. The gold is under redecoration." Lady Sophia answered absently as she cocked her head sideways, the better to view Mary's downturned face. "Not a bad face, but too tanned by far. The dress must go, of course."

"And here it's taken me all of two weeks to get her into one."

The duchess was shaken out of her absorption. "What? Do not be impertinent, young man! I'll not tolerate such talk. Any more of that and I'll toss the girl out in a trice."

"No, Grandmama." Ravenstoke shook his head gently, smiling down at the sleeping girl in a way that caused the duchess to stare. "You couldn't do that to little Mary. Do but let me put the child to bed, and then I will explain."

His grandmother considered this for a moment. "Very well. Take her to the blue room, and Maria will attend her."

"Thank you, my dear." Ravenstoke smiled. "I knew I could count upon you. I shall be down shortly."

"Yes, see that you are," the duchess said sternly. She lifted a minatory eyebrow and turned back to the drawing room.

Lady Sophia silently offered Ravenstoke a cup of steaming tea when he entered the room some fifteen minutes later. "So, she is Castleton's stepdaughter?" Her lips were pursed, her eyes sharp upon Ravenstoke, as he seated himself across from her. "If I am not mistaken, that would make her Julia Summerville's child."

"You are not mistaken."

"Julia Summerville set the *ton* on its ear the moment she made her come-out," Lady Sophia said, stirring her tea slowly. "She then ran off with the dashing Lieutenant Johnston and left many a broken heart after her—very noble ones, I might add. I always did have a soft spot for the chit. She was such a lively sprite."

"I'm glad to hear it," Ravenstoke said, testing his tea. "That will be the perfect story to put about when you present her to the *ton*."

The duchess's cup clicked sharply upon its saucer. "I beg your pardon?"

"I said that will be the perfect story—"

"I know that! But what do you mean, present her? Surely you jest."

"Indeed, no," Ravenstoke replied mildly. "I wish you to present Mary to the *ton* and see to it that she finds a suitable match. At my expense, of course."

"Why?"

"Why? Because Castleton will not."

"Alastair! What on earth have you done?" the alarmed duchess asked. "Never say you've ruined the girl. No, I absolutely refuse. I will not present your *chère amie*—"

"She is not my mistress." The duke's tone quelled Lady Sophia in midsentence. His eyes glittered dangerously. "She's a mere child, for all of her great age of twenty."

"Twenty! Lord, she certainly is no child," Lady Sophia said tartly. Ravenstoke's glance did not flicker. "Oh, very well. Do stop looking daggers at me, and for God's sake, explain yourself. You say she is Castleton's daughter and you found her in a tree. What in heaven's name was she doing in a tree?"

"She was looking for birds' nests, of course. She has a veritable fondness for birds, you see."

"Birds' nests!" The duchess's voice nearly cracked.

"Alastair, once and for all, do quit this teasing and tell me the truth. I swear my patience is at its end."

"Very well, she was in the tree in hopes that I would not discover her."

"Now that is more like it." The duchess nodded approvingly. "She is a lady of proper feelings after all."

"You wound me, dear. Of course, she was dressed as a scruffy boy at the time."

The duchess's cup smacked upon her saucer once again, this time with such force as to crack the fine china in two. The duchess slowly pushed her cup and shattered saucer onto the service tray. "Alastair," she said lowly, "if you do not tell me everything — and soon, you recalcitrant boy — I shall beat you with this cane. Don't think I won't!"

"Patience, Grandmama, patience, and I will enlighten you." Ravenstoke chuckled.

He proceeded to tell a captivated, if not scandalized duchess, the story of his meeting with Mary and all subsequent events, glossing over the details he thought unnecessary. "Come, Grandmama," he coaxed, as the duchess shook her head in astonishment. "You have often said how you wished for a granddaughter — now you have one. You can dress and coddle Mary to your heart's content. Confess it, dear, you have grown dull of late."

"Is it so noticeable?"

"Yes, dear," Ravenstoke said gently. "It will do you good to get involved with society again."

"So you went out of the way and plucked a girl from a tree expressly for my entertainment. How truly thoughtful of you."

"Then you will present her?"

"Perhaps . . . From the look of it, she will prove interesting."

93

"Do not vex yourself on that score." Humor leavened Ravenstoke's voice. "She will be presentable. She has a very neat figure."

The duchess quirked a suspicious brow. "Yes?"

He laughed. "My dear grandmama, do put such wicked thoughts behind you. It is nothing like that — only think on it! Even I would not treat the girl so shabbily after she saved me from the clutches of Lady Jane."

"I should certainly hope not," the duchess reproved. "If only for that, I will do what I can for the child. It sends me into proper shudders to even think of Jane Pelham as my granddaughter." She paused a moment, her eyes turning grave. "But, before I promise to help, I would like the true reason why you are doing this for the child. It is not like you to do such a thing . . . for a stranger."

"You mean, it is not like me to do such a thing at all," Ravenstoke said derisively.

"No, son," the duchess countered fiercely. "I did not mean that. With me you have always been wonderful. Always. But, you must admit, you do not worry overmuch about strangers."

Ravenstoke rose and stood before the fire. "I don't really know. Perhaps I have been bored of late as well." His lips twisted. "It can be very amusing to play God, don't you agree?"

"It can also be dangerous." The duchess studied him with worried eyes. "I fear this is folly, Alastair."

"Strange . . . that is what Mary said."

"I begin to have a fondness for the child. And pity, perhaps."

"Then you will present her?"

"Do I have a choice?" the duchess queried, her brow high. Ravenstoke merely smiled a slow smile in reply. "No, of course not. For you will do what you want regardless of what I say, so I might as well help you do it, rather than someone less qualified. The child seems to have enough trouble upon her plate without me casting a rub in the way. Though what else she can expect if she so forgets decorum as to dress up in boy's clothing, I couldn't say. Such foolishness! You are sure this Jameson person is out of the question?"

"Indubitably. He beats his dogs."

"I beg your pardon?"

"Let us just say that the squire is a tiresome individual with some . . . unhealthy traits. He covers his tracks well, but if one takes the time to look, one will find some very unsavory stories about the dear squire. Though not common knowledge, his wife died a rather sad death. . . . Mary has not yet figured out why Jameson wishes to marry her, but her fighting spirit is just the challenge a man like him desires. She ran when she could—her instincts were wise."

"And the old reprobate Castleton still plans to marry her off to such a creature?"

"Yes," Ravenstoke said, sitting down and stretching his long legs out before him. "But I believe he may be persuaded differently."

"Indeed," the duchess said, eyeing her grandson shrewdly. "I doubt not, if you have anything to say in the matter."

"Of course. I believe we shall be hearing from the man shortly. By the bye, Mary does not know she has silent bodyguards—I see no reason for her to. Just as she does not need to know I've met Squire Jameson."

"I see. Well, it appears you have everything and everyone under control—though your Mary sounds like she may yet kick over the traces if given half a chance."

"She won't. Her honor will bind her sufficiently."

"You truly are playing God, aren't you?" The duchess shook her head. "And I find that I must help you. The poor child cannot be tied to such a villain, and she certainly cannot become a governess. I've never heard anything so toddyheaded. But be warned, my son, the creator is often as bound by his creation as the other way around."

"Have no fear for me," her grandson replied, a sardonic glint in his eyes. "I am far, far too fickle to be bound by anything."

"You persist in ignoring your own true self, my boy. Well, we will see. . . . But first, we must attend to this poor child."

Mary opened her eyes to the morning light. She blinked, disoriented. The unfamiliar room around her was decorated in discrete, soothing blues and greys. Her eyes adjusted themselves, and then she started. In a winged back chair at the foot of the bed, a small lady, regal in purple silk, sat quietly, her hands resting calmly upon a cane. "So . . . you are awake?"

"Yes, ma'am," Mary said politely, masking her curiosity. "I do hope I haven't kept you waiting too long."

The apparition laughed and nodded her head in approval. "Plucky, aren't you? I'm sorry, my dear, I know I shouldn't, but I enjoy meeting people before their guard is up."

"You have succeeded in that, for I am never at my best in the morning." Mary smiled wryly, attempting to straighten her deshabille.

"Leave be, child. You look exactly as you

96

should—and your behaviour is exemplary. I'm surprised you haven't chucked your pillow at me yet. I'm Lady Sophia, dowager duchess of Denfield, by the bye."

Mary pulled herself up on her pillow. "Yes, I was beginning to suspicion that."

"Why was that?"

"Your love for the unconventional is very similar to your grandson's." Mary grinned, still a little sleepily.

"Oh, dear. I am never as bad as all that, I hope."

"No, no, I am sure you are not." Now that she was waking up, Mary found herself truly delighted with this woman. "I am very pleased to make your acquaintance, my lady."

"And I yours, child."

"Are you, my lady? I am sure my arrival could be nothing but a shock to you, and I do apologize. Especially since I was so ragmannered as to enter your house fast asleep."

"Lord, child, why should you apologize?" the duchess said, waving an imperious hand. "That was Alastair's doing. And no one, but no one, can stop Alastair once he has taken the bit between his teeth."

"Yes, he is rather . . . difficult to persuade," Mary observed.

"What a diplomat you are, my dear. He is positively overbearing and impossible." Lady Sophia studied Mary a moment. "You should never have played cards with Alastair, you know."

Mary started and flushed. "He told you?"

"Yes, he told me, as well as everything else. At least, I presume he did." Both ladies smiled in complete understanding. "He has been interfering odiously, I fear, which is not his usual style."

"I do not understand it myself," Mary admitted.

"Do you have any idea why he is doing this, my lady?"

"No," Lady Sophia said slowly, watching Mary closely. "But he did say it was from boredom."

"I figured as much. Why, oh, why, can he not find amusement elsewhere!"

"My dear, I assure you, he has tried amusements elsewhere. Too many, by far. Indeed, you must be considered the most innocent of his starts."

"I can imagine." Mary could not help but smile. Then she sighed. "Lord, what a coil he's put me in. My whole future hangs upon one man's boredom."

"I hate to repeat myself, but you should never have played that game with Alastair. That was your greatest mistake."

"My greatest mistake was ever coming down from that tree," Mary murmured to herself. "But, yes, I know that. Though up to that time, we seemed equally matched at cards."

"Really, then, you must have uncommon skill."

"So I had thought. . . . Even then, I would not have played, but the duke has a way of shortening one's options. Do you think he might weary of this diversion before much longer? Do say he will."

Lady Sophia looked at her oddly. "Most girls would be in alt over a season in London, with all expenses paid."

"I am not most girls."

"That is apparent. But in answer to your question: yes, Alastair bores easily, but no, I do not think he will lose interest in this case. He seems oddly resolute, in fact."

Mary sighed. "Then I am truly lost."

"Ah, yes, lost to parties and dissipation, what a frightful prospect," Lady Sophia nodded solemnly. "You mean to stand by the card game, then?"

"What else can I do? I am honour-bound."

"A sad defect in a woman when dealing with men. I suppose you are honest as well?" the duchess asked, disapprovingly.

"I'm afraid I am." Mary chuckled. "Another sad defect. Truly, I am totally beyond redemption. Why not tell Ravenstoke that you will not present me, for I'm unlikely to take anyway. Then I will manage it from there."

"But my dear, I do intend to present you," her ladyship apologized.

Mary looked astonished, then disappointed. "I had hoped you would not."

"Then you did depend on more than mere luck in the card game. I applaud you, my dear. Still, much as I admire your resources and gambling spirit, I must disappoint you. Alastair knew I would present you—you see, I have been terribly dull of late as well."

"Oh, no, not you too. A family trait, is it?"

"Yes . . . besides, you really could not become a governess. It is a thankless job, and quite below your station. And even if I turned you away, Alastair would only find another way to introduce you. The man is terribly inventive when he chooses."

"I have found that out, to my misfortune. But my lady, if you were to refuse him, it would take him time to discover another patron, and perhaps by that time, he might lose interest. He may weary of the opposition."

"More likely, it would goad him further," Lady Sophia returned.

"Are you sure you won't reconsider?"

"I'm becoming more and more positive by the minute," the duchess said, eyes sparkling. "I find you refreshing, child."

"I'm a shocking bluestocking, you know," Mary said quickly. "I even speak Latin."

"No, do you? How very enterprising. As long as you don't speak it to the gentlemen, I'm sure I don't mind. Why, I've even read a few books in my time and still avoided ostracism, if only by a step."

"I cannot sing," Mary said stoutly. "And have no ear for music."

"Excellent. Musical evenings bore me no end."

"I'm not beautiful. And quite a squab." Mary offered this as the clincher.

"Do you think so? I've had some experience with that myself—wait until Madame Cecile is finished with you. You'll be a pocket Venus, no doubt. Alastair says you will pass muster, and he is an excellent judge of these things—perhaps more so than he should be. True, one cannot call you a beauty, but you have a certain something—"

"Ah, yes, a cheerful disposition and amiability?"

"Good god, no! You are not insipid enough to fit that description, and I fear you are quite intractable, from what I hear. No, it is simply a certain something that draws one. And, of course, you have your mother's enchanting eyes."

"You knew my mother?"

"My dear, you will find that many knew your mother. It was a seven-day wonder when she ran off with your dashing father, rather than one of the dukes and earls who hung about. That was a grim settling day in the betting books, from what I've heard. Which delighted me no end, for I thought your father a very special man."

"He was that. And Mother . . . she did love him so much," Mary said, an odd tinge of regret in her voice.

"And that was bad?" the duchess asked gently.

100

"No, not bad. Never that. But I do not think I would like to love someone to such utter distraction. You would not have recognized Mother after Father's death. It totally destroyed her."

"I see. Then you are not in love with Alastair?"

Mary stilled. Her heart turned over, but she smiled at the duchess. "No, my lady. I would consider that to be certain folly."

"I'm glad," Lady Sophia said simply. "I love the boy dearly, but he does have a distressing habit of breaking our fair sex's hearts. I've often thought that if he truly loved . . ." Her voice trailed off, and she appeared to stare into nothingness. Then she clasped her hands tightly and said, brightly, "Oh, I don't know; I fear I am an old lady."

"Stuff and nonsense, my dear," Mary smiled. She hesitated a moment. "Might I ask what Lord Ravenstoke's mother was like?"

Lady Sophia seemed to jump slightly. Her brown eyes darkened. "How strange. Ravenstoke calls you a child."

"I am sure that to a man of his age and experience, I am. But in truth — no."

"I can see that. You ask questions far too pressing for that. Alastair's mother . . . she was a beautiful widgeon. No, that is too harsh — she was a butterfly. Always in need of attention and diversion. And my John, Alastair's father, I regret to say, was of a more serious and constant nature."

"What happened to them?"

"Only what one could expect," the duchess said tightly. "They fought tooth and nail, he taking her to task for her flirts, she complaining of his dull ways. Alastair didn't have a chance. He was shunted from school to school, for neither had time for a child who only wanted love."

"I see," Mary said, quietly. "I knew he rarely came home to visit—he said he spent the holidays with you."

"Yes. My husband and I tried to bring some sort of normalcy into his life. Do not misunderstand—Felicity loved Alastair as much as her flighty nature allowed. He, adoring her, always seemed to understand this. So it crushed him all the more when she finally left."

"She left?"

"Yes. She ran off with the Earl of Sedwick when Alastair was turned seven."

"My god." An inexplicable anger welled within Mary. "How awful for his lordship."

"Yes—and how awful for my son John," the duchess said sadly. "Like Alastair, he truly loved Felicity, but he was a man of pride and he never forgot her desertion. He became stern and reserved, and never married again. And Alastair is like you, my dear—he bears his mother's eyes. John had only to look into those green eyes and he would think of Felicity. Alastair could not do anything without John claiming he had Felicity's flighty nature or irresponsible personality. Every youthful exuberance was berated, every mistake lectured upon."

"Which only incited my lord to act more outrageously."

"Exactly." The duchess sighed. Both women shook their heads over the idiocy of men. "But all that should be in the past now—why can't Alastair lay his ghosts to rest? He no longer has anything to prove to his father."

"But he must still prove it to himself," Mary said gently. "What happened to his mother?"

"Felicity? Oh, she stayed with Sedwick fifteen years before the fever carried her away."

"Then she did remain faithful to the earl?"

The duchess looked stunned. "Why, yes, you could say that. Strange, I had never thought of it in that way. Hmm . . . Well, enough of the dusty past. It is the future we must attend to now. First we must turn you out in proper style. That brown dress I saw you in last night was an outrage. How are you feeling? Rested?"

"I'm fine," Mary assured the duchess. The old lady's eyes were crackling with excitement.

"Marvelous, child," the duchess said, rising briskly. "Then we will begin our foraging today. Meet me as soon as you are ready, my dear."

Mary closed the door to her room and headed towards the stairs. She found herself wanting to hum, and she smiled; despite her determination, she could not control the excitement budding in her. It was not even the new clothes as much as shopping with another woman that delighted her. She had missed that sort of female companionship since Manny had left. Mary walked down the steps in a daydream.

Suddenly she gripped the bannister, her step faltering. A slight gasp escaped her lips.

Her stepfather stood below, his angry purple face in counterpoint to his cherry red waistcoat. His hands flapped emphatically, and he spoke in high, enraged tones. Her gasp attracted his attention, and his eyes bulged at the sight of her.

"There you are, you ungrateful chit! Stap me if you aren't the most troublesome female. Wait till I get you home, you'll be sorry you put me through this." He galloped up the stairs, grabbed Mary, and shook her.

"Castleton!" Ravenstoke's voice sliced the air. "Unhand her!"

"Wh-wh-what?' Castleton's mouth fell open, and he swung confused eyes towards Ravenstoke. When they met the duke's rapier gaze, Castleton turned pale, his mouth snapping shut. He dropped Mary's arm as if he held a burning brand. "Uh . . . er . . . yes." His harried eyes swung to the duchess, who matched her grandson's glare. "I . . . I'm sorry, my lady . . . for such an outburst."

Mary's eyes flew to Ravenstoke. "So you brought him here after all?" she asked bleakly. He nodded. "If you wearied of the game, why couldn't you have let me go my own way?"

"See here, young miss," Castleton boomed, "how dare you speak to the duke that way?"

"Oh, she dares." Ravenstoke smiled, a dangerous edge to his voice. "She dares much, but often rashly. Your mistake, Mary. This is merely the opening play."

"Alastair! That is enough!" As Mary paled, the duchess pounded her cane upon the floor. Lady Sophia stamped up the steps and jabbed the cane into Castleton's ribs, getting a yelp of astonishment out of him. "You, sirrah, are a boor. I mislike your style immensely. Be pleased to control yourself while in my house, or I will have you tossed out on your ear with the greatest of pleasure. Come, Mary; we will leave the men to their discussion and be on our way."

Mary stood immobile, her eyes frozen upon Ravenstoke. "I'm sorry, my lady, but I would prefer to be present when I am disposed of between the two . . . gentlemen."

"You will never trust, will you, little Mary?" Ravenstoke's eyes were hooded. "You have a very wise stepdaughter, Castleton."

"Wise!" Castleton sputtered. "She's daft—touched in her upper works."

"No, merely stubborn beyond what is healthy. Come then, Mary. But you will not enjoy hearing what will be said, never doubt that."

"I did not expect otherwise," Mary said quietly, walking slowly down the stairs.

"Alastair!" the duchess said sternly. "Don't let the child hear this."

"I am not a child," Mary said as she stood before Ravenstoke. "And I prefer to be at my own sentencing."

"You are determined?" Ravenstoke asked.

"I'll but be listening at the door, otherwise."

"One never hears good of oneself that way."

"True, I never have—but at least one knows."

"Very well," Ravenstoke said coolly. "Come along."

"Alastair, don't!" Lady Sophia exclaimed. "You can spare the child this."

"I merely speculate, Grandmother. . . . Castleton, let us repair to the salon."

"Huh? What?" Castleton had been watching the three in bemusement, his mouth open like that of a fish upon land. "Oh—uh—certainly. Stap me if I know what this is all about, but no need to have the girl in, I'm sure."

"Ah, but she thinks there is a need." Ravenstoke bowed in irony. "This way."

A tense silence cloaked the room as the four entered the salon and took their seats. The duchess settled beside Mary upon the settee. Castleton plunged into the chair opposite. Ravenstoke remained standing.

"Here now, what's all this about?" Castleton

shifted in his chair, refusing to look at the ladies. "How did Mary come to be here? Your note explained damn little."

"By a . . . quite devious route," Ravenstoke said with a slight smile. "We need not discuss the matter. It is not your concern."

"What? My girl's doing ain't my concern?"

"Not anymore."

Here now. You go too far, Ravenstoke!"

"And will you stop me?" Castleton stared a moment, then his eyes fell to the floor. "Exactly. What is your concern is that my grandmother will present Mary to the *ton*."

Mary gasped and her eyes flew to Ravenstoke. He had not changed his plans! The duke bowed sardonically.

"Well, bless my soul." Castleton trained suspicious eyes upon Mary. "What's the little minx done to get you to do this?"

"I am doing this in memory of Julia Summerville," the duchess said haughtily.

"That explains it." Castleton nodded agreeably, and Mary smiled. Her stepfather gladly took things at face value when it benefitted him. Suddenly, his beaming face took on an arrested look, and he ran a finger around his cravat. "Ah. Well. Now that I think on it, I thank you for such kindness towards my little puss, but the thing is, she don't need a presentation. She's already betrothed."

"So I've heard," Lady Sophia said in bored accents. "To a Jameson person, I believe. He will not do."

"What?" Castleton stuttered, alarm suddenly stamped on his features. "You don't understand, my lady, the deed's done, all right and tight. Why he's — he's a fine man. Best I'll ever find the girl."

"Best *your* efforts will find." The duchess sniffed. "But I am presenting her now, and I will, indeed, find a more promising match than that!"

"You're bamming—er, roasting me. Why, the child's been on the shelf for an age."

"Thanks to your kind offices," the duchess said. "Rest assured, I will find her a more suitable match."

"You think you can?" Castleton sat up in his chair, enthralled. Then his face took on the same, alarmed look as before, as if he had eaten a sour lemon. He slumped back in his chair. "No, no. Nothing can be done. She's betrothed to Jameson, and she's gotta stay that way."

"You persist in believing you have a choice in the matter?" Ravenstoke asked silkily.

Castleton whitened; perspiration dribbled down his forehead. "You . . . you d-don't understand, Ravenstoke. The papers are already signed. I . . . I can't go back on my word. Surely you wouldn't want me to do that?"

"So now you are a man of honor?" The duke seemed amused. "Then you would certainly want what is best for your stepdaughter, wouldn't you?"

"But Jameson is the best." Mary's stepfather averted his eyes like a surly schoolboy caught in a misdeed.

"Is he?" Ravenstoke asked sharply. "Why?"

"Why?" Castleton repeated, nonplussed. "Why, because he—" He paused a moment, evidently unable to find a reason. "Well, he just is. That's why!"

"It couldn't be that you are in debt to him?" Ravenstoke asked.

Castleton swallowed convulsively. "How . . . how did you know?"

"I only assumed. Now I know. How much?"

"How . . . how much?"

"How much."

Castleton coughed. "Five hundred pounds."

"Five hundred pounds!" the duchess exclaimed, her face working. "For that you sold your daughter? Pah! You are a toad!"

"He was going to settle two thousand more on her—"

"Good gracious God!" The duchess rose angrily. "Alastair, settle this business. I am leaving before I squash that insect with my cane. Mary, do you come?"

Mary shook her head mutely, her face pale. The duchess sighed and raked both Ravenstoke and Castleton with a scathing eye. "Men!" she snorted, then left, a stiff, regal figure.

"What did I do to put her in such a pucker?" Castleton asked, bewildered. "Never does to have the womenfolk around for financial matters, my boy. They simply don't understand."

"Understand this, Castleton," Ravenstoke said curtly. "I will pay you the two thousand and five now."

Both stepfather and stepdaughter looked at him in surprise. "What?" Castleton gasped.

"I will give you the money on the condition that you pay Jameson directly and break the agreement. I will, furthermore, pay you a thousand if you will cease your gaming and wenching until Mary has contracted a match. You are to play the fond and loving stepfather during the season—and if you are smart you will not try and batten upon any of Mary's suitors until after the wedding."

"But the gal won't take, I tell you!"

"You will still be a thousand pounds heavier. I doubt that Jameson will make a felicitous son-in-law in any event."

108

"Don't I just know." Castleton sighed. "He's got a devilish mean way about him."

"Then we are agreed?"

" 'Pon rep, if I don't just think I'll take you up on it," Castleton exclaimed after a moment, brightening. "Yes, indeed, you've got yourself a deal. Jameson's been nothing but a curst millstone of late, anyway. I don't have the least notion why you'd want to help my Mary, but, as you say, that's none of my business."

Castleton sprang from his chair exuberantly. "Well, best be on my way. Gotta open my townhouse and see to old Jameson. Hmm, won't this just send him into the boughs, but it can't be helped. Well, Mary, you seem to have fallen into clover, though stab me if I know how. You're a very lucky girl, and don't you be giving the duke any difficulties now. You do whatever he wants you to do, do you hear?" Shaking hands with Ravenstoke, he strode from the room with a bounding stride.

Mary did not attempt to say goodbye; she sat quietly, gripping her hands together, trying to stop them from shaking. She refused to look at Ravenstoke.

"I warned you, you would not like to hear it."

Mary looked up at him, her eyes hard. "What, and miss the grand total of my worth? Never! I'd never have known I was worth as much as two thousand, five hundred pounds."

"Stop it, Mary."

"Oh, but I forget. We must add another thousand. Sold to the bored lord who lacks diversion! Only beware, my good lord." Mary rose from the settee to stand before Ravenstoke, eyes glistening. "The game you play becomes more and more expensive for you. I know how you hate to lose, but you have laid your blunt on the wrong horse this time."

"No, Mary," the duke said quietly. "I never lose."

"That's it, isn't it? You will see me married, no matter the consequences."

"No matter the consequences," he repeated in a strange voice.

Mary drew a shaky breath. "Very well. You have paid your money; I will do my level best to entertain. Bring on your fops, coxcombs, and simpletons, just as long as they are wealthy. For I will wed before the season is out, and pay you back every groat you've spent. Then, my lord, you and my stepfather can be damned." She spun on her heel and walked from the room.

"Wrong, sweet Mary." Ravenstoke stared into the fireplace, his face taut and closed. "I am already damned."

Chapter Six

MISS MARY CASTLETON—
THE TOAST OF THE TOWN

"Damn 'er—'pon rep, Duchess, it's a bloody marvel. If she don't begin to look more like her mother every day. How in blazes did you ever do it?"

Castleton, Lady Sophia, and Ravenstoke watched Mary whirl by upon a glittering dance floor. Her ill-cut crop of curls was now a burnished halo, beautifully arranged in the latest of fashion. Her skin was a pleasing cream color, her distressing tan a thing of the past. Nought but a few freckles still flirted upon her small nose, and a champagne silk clung to a small but delectable figure.

"Yes, isn't she beautiful," Lady Sophia said, pride lacing her voice as she laid her hand upon Ravenstoke's arm. "You were absolutely right, Alastair; she is taking the *ton* by storm."

"Stap me if I know how you managed it," Castleton said. "Why, she's behaving like a proper female for once! How'd you get her to do it?"

"Not by beating her," replied Ravenstoke coolly.

Castleton reddened, coughing. "Er, yes, well . . . I see that ain't the way to handle the gel—now. But, blister it, I was at my wits' end. She'd never given you the trouble she's given me."

"Indeed?" Ravenstoke asked.

Lady Sophia chuckled and rapped Ravenstoke upon the arm with her fan. "Alastair, do not tease so. You are certainly in a strange mood tonight—lud, you should be exuberant. What more could you want? The young men are smitten with our little Mary, and she not on the town a little over a sennight!"

"Expectin' offers any day now." Castleton nodded. He snatched a drink from a tray a servant carried by. "Well, now"—he sighed, taking a smacking sip from the glass—"guess I'll just take a peek in at the card room. Don't worry, Duchess; I said peek—wouldn't dream of playing. They play for mere pittances anyhow," he muttered under his breath as he strolled away.

Lady Sophia watched the man's retreat with narrowed eyes. "I do hope he does not ruin Mary's chances."

"He's caught a whiff of a good thing," Ravenstoke said, a twist to his lips. "He'll not destroy it. Faith, he may yet repair his fortunes during this period, so well has he behaved."

"Oh, look, she's dancing with young Sedberry," Lady Sophia said, pleased. "He's an excellent catch, you know, though I fear his flights of fancy might drive Mary to distraction. He writes such abominable poetry—calls her his summer rose. Quite unoriginal. I dare swear any other man would do the same."

"And does she quote Plato in return?"

"Hush," Lady Sophia said sternly, looking swiftly about her. "She's being wondrously circumspect about that, I am proud to say. Though I own I almost fall into whoops just watching her expressions when a subject of moment arises. They are truly a sight to behold, but the gentlemen don't seem to notice, thank

God. You should have been there when that fool Tarrington opened his budget upon the Corn Laws, which, you own, he doesn't understand in the least. Poor Mary lasted but a few strained minutes before she fled the room. She would have surely set him down otherwise."

"Yes," Ravenstoke drawled. "She presents the perfect picture of the vapid young miss."

"How can you say that, Alastair? After all, it was you who tutored her in the proper deportment."

"Another sin laid at my door." Ravenstoke watched Mary, his eyes unfathomable. She could be seen laughing up at a beanpole of a youth, who pushed her around the floor with far more vigour than grace. She had apparently flustered the lad, for he suddenly flushed bright red, trod upon her foot, and careened her into a nearby couple. Ravenstoke grimaced. "I'd best go rescue Mary before that clod ensures she will be unable to dance again for the whole of the season."

Lady Sophia sighed as she watched her grandchild weave his way through the crowd, his tall, easy figure a compelling magnet for the feminine eyes in the room. "Oh, yes, rescue Mary, by all means," the duchess whispered. "And throw that poor boy, as well as any other man here, into the shade in Mary's eyes." She cast her own eyes to heaven. "Lord, those two foolish children," she murmured; then she left to find Lady Garfield, a favorite crony of hers.

"Hello, Sedberry." Ravenstoke greeted the young man in his deep voice, just as Mary and her partner were leaving the dance floor. Sedberry, looking up at the older, sophisticated man, flushed, gulped, and murmured an incoherent response. His prominent Adam's apple bobbed alarmingly.

"Mary, my dear, I believe Grandmother is looking for you."

"Is she?" Mary asked brightly. She turned to Sedberry with what she hoped was a pleasant smile. "Thank you for the dance. I must go now." She grasped Ravenstoke's arm, grateful for its strength, and, attempting to hide it, leaned heavily upon her support as she walked away. "Thank you, my lord," she gasped, her voice filled with gratitude.

"Ah, my little summer rose, never say you wilt?" Ravenstoke teased as he eased her down onto a nearby chair.

"I'm no summer rose tonight." Mary smiled impishly, and Ravenstoke quirked a brow. "I'm an orchid tonight."

A pained expression crossed Ravenstoke's face. "No doubt in honor of your charming dress."

"With its charming neckline."

He laughed. "It is perfectly proper, as I assured you when we had it made up. Only look about you — there are dowagers with lower décolletage than yours, my dear. You would surely not wish to appear a country dowd, would you?"

"Heavens, no," Mary said, sweetly. "I am here to attract attention, am I not? I only hope that it leads to a decent offer of marriage and not a carte blanche."

Ravenstoke's eyes gleamed. "So this is the conversation that draws the young men like flies."

"No, you odious man." Mary could not help but smile. "That consists of 'Lud, you flatter me' and 'Yes, my lord' and 'No, my lord,' and 'How clever you are, my lord.' " Mary fluttered her lashes at Ravenstoke and then cast him a glance from under half-lidded eyes.

"Minx." Ravenstoke smiled. "You stun me with such scintillating conversation. But do watch that last look. It will only draw the incorrigible rakes, like me."

"Yes, my lord," Mary said. She widened her eyes

with dewy innocence. "Is this better?"

"Much." Ravenstoke nodded, grinning.

Mary flicked open her fan and raised it to her face, only her sapphire blue eyes peeking over. "La, my lord. Do not worry your brilliant, most awesome brain over me. I assure you, not an acid word trips from my tongue or a solitary idea from my lips."

"Excellent." Ravenstoke reached over and pulled the fan from her face. "But save the tricks I taught you for other men. I am odd enough to enjoy seeing the whole of a lady's face." He smiled suddenly. "Especially the lady's lips, when they purse in surprise as yours do now."

Mary, overset, took her fan, and cracked him upon his knuckles sharply. "Tut, tut, Mary. You are to rap the man lightly upon the hand, not break your fan."

Mary looked down at her fan in dismay. Its delicate sticks hung in two and telling red marked the duke's knuckles. "Oh, Lord, will I never get the knack of it?"

Ravenstoke chuckled. "Never mind, sweet Mary, you have done extremely well. Now, here is the supper dance. Let me but cross off young Graystoke's name from your card and we will dance. And then, my dear, you can whisper all the most shockingly erudite things you wish in my ear, and cast me all the level looks you could desire."

Mary stared at him; then she smiled slowly. An undeniable delight coursed through her at the thought, for only with Ravenstoke could she be herself and say what she wanted without drawing disapproval. "My lord," she said, her eyes sparkling, "I accept. You are far too tempting to resist."

"So I have been told." He lifted her to her feet; Mary groaned, and shifted quickly off the foot that Sedberry had danced upon for most of the night. "Come along, little Grandmother," Ravenstoke murmured in her ear.

She shook with silent laughter as she felt his arm direct her—but suddenly she froze, fear coursing through her. Squire Jameson was advancing towards them, his hawk eyes trained unwaveringly upon them.

"What is it?" the duke asked as she stiffened.

"Squire Jameson," Mary said softly, trying to control the quiver in her voice.

"Yes, so it would seem," Ravenstoke said, as he, too, spotted the squire. "I would have thought the Suffolks much more discerning in whom they invited to these affairs. They shouldn't allow such riffraff in, don't you think?"

Mary drew a steadying breath at Ravenstoke's calmness. She chuckled, then, and, squaring her shoulders, consciously loosened her death grip on the duke's arm.

"Excellent," he said. "Take your fences flying. It's the only way."

"Good evening, Mary." Jameson greeted her with a wide smile as he came to stand before them. He performed a courtly leg and reached for Mary's hand to kiss. Mary, her face calm but her heart beating, held her hand back, as if she did not see him reach for it. His eyes darkened, but he only smiled. "It is a true pleasure to see you once again, dear lady."

"Is it?" Mary's insides seemed to jell.

An ugly look entered Jameson's eyes. "But of course, my dear. I was utterly shocked when your father told me that my suit was unwelcome. Believe me, dearest lady, the last thing I would ever have wanted was to cause you the slightest embarrassment. Had Castleton but told me, I would not have pressed my hand."

"Indeed?" Mary said, her chin up. Her insides tightened even more to hear the man lie with such smoothness.

"Certainly," Jameson nodded. "I would never wish to cause you pain at any time."

"I am glad to hear it." Mary turned to leave.

"To prove you forgive me," Jameson said quickly, "may this humble servant be allowed this dance?"

"I am sorry, Squire," Mary said frigidly. "I am promised to my Lord Ravenstoke."

A discomforting flicker passed through Jameson's eyes and he turned them toward Ravenstoke. "Ah, yes, Ravenstoke. I am sure you would not mind giving me this one dance with the lady?"

"Sorry, old man, but I would," Ravenstoke said blandly. "I had the devil's own time getting close to the elusive lady myself."

A muscle twitched in Jameson's cheek. "I only hope so. Strange, Ravenstoke, you told me you didn't know Mary the last time I saw you. In fact, I am positive you said you had never met her."

"I hadn't." Ravenstoke smiled, his eyes laughing. "Only imagine my surprise to discover her residing safely here with grandmother when I arrived in London. Faith, how was I to know that she was a favorite of hers?"

"Indeed," Jameson said, eyes narrowing. "It is . . . uncommon . . . how things turned out."

"Yes." Ravenstoke smiled again. "But then you've heard of my infamous good luck, haven't you, Jameson?"

"We'll just see about that?" the squire said darkly. "Don't think I won't get to the bottom of this all, Ravenstoke. Things are too smokey by far, but don't think I won't see through it. And then, my interfering lord—"

"And then what?"

"We'll see who wins the hunt," Jameson said angrily, his hands clenching.

117

"The dance is beginning," Mary said tensely before Ravenstoke could answer. "I am sure you will excuse us, Squire." She stepped between the men, blocking their glares, and pulled at Ravenstoke. "Come, my lord."

"Certainly, my dear. I am yours to command." He put his hand over hers in a slow, obvious movement, and nodded sardonically to the angry squire. "You will excuse me, Jameson, but the lady does demand."

Mary maintained a silence until they were upon the dance floor. "Enjoying yourself, my lord?" she asked as he swung her about in a waltz.

He looked down at her through lidded eyes. "Of course. Mary, did you not find it diverting?"

"No, I did not," Mary said angrily. "But then, I was only the bone in the fight, wasn't I? Next time do leave me out of it when you choose to bait him."

"You ruin sport, my dear." The duke smiled coolly. "If you had just given me a moment more, I am sure I could have insulted the squire enough to bring him to action. Surely you would have enjoyed a duel fought over you?"

"A duel?" Mary said scornfully. "I cannot picture you duelling over me."

"Can't you, my dear?" He pulled her imperceptibly closer. "Tsk, Mary, surely you've heard what a fine duellist I am?"

"They say you wound your quarry wherever you wish."

Ravenstoke shrugged. "Death seems so very heavy-handed. Pinking them suffices."

"I am sure," Mary said, looking away from him.

"Oh, cheer up, Mary. Things could go differently, perhaps. Think how your troubles would be over if either Jameson or I were to accidentally put a period to the other's existence. It would be one less pestilent male on the face of the earth to plague you."

Mary stumbled. Ravenstoke held her to him a moment; then he righted her, twirling her about. Her breath caught in her throat. She remained silent, though her mind wanted to scream for him never to dare jest about his life like that. She looked up at his face, but his eyes told nothing. "Why didn't you tell me you'd met the squire?"

"It was a fatiguing conversation. I saw no reason to repeat it."

"I see," Mary said, her voice shallow.

"Do you?" There was a bitter smile on the duke's lips. "But of course, you know so much about men, don't you?"

"I am learning, my lord."

"And so fast, my dear. Why, I know of three men who are sure to propose to you before the fortnight is out."

"Only three?" Mary asked, feigning lightness. "I thought it would be more. After all, you have turned me out in such a style and lent me such prominence, surely there should be a score or more."

"My dear, does your conceit know no bounds?"

"Why should it? Faith, I am no longer a bluestocking or a country quiz. I neither say the wrong things nor act the wrong way." Mary's anger suddenly drained into weariness. "In fact, I have become a perfect ornament of society, wouldn't you say?"

Ravenstoke scanned her face, and spoke more gently. "Of course, my dear. And you shall marry and live happily ever after, just as all good girls do."

"And what of you?" Mary asked softly, her eyes foolishly stinging.

"Me?" Ravenstoke quizzed, with only the slightest hint of mockery. "Why, after you have righteously thrown my foul money back in my face, as you have sworn to do, I will go to perdition—as all bad boys do."

Mary smiled a small, sad smile. "What a charming life we two have to look forward to."

Ravenstoke did not reply. He merely held her closer. They danced in silence. Mary closed her eyes, blocking every thought from her mind, the duke's arms about her the only reality.

The music's strains drifted to an end. Sighing, Mary opened her eyes reluctantly. She and Ravenstoke walked from the floor, each holding onto the silent moment and the words not spoken.

Mary froze then, and a hysterical giggle rose to her lips. "Oh, no, not again. And before dinner, too!"

Lady Jane stood not four feet away. She seemed in a daze, her eyes fixed upon Mary in disbelief. "You!" she exclaimed dramatically. The glass she held dropped and shattered upon the floor, and the lady walked towards Mary and Ravenstoke in a perfect Lady Macbeth trance. "It is you!"

She, Mary thought wryly, certainly knows how to create a scene. She shook herself mentally; she'd not let Jane Pelham get the best of them in this encounter. Pinning a blank expression upon her face, she asked in pretty confusion, "I beg your pardon? My Lord Ravenstoke, is this a friend of yours?"

"This is Lady Jane Pelham, my dear," Ravenstoke said smoothly. He bowed. "Lady Jane, may I introduce you to Miss Castleton?"

"How do you do?" Mary smiled, curtsying to the gaping Lady Jane. "A pleasure to meet you." Lady Jane, her mouth working, said nothing. Mary cast Ravenstoke a delicate look, suggesting she feared for the woman's sanity. Then she turned gentle, concerned eyes back to Lady Jane. "Excuse me, my lady, but is something amiss?"

"But . . . but you're him! Aren't you?" A shaking finger pointed at Mary.

"Him who?" Mary widened her eyes and cast Ravenstoke another look, one that clearly said she thought Lady Jane unhinged.

"Yes, him who?" Ravenstoke repeated, his tone expressing nothing but irritation. He then lowered his voice. "What game are you playing, Lady Jane? I swear, if this is a ruse to embarrass Miss Castleton, I'll have your head. Do not bring her into our little disagreement."

"Me? Ruse?" Lady Jane sputtered, an unbecoming flush spreading down to her daring décolletage. "But it's him—isn't it?"

"Dammit! Him who?"

"My lord," Mary said blankly, "who is she talking about?"

"I don't know," the duke replied, patting Mary on the shoulder bracingly. "Enlighten us, Lady Jane, or stop this nonsense. You are frightening poor Miss Castleton with your queer behaviour."

Lady Jane could only stare in the faces expressing bafflement. She looked wildly about her to see people raising quizzing glasses and disdainful eyebrows in her direction, and she faltered. "I . . . I am sorry. I seem to have . . . made a mistake. Do . . . do you perhaps have a brother?"

"A brother?" Mary frowned. "No . . . Oh, that is what this is about. You think I look like someone else?"

"Yes, that is it," Lady Jane said quickly, happy for an escape. "That is it—it was all a silly mistake."

"I quite understand," Mary said, though she made her smile weak. She looked around at the curious faces and turned beseeching eyes to Ravenstoke. "My lord, everyone is staring so," she whispered, pitching it so it carried. "I begin to have the headache."

"Certainly, my dear." Ravenstoke's tone was all sympathy. He levelled an accusing look at the blushing Jane Pelham. "Excuse me, Lady Jane, but Miss Castleton suffers from delicate sensibilities. Come now, Miss Castleton." He turned his back upon Jane and put a supporting arm around Mary's shoulders. Mary accepted his support, adding a feebleness to her walk.

They reached the foyer door and Ravenstoke ordered the carriage while solicitously placing Mary's wrap about her shoulders. "One moment," he murmured into her ear. "I must tell Grandmother. Go ahead to the carriage; I will join you in the nonce."

Mary nodded acknowledgement and walked swiftly to the carriage. She climbed in and closed the door, grateful for the refuge, trembling in aftershock. Lord, what a dreadful night! She laid her head back up on the squabs and closed her eyes, shutting out the twin confrontations.

The door opened and she sat up quickly. Ravenstoke climbed in. "It is only I," he assured her. There was a basket between his hands.

Mary's eyes widened. "What is that, my lord?"

"Why, dinner. I knew you despaired of having any."

Mary simply stared at him, then broke out in peals of laughter. "Oh, lud, you are the most astounding man!" She was brushing tears from her eyes. "You think of everything, absolutely everything."

"Of course, my dear. It never pays to miss details. Whereas any other lady would be wanting her smelling salts at this time, I knew you would prefer your supper."

"Indeed!" Mary said. "I know Lady Suffolk lays a wondrous spread." She stifled a giggle and put a hand to her aching ribs, then smiled contritely. "We were very cruel to Lady Jane, weren't we?"

"No, we were simply superb." Ravenstoke pulled a bottle from the basket and signalled for the driver to set the carriage in motion.

"Did you see her face when you accused her of a ruse? You were absolutely heartless."

"Me? And how about that masterful little look of yours when she accused you? Lord, you made her look like a crazy fresh from Bedlam." With a smile, the duke poured Mary a glass of champagne.

"No, I think you still topped it when you out-and-out told her to stop her queer behaviour before she frightened me." Mary took the glass he proffered. "My, we have all the elegancies."

"Certainly. A toast," he said, raising his own glass, "to the lady with the steadiest nerves and best acting abilities I have ever had the pleasure to behold."

Mary flushed. "Steady? I was positive I would faint. Only the horrible thought of what you might do if I swooned to the floor kept me standing upright. In fact, part of me was just dying for Lady Jane to faint as she looked to, for I would gladly have followed."

Ravenstoke laughed deeply. "You're fortunate you didn't. I would have killed you if you'd left me with the two of you cluttering the floor."

"Oh no," Mary said without thought. "I am sure you are quite accustomed to ladies swooning away dead at your feet."

Ravenstoke fell silent; even in the darkness, she could feel his eyes upon her. She took a quick drink and said, "What is the first course, my lord?"

"Very wise, little one," he replied, almost tenderly.

Mary blushed, glad of the cover of darkness. His voice sent warm trembles circuiting up her spine where cold chills had been before. She took another quick sip from her glass.

"We have lobster pâté and other dainties for my

lady," Ravenstoke said, offering her some. She reached forward, only to spill her drink.

"Oh dear — now I shall smell of champagne."

"Far better than semlling of ale; indeed, the French would consider it a perfume. But it's quite ill mannered to reach for your food — allow me." He shifted to the cushion beside her. She, silent, took another sip.

"Now, let us see if we cannot satisfy your appetite." Mary did not know why, but she blushed. "You will feel better after you have eaten."

"Yes . . . I hope so," she said weakly.

They settled down to eat in companionable silence. Mary drank more champagne than she knew was wise; but the dark was a comforting blanket, and the warm strength of the large body beside her was lulling. She could feel her tension draining away. Ravenstoke opened the shade, and silver moonlight spilled into the carriage. Mary finished her last bite of chicken and, looking out, asked in curiosity. "My lord, we have not arrived home yet. Where are we?"

"In the park. I thought you'd best finish your repast before you arrived upon your doorstep."

Mary chuckled. "No, it would not do to enter the house gnawing upon a chicken bone. Only consider what Adams might think." She reached her hand into the pool of moonlight upon her lap and said in musing tones, "Strange . . . I have always found moonlight one of the loveliest things."

"While I have been a creature of the night for far too long," Ravenstoke responded, "I have begun to admire the dawn of late."

"Indeed, my lord," Mary murmured, laying her head back against the cushions. "I take the dawn for granted."

"Which is as it should be. I hope you always will."

"And I hope you will begin to love the moonlight

again," Mary yawned, her head finding a comfortable place upon the duke's shoulder. "You really should, you know, dark angel. Moonlight and you go together."

The body next to her tensed. "Dark angel?"

"Hmmm?"

"You called me a dark angel—of course. For a brief moment, I'd quite forgotten . . . how fortunate you reminded me. It is time for us to go home."

"Must we?"

"Yes, we must."

"But I don't want to." Mary sighed, closing her eyes again. "Wouldn't it be lovely if we could ride in the park forever. To have no Squire Jameson . . . no Lady Jane . . ."

"Yes, my dear . . . it would." His voice seemed to be coming to her through a pleasing mist. She heard a warm chuckle and felt a comforting arm wrap about her. It seemed there was a kiss upon her hair and a murmured "Rest, sweet Mary . . ." She smiled to herself. What a pleasant dream it was!

The lulling rocking of the carriage stopped, and she was held closer as strong arms lifted her up. Mary forced groggy eyes open as the night air hit her. Ravenstoke was carrying her up the steps to the duchess's townhouse.

"My lord. . . ?" she said, sleepily. "You may set me down now."

"Why? I am quite accustomed to it now, child."

"I am not a child," she said sternly.

"I know." He gently set her down, supporting her with a steady arm. "You more than proved that tonight. Still, it is best that I call you so."

Mary swayed and put tiny hands to his chest for support. She frowned at him, her blue eyes inquiring. "Definitely best," he repeated to himself. "Now, run along to your bed." His hands encircled her waist and gently turned her towards the door. He gave her a slight push. "Go."

Mary walked up the stairs, feeling suddenly wide awake, and strangely bereft. She turned at the door and looked down at the silent duke. Moonlight shone upon his raven hair and seemed to glitter in his eyes. "My lord?"

"Hush. Not a word, Mary."

"I . . . I only wanted to express my gratitude." Her voice quavered unaccountably.

"Yes, I feared that is what you would say," he replied coolly. "Well, I don't want your gratitude. Always remember that. Now take those wounded eyes away and run to your bed. At least you are still safe there." He bowed stiffly, and was gone.

"To what do I owe the honor of this visit, sir?" Jane Pelham asked politely of the man who sat across from her.

"It is in regard to an interest we both share, my lady." Squire Jameson eased back into his chair with a smile.

"We share a common interest? I find it difficult to credit, since we hardly know each other."

"Let me rephrase myself. Rather let me say, it is acquaintances of ours in whom we share a common interest."

"Indeed?" Lady Jane's eyes narrowed. "Do tell."

"Perhaps we should discuss this matter in private." He nodded toward the small, quiet companion sitting across the room.

Lady Jane laughed. "But we are in private. Do not mind Margaret — she knows far better than to discuss my business."

Jameson studied the silent woman, and a pleased

grin formed on his thick lips. She had the dulled eyes of an animal caught too long in a trap; it was a look he knew well, and always took pleasure in. "Yes . . . just so. I have come here in regards to Lord Ravenstoke."

"Yes?"

"And his tedious interest in little Miss Castleton."

"Go on."

"It appeared, last evening, that Miss Castleton gave you quite a start. Had you seen her somewhere before?"

Lady Jane flushed. "What is your interest in the matter? If you have come for gossip, I assure you, you will gain none."

"I do not ask in idle curiosity—may I speak plainly?"

"Please do. I find this roundaboutation boring."

"Then let me liven it up for you." Jameson smiled. "As I understand it, you would like the Duke of Denfield for a husband. I, in turn, would like Mary Castleton as a wife."

"So I have heard—indeed, I'd heard you were affianced. Yet here she is, doing the season and obviously hanging out for a husband."

"Just as Lord Ravenstoke is still unfettered and dancing attendance on Miss Castleton, not you," Jameson replied smoothly.

"I believe, Squire," his companion said stiffly, "that this discussion is becoming too dull to continue."

"In another moment you will not find it so." Jameson's face became grim. "As I said, I find the duke's protection of Miss Castleton cumbersome. I cannot imagine that you find it any more pleasing—"

"Miss Castleton is not a threat to me!" Lady Jane snapped.

"Do not be too sure, my lady. Do you know that when Ravenstoke is not in attendance on her, she has her own personal bodyguards—employed by him? Does that sound like disinterest?"

Lady Jane gnawed her lower lip with perfect white teeth. "Proceed."

"I fear, my lady, that Miss Castleton has duped society."

"Why do you say that?"

"Because I know the date she left her stepfather's home, and there is more than two weeks unaccounted for between that date and her appearance in London. Where was she? Had you perhaps seen her during that time? You reacted last night as if you had."

"I . . . I mistook her for another," Lady Jane said guardedly.

"Who? It might help."

"I doubt it," she said dryly. "I mistook her for Ravenstoke's young cousin, who stayed with him a while ago. A boy."

Jameson sat bolt upright. "Damn his rotting eyes!"

"Sir, your language! Surely you don't think—"

"Yes, I do. Mary was Ravenstoke's cousin! That's why she disappeared beyond my finding. We weren't looking for a boy!"

Lady Jane sat frozen, her eyes glittering with feral anger. "Why, the bitch! The jade! Acting as if butter wouldn't melt in her mouth last night, and all the while making me the laughingstock of the *ton*. She's doubly interfered with me! I'll make her pay in turn, see if I don't. When I'm through with her, not a hostess will receive the little tart!"

"No," Jameson said curtly. "That will not help you."

"Why not? You're not suggesting I just let the little trollop parade about town?"

"I'm suggesting we use our heads! It's too dangerous to attempt exposing her. She has Ravenstoke's patronage—and that of the Dowager Duchess of Denfield.

They may very well be able to brazen it out, as they did last night, and where would that leave you? Worse still, if perchance we did succeed, we might only force Ravenstoke to marry her to avoid a scandal."

"Ravenstoke forced by convention?" Lady Jane laughed snidely. "That will be the day."

"Don't be foolish. For some reason he is taking care of the girl, and watching out for her good name."

"You're not suggesting he has a *tendre* for that little bland squab, are you?"

"I don't know what he has, and I don't care. But I do know he will not have Mary if we play our cards right."

"What do you mean?"

"It's very simple, my dear." Jameson smiled, slowly and cruelly. "We merely remove Mary Castleton from Ravenstoke's care. Once she is gone, I feel sure you can console the duke."

Lady Jane smiled. "Yes . . . I am sure I can. There won't be any mistakes next time."

"Precisely. And I promise you, I will take care of little Miss Castleton." Their eyes met, and they both began to laugh.

Mary sat in solitary splendour within the breakfast room that same morning, having arisen much later than the rest of the household. Adams appeared and inquired what she desired to eat; he allowed a shade of disapproval to show when she asked for only tea and toast. For some reason, that oh-so-correct butler had taken Mary under his wing, making her his own personal responsibility.

Mary stared into space as Adams left. Her head pounded, and her stomach felt terribly hollow. This she could manage, but the gnawing pain within her heart was far harder to ignore. She wished she could blame that, too, on the champagne, but she knew better. It was a pair of green eyes in the moonlight that caused this illness.

Deep in contemplation, she sipped gratefully at the tea Adams brought. When he returned abruptly, she started.

"Excuse me, Miss Castleton. My Lord Sedberry wishes to have words with you."

"Does he?" Mary's heart sank even further. She did not feel up to the enthusiastic youth that morning. "Where is the duchess?"

"She is out, Miss. I took the liberty of informing Lord Sedberry of the fact, but he said he must speak with you nonetheless. He appeared greatly agitated."

"Oh, no. He must have written another ode." When the grand muse struck him, Lord Sedberry was wont to rush immediately to Mary to offer her his creation, no matter the hour or the day.

"I fear it must be an epic, miss. He appears more agitated than customary for him."

Mary's brows rose. "Where is he now, Adams?"

"In the hall, miss."

"Heavens, and he still did not take the hint?"

"No, Miss Castleton, I am sorry to say."

"There is nothing for it, then," Mary sighed. "I will have to see him, lest he moon outside the townhouse again." Sedberry was not above pacing wildly outside the house if turned away, quite scaring the passing horses and pedestrians with his energetic manner. Mary rose in resignation and walked into the hall.

"Miss Castleton! Dear Miss Castleton!" Lord Sedberry gasped, springing from his chair and sending it screeching across the marble floor. He rushed to her and grabbed her hands dramatically. "I must speak to you before my heart bursts!"

"Certainly that would never do," Mary said soothingly. "Do let us adjourn to the library."

"Oh, thank you, Miss Castleton," he exclaimed as they entered that room. "I knew you would not be so cruel as to turn me away, sweet angel of mercy."

Mary bit back a smile and sat down. "Now, my lord, what has you in such a state? Have you written another verse?"

"No, it is far greater than that, far greater, Miss Castleton." His voice rose to a squeak and he coughed, reddening. "Miss Castleton, I can no longer withhold my — my deep emotions!" He stumbled forward and lunged down on one bony knee.

Mary looked down at her wobbling admirer in astonishment. "My lord, do please get up. That is not necessar —" She froze in midsentence and sniffed suspiciously.

The ardent Sedberry seized the moment and grasped her unresisting hands. Mary sniffed again, too intent on the smell to notice. It was smoke, smoke from a cheroot. And there was only one who dared to smoke in the duchess's house.

She scanned the room piercingly, until she came to the curtained French doors leading to the veranda. They stood slightly ajar, and a sinuous coil of smoke snaked its way in. "Most definitely get up!" Mary said quickly. "Do not say any more."

"Please do not deny me, Miss Castleton, my fair torment. You are all that I dream of, live for, breathe in —"

"Yes, indeed, but please do get up!" Mary was sure the curtain had moved.

"My dear . . . I love you!"

"I am sure," Mary said distractedly, "but will you now rise?"

"I cannot rise until you are mine! I cannot survive without you! Marry me!"

"What?"

"Please, Miss Castleton, make me the happiest man alive; only say that you will be mine!" His eyes shone with puppylike devotion.

"No—no. I am sorry, sir, you have taken me by surprise—I am deeply honored, but no, I fear I must refuse you. Now please rise!"

"Do not cast me off so quickly!" Sedberry jerked her aching hands to his bony chest, clutching them even tighter. "I see that I have frightened you with my bold announcement. How clumsy of me, my tender love. Never fear, I will wait—give you more time."

"I do not need time," Mary said quietly, struggling to reclaim her hands. "I am sorry, my lord, but I fear we will not suit."

"There is another?"

"Another?" Her eyes unwillingly flew to the French doors. They seemed to be inching open ever so slightly "No, indeed, there is no other. Now will you please rise?"

"But how can you refuse me, when my heart burns for you? I cannot eat for love of you, I cannot sleep or think, I grow faint from longing—"

"My lord . . ." Mary didn't know whether to laugh or cry. "Please lower your voice." She beckoned him closer; he leaned over at an alarming angle, eager for her words, which were delivered almost in a whisper. "I have said I am deeply honored and I am. But I am sincere when I say we shall not suit. Now, my lord, let us not hear another word on that head."

Mary stood with determination and motioned Sedberry to rise, feeling rather like a bishop with a congregation. Her gallant's face fell, and he beat his chest with a groan. "Miss Castleton, fair fatality, do not do this!" He snatched up the skirt of her dress and kissed the hem madly, so frantically he looked very

132

much like a chicken pecking at grain. "See, I abase myself, I am at your feet. Have mercy upon me — do not destroy my heart, my soul!"

"My lord, do get up this instant!" Mary said sternly, finally losing all patience. She twitched her skirts from his grasp.

In the throes of passion, Lord Sedberry did not release the material in time. He toppled over with a squawk, his elbows smashing the floor resoundingly.

Mary flushed, totally embarrassed for the boy. "Dear sir, please, please do not do this." She bent and assisted him to his feet, then half-dragged him towards the door. "I . . . truly do not deserve such devotion, my lord. I will . . . will always remember you with fondness and gratitude."

Sedberry stood, bewildered, at the door, and finally bowed dejectedly. "I . . . I am forced to accept your refusal, then. I shall never love another."

"That would be a shame. You will break the hearts of many other ladies if that be so."

"Other ladies?"

"Yes, indeed." Mary nodded. "Don't think I haven't seen the languishing looks they send your way."

"They do?"

"Why, yes. If you settled down so fast, you'd cut up all their hopes."

Lord Sedberry looked at her in astonishment, but slowly his eyes became more starry and his chest puffed up. "Well, now . . . perhaps you are right. Yes, perhaps you are right." He bowed absently and, straightening his shoulders, walked away, practicing a Don Juan attitude.

Mary smiled slightly, shaking her head. The smile slid from her face as she closed the door, and she walked quietly over to the French doors. "You can come out now, my lord. He is gone."

Ravenstoke, a saturnine expression on his face, stepped out from behind the doors, cheroot still in hand. "I thought you had tumbled to my presence. Especially when you started whispering to young Sedberry for no apparent reason. It was the smoke that gave me away, wasn't it?" He threw the cheroot out the door. Mary sat down, and he sauntered over to sit across from her.

"I rarely mistake the odor," she said. "And only you smoke in this house."

The duke smiled in amusement at Mary's clipped tones. "Displeased? I did not intend to be a third party. Your poetic admirer was well in full blast before I could make myself known. Besides, you of all people can hardly rake me over the coals for eavesdropping."

"I knew you would say that!"

"You were quite correct, eavesdropping can be diverting. Though young Sedberry was far too dramatic for my taste. And he never could quite decide whether you were the cruelest woman on earth or the sweetest — he made you sound rather like a terrible disease, in my estimation."

"Stop it!" Mary rose from her chair angrily. "You should never have witnessed that poor boy's proposal."

"Or your refusal? Sedberry is well situated from what I hear . . . yet you turned him down."

Mary turned her back on him and walked to the window. "He is a mere boy. I will not rob the cradle." She refused to meet Ravenstoke's eyes.

"He is only three years younger than you."

"Yes, and he deserves some young, impressionable thing who will fly into raptures over his poetry and think him the center of the universe," Mary said fiercely.

"And for that you turned him down? How utterly

mawkish!"

"No." Mary turned around, lifting her chin. She wouldn't — couldn't — allow him to taunt her anymore. "I turned him down because I am sure I can snag much larger game. After all, I really should make the most of your — and the duchess's — effort, don't you think? Faith, I am the toast of the town; why should I accept the very first proposal when I shall receive better offers, and from men I find more alluring?"

Ravenstoke's jaw tightened, but he said, lightly, "Heavens, it seems I have created a monster."

"Oh, no, my lord. You have only created a woman in the image of your likeness. A woman that should marry a man, grateful to him for his money and protection, only too glad to become his chattel, to become one more trinket thrown on his stockpile of possessions."

"My god, such bitterness!" Ravenstoke said roughly. "And for what? Because I have given you what any normal girl would dream of?"

"Ah, yes, here it comes! I am not normal; I am strange!" Mary said angrily, hurt welling up inside her. "Well, I am strange. I don't want what you've given me. I don't like what you have forced me to become."

"What is that? A woman?"

"No, I am that. God forgive me, I'm just not the woman you decree I should be, happy to live under some man's rule."

"Rule? You could have married Sedberry, for God's sake! He certainly would not have ruled you — you could have held the reins!"

"And made his life miserable. What enviable choices you offer me."

"I offer you life, real, ordinary life," Ravenstoke snapped. "Not some make-believe fairy tale. Don't run away — face up to the truth! I offer you what most women would kill for, so spare me your tragic airs and don't be such a little fool."

"Perhaps I am a fool. But I should be allowed my folly."

He laughed harshly. "Stubborn to the end. No, Mary, you won't ever be normal. That's an impossibility."

Mary's face whitened, her expression showing the depth of the wound he'd inflicted. "And still you will foist me off on some unsuspecting man?"

"If it is the last thing I do."

"Do so, and I will hate you for the rest of my life," Mary said softly. "And I will hate myself, as well."

"No. Someday, when you are settled with your children about you and a loving husband by your side, you'll thank me."

"No, my lord, I will never be that comfortable." Scorn dripped from her voice. "Do not deceive yourself. I will hate you, my lord, I will surely hate you." She curtsied deeply enough to honor royalty and walked slowly from the room. Ravenstoke did not call her back.

Chapter Seven

FOUL DOINGS

Wilson entered his master's chambers to prepare the duke's clothes for the evening. He stopped in the doorway, in surprise.

The dim shadows cloaked a solitary figure lounging before the fireplace. A bottle sat on the table beside the man. The tip of a cheroot glowed red in the dark.

Wilson sighed. The duke had not been in such a condition since his return from the country. Wilson was not pleased it had happened now. Lord Ravenstoke never became ape-drunk like other men, he only became dangerous. "My lord?"

"Wilson? What is it?"

"You said you wished to attend the Rathford ball this evening."

"Did I?"

"Yes, my lord."

"Prepare my clothes, then."

"You . . . still wish to attend, my lord?" Wilson pitied anyone who dared cross his master's path tonight.

"Of course. I must be present to watch my protégé

capture hearts she has no use for."

"My lord?"

"I called her a fool, Wilson," the duke said, as his man crossed to the wardrobe. "I am the larger one, though. Grandmother was right, you see."

"Indeed, my lord?"

"Indeed." Ravenstoke laughed harshly. "Never play god, Wilson. It's a thankless job and one comes to — to care too damn much."

Wilson looked at his master in concern. What demons drove his lordship now? He cleared his throat. "My lord, we must hurry if we are to turn you out in proper style."

"Certainly we must appear in proper style," Ravenstoke murmured ironically. "Always in proper style."

Mary's fingers clutched the chicken-skin fan she held. The duchess stood in amiable conversation across the room, and people flirted and gossiped between them. Forcing her eyes away from the dance floor where a tall, loose-limbed Ravenstoke now trained glittering green eyes upon a blushing debutante, Mary stood tensely.

The duke had arrived late at the ball, sauntering into the room, resplendent in black. Even at a distance, Mary could feel a dangerous energy emanating from him. Like a panther on the prowl, she thought.

He had not approached her once. Instead, he had partnered the most beautiful ladies in the room, be they debutantes or matrons.

"The man is an absolute devil tonight, Lucille."

Mary jumped, for the words echoed her very thoughts. She turned slightly to see the speaker. Two patrons stood a distance away, their bright eyes trained upon the dance floor. "It appears my Lord Ravenstoke is once again back in form," the speaker was saying.

"Lud, but he is beautiful," her companion breathed. "It appears the little Miss Castleton has loosed the reins on him."

"My dear, surely you never thought she held them, did you? The duke was merely lending his support to the dowager duchess's presentation of the girl. Lady Sophia said so herself. And you know she may call on her grandson for whatever she wants."

"A lucky woman—I dare say the only one who has ever been able to claim that. Well, I thank her for bringing him back to these functions. Why, we haven't seen him at a ball in years. And now here he is, setting the *ton* on its ear again. There will be fear in more than one fond mama's breast tonight."

"They say he is between *chère amies* at the moment."

The second woman laughed. "He won't be for long."

They drifted away, and Mary could hear no more. Then she discovered Sir Percival mincing across the floor toward her, a glass of lemonade held out before him—apparently to avoid spilling it on his chartreuse ensemble. Mary stifled a sigh, then turned on her heel. She walked swiftly to the balcony doors and out into the quiet night. She couldn't face the lisping fop as yet.

The alcove was silent as she sped down the stairs and into the garden, wishing to escape the conversation that now ran round and round in her head. She found a stone bench beside a picturesque fountain, and sat down with a tiny sigh.

"Oh, Mith Cathleton," a nasal voice shrilled out. "Yoohoo, where are you?" Heels clicked upon the pathway, and Sir Percival, glass still out before him, tripped out from amongst the shadows. "Naughty Mith Cathleton. You had but to thay you withed freth air and I would have obliged. Your lemonade, madame." He flourished it, handed it to her, and sat down beside her.

"Thank you, sir. I feared I was about to be overcome by the heat."

"No exthplanation required, my dear," her companion smirked. "I underthtand. I, too, found the crowd unbearable when I only wanted to be alone with you." He laid one beringed hand possessively upon her arm.

Mary rose swiftly as Sir Percival sidled closer. "Sir, I fear you mistake the situation."

"No need to be coy, dear heart." He sprang up and rushed over to her, then wrapped his bony arms around her waist.

"Sir, watch what you are about!" Mary held the endangered lemonade in one hand while fending off the amorous fop with the other. "Stop it this instant—you misunderstand."

"My dear, I fully underthtand. Little butterc— Oof!" Mary's small fist had slammed into his chest. "You . . . you are divine, thweet goddeth."

"Let me go, this instant."

"Ah, your eyeth, they are jewelth." He pulled her close and clamped his wet lips to hers.

Mary let out a muffled protest and hit him upon the shoulder with her free hand. When that proved futile, she slowly raised the lemonade glass and poured it over the unsuspecting gentleman's head.

Sir Percival's closed eyes flew open, and he yelped and flung Mary away. "What? What?" Sticky lemonade trickled over his coiffure and onto his shirt points.

"I'm sorry, Sir Percival," Mary said sweetly. "I spilt the lemonade when you took me so much by surprise."

"My new jacket!" exclaimed Sir Percival, turning purple. "You've ruined my new jacket!"

"Do let me help you—"

"No! Thtay away! Do not come near, I mutht thave my jacket, I mutht thave my jacket." He turned away and fled, his heels clicking in retreat.

Mary stood a minute in amazement, then chuckled. The sound of applause from behind made her stop abruptly and spin around.

Ravenstoke stepped from behind the bushes. "Excellent, Mary. You routed him with such inventiveness."

"How long have you been here?"

"From the beginning of the act, of course. Grandmother sent me word the minute she saw you leave the ballroom. Didn't she warn you not to wander off by yourself?"

"Yes, and now I know why. I still do not think it warranted such odious behaviour from Sir Percival."

"You did not enjoy the kiss?"

"No. I do not enjoy being importuned or mauled." Disgust laced Mary's cool voice.

"He was rather inept," Ravenstoke agreed, an unfamiliar note in his voice. He stepped closer and took the empty glass from Mary's hand. "First of all, one must always be sure that the lady holds nothing dangerous in her hands." He threw the glass into the bushes.

Mary looked at him in surprise, and stepped back warily. "My lord, what do you think you are doing?"

"Doing?" Ravenstoke smiled and followed her move. "Teaching you, of course. You seem to draw the most incompetent suitors; I can't depend on

141

them to teach you anything."

"I have learned everything I need to know," Mary said stiffly.

"No, Mary. You've only learned the wrong things. For example, an experienced man wouldn't pounce on you or grab you like a sack of grain." He placed his hands upon her arms and slid them gently upwards until they rested on her shoulders. His thumbs caressed the hollow of her neck.

"My lord, you are drunk," Mary protested as he drew her nearer.

"Hush, Mary." His voice was like liquid silver as his arms enfolded her. "You're interrupting the lesson. Now, a man is a fool if he holds you in his arms and calls you a buttercup or a sweet goddess. For you are not." His lips brushed lightly upon her hair. "You are a witch caught in her own spell of innocence." His mouth sought hers, and Mary closed her eyes against the glitter in his.

She was wrapped in a world of only Ravenstoke, his arms, his scent, his lips. Mary shuddered as strange, warm tremors radiated through her, and she reached, desperately, for every moment in his arms. She stretched, molding herself to him, marvelling at every sinew of his form. Her senses whirled as a warm, glowing ache filled her.

Suddenly, she was torn from the warmth. She stood, shivering in the night air as Ravenstoke pulled away and held her at arm's length, his fingers digging into her shoulders.

"You take well to instruction." His eyes were lidded.

"How could I not, with you as my teacher." Mary managed to say it calmly, though she felt the earth was shaking beneath her.

"Touché, my dear." Ravenstoke bowed. "But one

cannot teach passion like yours. That must come from within."

"You are foxed, my lord—and I believe I have had enough education on the ways of men for one night. I will return to the ballroom now." Mary brushed past him, heading down the path.

"Mary." The duke's voice stopped her. "Drunk I may be, but I still suggest you not display that side to any other man than your husband. You could drive a man crazy."

"Only an intoxicated man, I am sure. But never fear—I have learned enough. It will not happen again. Good night, my lord."

Mary sighed. She was tired of the endless social rounds. Soiree faded into drum, drum into rout, and rout into the interminable ball, all deathly boring. All missing the presence of Ravenstoke.

Mary waved her fan against the heat of the room. Castleton was glowering at her from the opposite wall, evidently displeased that she sat the dance out. She did not care; she was glad she had sent Randall, one of her many young admirers, after a glass of punch. It gave her a respite.

At least tonight, the duchess was not present, she'd been laid low by a migraine. Mary did not have to act happy, or avoid Lady Sophia's discerning gaze. It had been three weeks since the Rathford ball, three weeks since she had seen Ravenstoke. She had not asked the duchess about him, and Lady Sophia seemed tactful enough not to raise the issue. What the duke might have told his grandmother, Mary did not know.

Mary's fan-waving faltered. Jane Pelham was approaching, punch glass in hand.

"My dear Miss Castleton. Here is your punch. Randall was detained, and I assured him I would be delighted to deliver it for him."

"How kind of you," Mary said calmly, and took the glass. She sipped the drink, wishing it were stronger, for Lady Jane was sitting down beside her. The woman seemed bent on friendship, and Mary's nerves rang out a warning.

"I just knew you would be dying of thirst. It's so wickedly hot in here, isn't it? A pity the punch is so dreadful — I could only handle one glass." Sipping the bitter liquid, Mary nodded agreement. "I was pleased to bring it, though, for I wished to apologize for my odd behaviour upon our first meeting. You must have thought me insane." Jane Pelham's smile did not reach her eyes.

"No, my lady. Not after I realized that you mistook me for another. I'm sure all of us have made that sort of mistake at some time. Though I own I have never been mistaken for a boy before."

"I'm sure you haven't." Lady Jane trilled a sharp laugh. "Why, it is quite clear you take the men's breath away. They swarm around you like bees."

"You flatter me, I'm sure." Waiting for the woman's next words, Mary sipped her punch.

"It seems you have Ravenstoke under your spell."

Mary winced internally. "I'm certain you jest. The duke is merely aiding his grandmother; surely you know, he is not the man to be caught by any one female."

"Indeed . . . and where is the dear duke tonight?"

"I am sure I do not know," Mary said quietly, blinking. A wave of fatigue seemed to wash over her, and she took a deep, refreshing drink.

"Oh? Perhaps you were right. Lord Ravenstoke is not to be caught by you after — my dear Miss Castle-

144

ton, you look pale. Is something the matter?"

"It is . . . only the heat, I am sure."

"I see. Perhaps some fresh air will help you. I know just how you feel—do let me assist you."

"No thank you." Lady Jane's air of excitement disturbed Mary in some way. She arose, only to wobble on her feet. "I . . . I am sure I can manage by myself."

"But, my dear, you look positively hagged. Here, let me help you."

"I . . . I am fine, thank you."

"My dear, you are ill." Lady Jane took hold of Mary's arm, directing her firmly toward the garden door. "Fresh air will revive you."

"I believe I would rather go to Stepfather," Mary said shakily. She could not understand what was the matter . . . or why Lady Jane's aid worried her. Was she going crazy?

"No. He is nowhere in sight. Isn't that just like men?"

"I . . . do not wish to go into the garden," Mary said, as firmly as possible, as Lady Jane steered her towards the door.

"Now, now. You will feel much better with some air. See, you are trembling."

"But I don't—"

"You there!" Lady Jane called to a passing footman. "This lady is faint. Help us."

The footman stopped in obvious surprise, but rushed to aid them. Somehow his presence soothed Mary's fears, and she allowed them to lead her out into the night air.

The cool evening did clear her senses for a second. "Thank you," she smiled numbly at the footman.

"Fetch the lady some smelling salts," Lady Jane commanded.

"No!" Mary said before the footman could leave. "I am sure . . . I will be much better in a moment."

"Fetch them now," Lady Jane said.

The footman stood in obvious indecision. Feeling foolish, Mary smiled. "Perhaps a glass of water will help."

"Certainly, miss." He bowed and left. Mary watched him go with an odd regret — what was the matter with her? She yawned and shook her head in confusion.

"Here, drink this." Lady Jane lifted Mary's punch to her lips. "It should help."

Mary drank obediently, then looked up from her glass. Her heart froze as she caught the glitter in Lady Jane's eyes. "Th-thank you." She walked slowly over to the stone wall surrounding the terrace and leaned against it for support. "What was . . . in it?"

"Ah, very smart, Miss Castleton. Only laudanum. I'd have preferred poison myself."

"Why? The laudanum, I mean. I could understand the poison."

"My God, you are a cool one. . . . The laudanum is Jameson's idea. I doubt you'll be so cool after he gets done with you."

"Jameson . . . You are in league with him?"

"Of course. You and Ravenstoke managed to fool me. It took the squire to connect certain . . . events. You'll be sorry you ever interfered with my plans."

"I . . . believe I will." Mary could spy two dark figures standing in the shadows. "Your men are here on time — I presume they are not the gardeners?"

"They are Jameson's. Here to escort you. I do hope you do not intend to make a scene, or things will go worse for you."

"Of course not." Mary managed to smile as she walked up to the other woman. "I wouldn't dream of interfering with you again, but . . . I would like to say this." She lashed out and delivered a ringing slap to the woman's face. "I do not like your style, Jane Pelham."

Lady Jane reeled back, stifling a screech, her hand clasped protectively to her face. "You bitch!" She lowered her hand and saw the blood on it. "You scratched me!"

"My . . . ring . . . I suppose," Mary said, blinking. Two rough hands latched onto her arms. "I only wished to even matters up."

"Why, you trollop! I'll teach you to slap me!"

"For the love of God, lady!" one of the men growled. "We ain't got all day for you morts to fight. Someone might come. Let's get out of here, Mike." The two men dragged Mary backwards.

As she relaxed into the men's arms, Mary laughed at Lady Jane's astonished face. "Pity, they are much smarter than you. . . . I'd like to stay and talk, but . . . I fear I cannot. . . ."

Castleton's face darkened as Lady Jane entered the ballroom without Mary. "Blast and damn the chit!" He headed for the door in irritation. The girl had acted strangely all night, first sitting out dances, now staying outside while Lord Darlford, who commanded thirty thousand pounds per annum, looked for her for the next dance.

He stormed onto the terrace and looked about in confusion; Mary was nowhere in sight. He cursed again and headed down the path, rehearsing the trimming he planned to give the girl.

The path lengthened and darkened. "Mary? Where the hell are you?"

A muffled noise drifted back to him. "What d'you

say? Can't hear you."

Suddenly, an obvious male voice yelped as if in pain. "What the devil?" Castleton cursed.

"Help!" Mary's voice.

"Mary?" He charged through the bushes; the path only grew darker and silence settled over him. He thought he heard a rustle from behind, and spun around. "Mary?" Nothing. Backing up cautiously, his eyes peering into the darkness, his legs hit stone, and with a curse, he toppled backward. A splash followed.

Castleton surfaced from a decorative fish pond, sputtering. Dragging himself from the water, he stood one minute in contemplation. "Damn, don't like it. Best get Ravenstoke."

The footman at that exclusive club, White's, showed obvious surprise as a sodden Castleton clambered down from his carriage and charged up the steps. "Make way!" Castleton bellowed to the staring servant, and sloshed past him. "Important business."

"Here, gov, you can't go in there like that!"

"Dammit, ain't got the time to waste, I tell you. Let go my arm."

"Ye can't go in like—"

"Ravenstoke's here, isn't he?"

"Yes, but—"

"Then I got to see him." Castleton nodded and brushed the footman away.

"Jake, grab the bloke!" the footman yelled as he narrowly missed grasping Castleton's dripping coattails.

Heavy feet thudded, and a man of imposing build thumped into sight. His bovine expression changed as he saw Castleton dripping on the best carpet, and he charged. Castleton dodged the heavy body, galloped past lounging club members, and strode into the card room.

"Ravenstoke!" Out of breath, he leaned against the wall, just inside the door. "The chit's—gone!"

All heads turned in the room, no matter how deep the play. A murmur arose as the members saw the wild-eyed, soggy intruder. The two footmen appeared at that moment and, with snarled threats, dragged Castleton out of the room.

"Castleton's in his cups again," one lazy dandy murmured. "Your turn, Chancellor."

"The man's queer in the attic, if you ask me," Chancellor said, studying his cards.

"Damn, a man can't even find a quiet game of cards in his own club anymore," another player grumbled.

The five men sitting at the back table with the Duke of Denfield kept their eyes on their cards. "I raise you a thousand," Tyndale said with a drawl. "That is, if you wish to ignore the man, Alastair."

"No, Jonas, I fear I must be excused. Castleton is no doubt in his altitudes, but curiosity compels me, nonetheless."

"Excellent," Andover smiled. "My hand was useless anyway. Do find out what that lunatic wanted."

"Something about a chit," Tyndale said, eyeing Ravenstoke as he rose from the table and bowed to them gracefully. "Farewell, Alastair."

"Gentlemen." Ravenstoke smiled politely and exited.

The duke's face showed nothing as he wove his way through the tables and into the deserted hallway. There were shouts from the front steps, and he followed them.

Three men lay in a muddled heap at the bottom of

149

the steps. Groans and curses arose from the mass. "Damn," Castleton bellowed, "ye've broke my leg!"

Ravenstoke strode down the stairs, bent over, and with startling ease rolled the footmen away from Castleton. "What's this about, Castleton?"

The squire bent to nurse his injured leg. "Someone's got Mary."

"Explain yourself." The duke's voice was suddenly chilling.

"I said, someone's got Mary. Abducted her from the Sewells' ball."

"How?"

"How? Damn it, man, I don't know. The foolish chit had to go wandering out in the gardens again."

Ravenstoke's eyes were green fire. "She went out by herself?"

"Well, no — at least she wasn't as silly as that. She and that Lady Jane got to gossiping —"

"Lady Jane. Pelham?"

"That's what I said. They got to gossiping, and then the two went out the balcony doors. Mary was acting queer."

"Queer?"

"She was quiet all evening and kept sitting the dances out. Then she and the Pelham chit got to talking and soon after Lady Jane had to help Mary out the door, it seemed."

"Then what happened?"

"The lady came back, but Mary didn't. So I went to find her. I thought she was going off by herself like she always does. I walked through the gardens to find her — and when I called her, I heard a man shout instead."

"A man?"

"Never was more flabbergasted. Then I heard Mary yell for help. I ran after her, but never found

150

her. I came here as fast as I could."

Ravenstoke stared off into space. "If she's harmed her, I'll kill her."

"She who?" Castleton asked in bewilderment. "Kill who?"

Ravenstoke stood up swiftly, his face dark and thunderous. The footmen, who had sat, listening to the dialogue, now backed away in fear. "Are you coming, Castleton?"

"Coming where, blast it?" He started to rise, then fell back to the ground, swearing. "Stap me — my confounded leg!"

"Damn. I must leave you here, then." The duke's eyes raked the two footmen. "You two fools help this man — and I'd better not hear a word of this mentioned, or I'll have your posts, do you hear?"

"Yes, m-my lord."

"N-never, my lord. It . . . it was all a mistake."

"See that you do not make another one." He left the three men staring at his dark, departing form.

Lady Jane started when she looked up and found Ravenstoke bowing before her, his tall form towering over her other admirers. A frisson of apprehension passed through her, until she looked into his eyes. There was nothing there to see except admiration. "My Lady Jane." He took her hand and bent over it.

"My Lord Ravenstoke, what are you doing here? I had heard that you were not attending tonight."

"Did you? One must never listen to gossip, especially rumors in conjunction with me. May I have a word with you, my lady, away from all these admirers?"

"Here now, Alastair. You can't just waltz in here and steal the lady away," one of Lady Jane's admirers protested.

She drew a breath. "What do you wish to discuss?"

"A matter we have discussed before, but one I have never seen reason upon previously."

"Indeed, my lord." Lady Jane flushed with the thrill of success. "By all means, let us discuss it. I hope you will excuse me, gentlemen . . . ?"

"My lady, you're not going to let Ravenstoke commandeer you like this?"

"Oh yes, I will." She laughed and rose swiftly, to walk with Ravenstoke from the group. "So you have seen reason, my lord? I am intrigued."

"I thought you would be," the duke smiled, taking her arm. "I feel that we need a more private setting for this . . . discussion."

"You are naughty tonight? Where is your conscience?" Lady Jane laughed again, in delight.

"That is what I do not know. I thought I might enlist your aid in finding it." He smiled down at her.

"There is a private room this way. . . ."

"I knew I could count upon you."

"Isn't that what I have been telling you?" They slipped into an anteroom, and she sat down gracefully on the settee, then patted the seat beside her invitingly.

For a silent moment, her pulse raced; then Ravenstoke sat down next to her and took up both her hands. Looking steadily into her eyes, he said, slowly, "I want to know where Miss Castleton is."

Lady Jane felt as if she'd been doused with cold water. "What?" She tried to pull her hands away, but Ravenstoke's grip tightened until it hurt. "Let me go, Alastair, you are hurting me!"

"I will do worse if you do not tell me what happened to Miss Castleton."

"You . . . you asked me in here to talk about another woman? You tricked me in here, playing upon all my hopes, merely to ask me where that little daub is?"

"Forget the dramatics, Jane." His smile chilled her to the bone. "Just tell me where Miss Castleton is."

"I don't know—how should I?"

"You were the last one at the ball to see her. You escorted her out to the balcony."

Her ladyship paled. "How . . . ? I did not see you there."

"Castleton told me. He also told me that when you returned, Mary did not. Why was that?"

"I don't know! She said she wanted to be alone for a while! She . . . she wasn't feeling well and wanted to rest quietly. Perhaps she went home then . . ."

Ravenstoke studied her intensely. He raised one hand to the scratch on her cheek. "You have a scratch, Jane."

"I . . . scratched it this morning. On a branch, while riding."

"In the park?"

"Yes, in the park."

"It does not seem to be that old." He sighed. His hand slid to her neck, his thumb covering the pulse point. "I think it is time for plain speaking. I do not believe you. Now tell me where Miss Castleton is, or I will choke it out of you."

"You wouldn't dare!" But though his hand did not increase its pressure, she quaked inside. His eyes glowed with a wild, green light, too wild for safety.

"I wouldn't doubt it if I were you. You've courted my power and position, and I will gladly show you its full extent. Tell me, did you never stop to ask yourself why I have a reputation?"

"I don't know!"

153

"I grow impatient, Jane."

"I mean . . . I only delivered her to Squire Jameson's men on the balcony." The hand on her neck remained tight; she was beginning to gasp. "Ravenstoke!"

He shook himself and withdrew his hand from her neck. "You gave her to Jameson." His voice and manner were deathly calm. "My God, I should kill you."

"She . . . she was betrothed to him, after all."

"What a vindictive cat you are, Jane. Why did you do it? Wasn't it enough that you sent your boys with the slingshots?"

"Ah, but you see, that was meant for your cousin!" Jane snapped, unable to control herself. "This was meant for Mary Castleton, who deceived us all and acted like a proper miss when all along she was your—"

"Say it and you'll regret it."

"Very well," Lady Jane replied, realizing she had almost made a terrible misstep. "I suppose you're going to tell me you plan to marry her?"

"Marry her? No. . . . You see, Mary is much finer than either you or I will ever be—and people like us can only hurt her. The cream of the jest is that if you had not sent your boys to harm her, I would never have brought her to London for the season." Lady Jane burned in frustration at his words. "Now, where is Jameson taking her?"

"To a run-down house of his, not far from town." The game was up, and she realized she didn't like dealing with this new, dangerous Ravenstoke. "You'll be too late to help her."

"You'd better pray that I'm not, for your sake," the duke said in silky tones. He rose to leave and turned at the door. "I suggest you convince your parents to take you to the continent; I wouldn't like to be you if I see your face in town during the next few months. Do I make myself clear?"

Lady Jane looked into his merciless eyes and nodded, her face paling. She understood all too clearly.

Chapter Eight

CHIVALRY TO A HIGH DEGREE

Two men sat huddled over a small fire in a stable, morosely swilling blue ruin from a communal bottle.

"Queer mort," the weasel-faced thinner man observed, scratching the scruff about his neck. " 'Twas mighty queer, wouldn't ye say, Jake?"

"Stow it, Eb," his beefy, taciturn companion growled, grabbing the bottle for a noisy gulp.

"Mighty queer if ye ask me." Eb shook his shaggy blond hair as he gazed into the anemic blaze. "Cool as a cucumber the mort, but 'gads, didn't she come one over t' a other, turned right scrappin'."

"I said shut yer gaff!"

The two men sat in sullen silence until Eb ventured to ask, "What ye suppose she meant about a dark angel comin' fer her?"

An ugly expression descended upon Jake's face. "She was daffy, ye lummox! Doped! She didn't mean nothing. Now, stubble it!"

"Might be she's a witch."

"Ah, fer God's sake muffle it, or I'll make ye." Jake unconsciously clutched his bandaged left hand closer. "I don't want to hear no more about the daff mort."

"Gore, I'd never thought ta see a gentry mort fight like that — an' she just a mite of a thing. Don't know, Jake, that queer talk about a dark angel comin' fer her gives me creepin' feelin's."

"Stow it ye bloody looby, there ain't no such thing as a dark angel —"

"I would not be too sure of that, my common friend," a cool voice murmured quietly. A large caped shadow danced across the wall, flickering with the flames.

Eb jumped in his tattered coat and cut his lip with the bottle he was just lifting to his mouth. He turned quickly to discover a tall, imposing gentleman standing before them, green cat's eyes a-glitter. "Holy Mother of God!"

Jake was made of sterner stuff. "What the hell do ye want?" he growled, and lumbered to his feet, legs spread apart in defiant belligerence.

"I want the lady you gentlemen so kindly escorted here."

"We don't know what yer talkin' about, do we, Eb?"

"But of course you do," the gentleman returned urbanely. "And I'd advise you to tell me where she can presently be found."

"Tell him Jake!" Fear mingled with awe upon Eb's weasel-face.

"Shut up, ye bleedin' idiot, no man's goin' to tell Jake Sumter what to do!" Clenching hamlike fists together, Jake plunged wildly at the caped man. Eb swallowed and winced painfully as the stranger calmly met the raging ruffian with two stunning blows that sent him spiralling to the ground, all consciousness lost. Eb, looking up from his fallen crony, wheezed and gurgled. He found himself staring into the end of a healthy-looking duelling pistol trained, with a deadly precision, upon him.

"What about you?" the stranger said with unnerving calm. "Do you choose to tell me the lady's whereabouts or must I convince you as well?"

"Not me, guv! No need to go aimin' that popper at me," Eb stammered, his hands creeping up in open surrender. "I'll tell ye. The master's got her in the house, but ye best hurry—she's doped up, ye see."

"I see." The man's voice had turned deadly.

"N-now take it easy, guv. 'Tweren't my notion, nohow. I'll just be slippin' ye in the house quiet like—that's my real lay, see. I didn't hold with this business, so do ye think ye might see yer way to pointin' that barkin' iron elsewhere?"

This gained a slight smile from the stranger. "Perhaps . . . Now, let's go. First, tie your partner up."

"Right, guv. That's the barber. No flies on you." Eb's look grew speculative, and he grinned slowly. "Well, hang me if you ain't him."

"Him who?"

"Her dark angel. She said you'd be comin'."

"Nothing would have stopped me."

"I reckon you're right." Eb's expression was almost comical as he looked at his gagged, insensible partner. "And if ye don't mind me sayin', yer lady ain't no angel herself, so we'd best be hoppin' before the master tangles with her. He ain't a good man, he ain't."

"My exact thoughts. If he values his life he had better not have harmed her, for it would cause me immense pleasure to send him straight to hell."

"I reckon so—by the bye, guv, me name's Eb."

"Eb?"

"Short for Ebacaneezer. Me mum was a fanciful sort."

"Indeed," the man said, smiling. "And I'm Ravenstoke."

"Gore, Rake Ravenstoke? The Dook?" Eb asked. Astoundingly, he doubled over in laugher. "Blimey, don't that beat all hallow! And that nodcock Jake said there wasn't no such thing as a dark angel."

Mary opened groggy, sleep-laden eyes. There was a dimness all about, except for a faint glow to her left. She turned her head slightly, wincing, and found herself lying on a musty settee in front of an unfamiliar fireplace. Focussing her will, she pushed herself up into a sitting position. She shivered and blinked, urgently trying to marshall her dispersed thoughts.

Her chin was tender, and she rubbed it; a henchman had struck her there after she'd bitten him. Compelling herself to stand, she stumbled to the fireplace, desperately seeking its heat. A wave of dizziness assailed her and she gripped the mantelpiece.

"So you're awake?" a familiar and hated voice said.

Still clinging to the mantelpiece, Mary turned in distaste; Squire Jameson stood in the doorway. Laughing, he swaggered into the room in evident triumph. "You've been asleep much longer than I expected; but then, I heard you were a naughty girl and gave Jake a difficult time. I knew you'd put up a good fight—God, I can't wait to bed you."

All pretense of civility was stripped from the man, and he watched Mary with a strange lust in his eyes. Her stomach turned as the reason she'd always

159

dreaded the squire hit her in full force; here was a man whose passions fed upon fear and brutality.

She attempted to mask her revulsion, and said with a tenuous calm, "Perhaps you can tell my why you brought me here?"

"Why I brought you here? Don't play the fool, sweet Mary, you know full well why I brought you here. It was the only way I could get near my beloved fiancée."

"I'm not your fiancée," Mary said, shaking her head as if to rid herself of a bad dream. "Not anymore."

"Yes, you are. Just because your mighty Lord Ravenstoke bought your father off doesn't mean he bought me off. I have chosen you for my wife and I will have you. I've waited damn long enough and tolerated as much interference as I am going to accept."

"But why? Why want me when I don't wish to marry you?"

"Why? My dear, you hold your charms far too lightly. You are a rare one—a very rare one. I've watched you for a long time. Always distant and cool, you're headstrong with a will of your own. You've managed to elude and control your stupid stepfather long enough. He's no match for you. But I am. You're no namby-pamby weakling. Not like my first wife. The snivelling bitch died on me after only two years, and before she'd given me children."

"She died of pneumonia," Mary said in bewilderment, remembering how the villagers had shaken their heads over the death of the gentle, quiet woman who had been Jameson's bride. "You could hardly say it was her fault."

Jameson laughed derisively. "Pneumonia! That's rich!"

Fear seeped into Mary. "She didn't die of pneumonia? Wh-what did she die of?"

"The bitch killed herself!" Jameson's face twisted with rage. "Wrote some puling little note saying as how she couldn't stand her life with me anymore. But you're not like her, are you, Mary? You're made of sterner mettle. You'd not take the cowardly way out, not you—you'd fight and fight and still bear me children."

"I . . . I don't know, I might have done the same as she. I . . . I am not as strong as you think."

"Ha, there you go, trying to gammon me again. Don't you know you can't—and do you know why you can't? Because I know you, Mary Castleton. You think nobody will ever possess you. But I will. You think nobody will ever control you. But I will!" Jameson stepped closer, his breathing heavy and fast. "No matter how long it takes, I will own you."

"It would take a lifetime," Mary said slowly backing away.

"God, I can only hope so."

"You'll never force me to marry you. Ravenstoke will stop you before that."

"My, what trust you put in that man. But Ravenstoke will be of no help. He's prolonged the chase, I admit, and has proven a worthy opponent. It took no little work to slip past the guards he'd set on you, else you'd have been mine already. But I've succeeded at last, and I'll have you wed to me before he ever catches wind of it. Though my people tell me that he hasn't been sniffing around you of late, it almost makes me fear that those little strategies of Lady Pelham and myself were all for naught. What happened? Did you and your lover have a falling out? Don't worry, darling Mary, I'll help you forget him. I shall satisfy your every desire."

161

"Go hang yourself," Mary retorted, before her mind could restrain her drugged tongue.

Jameson looked stunned, and then his face darkened. He grasped her shoulders cruelly. "By God, I'll make you take that back!"

"But not now," Mary gasped, fighting the pain. "I feel sick — not a proper challenge for you."

Jameson chuckled and jerked her closer. "Always the sly one. Playing your tricks on me, aren't you?" He lowered his head to kiss her.

Mary twisted her mouth away. "I swear I feel sick . . . it is the laudanum."

"What's the matter?" Jameson shook her hard. "You've had Ravenstoke, but won't have me?"

"I've . . . had no one — and I'll have no one!"

"You'll have me!"

Jameson clutched roughly at Mary's bodice. She flailed at him, and her bodice tore in his grasp. She reeled backwards, desperately seeking a weapon; her hand contacted porcelain on the mantel, and she threw a small statuette at Jameson. He dodged it, laughing.

"Come on, little hellcat." He murmured it like a caress. "Come on, fight me!"

Mary backed away, horrified as sheer passion flared in Jameson's eyes. She had only inflamed him all the more. A cold determination entered her; she tensed and, in a flash, lunged for the fire iron. Jameson lurched forward and grasped her wrist crushing it until she dropped the iron. He slammed her to him, then bent her ruthlessly backwards, his thick lips seeking hers.

"Jameson — that's enough."

The squire stiffened, raising his head like a viper balked of its prey. Mary sagged in relief. She knew that voice, every pitch and timbre of it.

162

Jameson all but snarled and, as he swung round, shoved Mary in front of him as a shield. It proved a wise move, for Ravenstoke stood in the doorway, pistol in hand. "What are you doing here?" Jameson spat.

"I am here to escort Miss Castleton home, of course."

"Stay out of this, Ravenstoke. She's my fiancée."

"You still choose to think that? The lady refused your unappealing offer and so did her stepfather."

"Only because you paid him off! Don't think I didn't get that out of him. She must be one hell of a toss for you to have gone through all the trouble. But she's mine now, and I'm damn tired of you." Jameson snaked one arm about Mary's neck while pinning her right arm behind her back. Mary stifled her gasp of pain. "Now get out of my way, or I'll choke her to death right here."

"Don't be more of a fool than you have to be, Jameson," Ravenstoke said quietly. "I'd regret the inconvenience of killing you."

"You won't kill me. Not with the chance of shooting your precious Mary instead. Now, let us pass." He shoved Mary forward, bearing down harshly upon her pinioned arm. Mary stumbled ahead, her mind numbly crying out for Ravenstoke to stop them. Yet Ravenstoke stood paralyzed, allowing them to safely circle about him. Heartsick, Mary realized that Jameson had judged the matter correctly. Ravenstoke would let them go and wait them out, rather than risk endangering her. Her mind revolted at the frightening thought, and, regardless of the cost, she began struggling, throwing her weight against Jameson in an attempt to unbalance him. Only the deadening effects of the laudanum saved her from fainting as rending pain shot through her twisted arm.

Jameson cursed lowly. He hurled her from him and spun, striking the pistol from Ravenstoke's hand before the duke could safely fire. The two men clinched each other in a deadlock, their bodies crashing across the room in combat.

Mary, after one dazed moment, got up from where she had fallen. With single-minded determination, she staggered towards the discarded gun. Seizing it, she walked deliberately towards the grappling men, aiming it directly at them, awaiting her chance. The men appeared evenly matched, both delivering well-calculated blows, blows that reverberated throughout the room. Mary bit her lip as Jameson succeeded in landing a punch to Ravenstoke's stomach. Ravenstoke did not falter; in a rush, both men plummetted to the floor behind the settee, lost from Mary's sight.

She could still hear the sickening thud of knuckles driving into bone. There was an appalling silence, then a solitary figure arose. Mary gasped; Ravenstoke stood before her, casually dusting himself off. His cape was ripped and awry, and a bruise was darkening over his brow. He glanced up at her and stilled, gazing pointedly at the gun she held out before her, the barrel of which was level with his chest.

"I do hope that you intend to refrain from firing that thing. I did try to come as swiftly as possible, after all."

Mary looked confused and then shook her head dazedly. "No . . . you're not Jameson."

"A fact that I cherish most highly. Now, do you think, perhaps, sweet Mary, that you could bring yourself to lower that just a tad — but not too low, mind you."

Mary gazed blankly at the gun and nodded. The

weapon fell to her side as a mist of tears filmed her eyes. Ravenstoke was safe!

He trod softly over to her, prising the gun from her chilled fingers. "What were you going to do if it was Jameson?"

"Kill him."

Ravenstoke nodded, his eyes roaming over his dishevelled companion with intense compassion. He dragged his cape from about himself and wrapped it gently around Mary's bared shoulders. "Come, dear. We're going home."

Mary heard his words, but she could not take them in. She stayed rooted, unable to move.

Ravenstoke tipped her chin up, his tapered fingers gently stroking her jaw. The green of his eyes was deep and murky as he studied her. "Should I kill him for you, my dear?"

Mary forced back a sob, reaching for the protection of his arms. "No, just take me home. Take me home, my lord."

He swore softly and swept her up into a tight, urgent hold, striding from the room. Mary lay her dazed, heavy head upon his shoulder, but lifted it with a gasp as a figure stepped out from the dark. "Ravenstoke!" It was Jameson's henchman.

"Hush, it's all right," Ravenstoke whispered in her ear. "Mary, please meet Eb. Eb, this is Mary. Eb has decided to change camps, as it were."

"Sorry, missy," Eb apologized. "Didn't mean to scare ye. It's a pleasure to see ye safe, and I'm mighty sorry about beforetimes. As I told the guv'nor here, it wasn't my lay, nohow. So where's the cove?"

"You'll find him in the drawing room."

"Cocked up his toes, has he?" Eb asked cheerily.

"No, no," Ravenstoke smiled. "Only floored. So

please tend to him as we had agreed upon, and I shall see you tomorrow."

"It will be my pleasure, see if it won't." Eb grinned through his scruff. "Well, if you'll excuse me, missy, I'll be about me business."

Mary blinked as he went whistling away. "What— what is he going to do?"

Ravenstoke chuckled. "Tend to Jameson's sad condition, that is all. Now rest; we'll be home soon."

Adam's face registered extreme consternation as he opened the townhouse door. He did not even attempt to mask it as he surveyed Lord Ravenstoke; as once before, his lordship stood on the steps, holding Miss Castleton. This time, however, the hour was one at night, and Miss Castleton was not asleep, but awake and peering muzzily at him from behind a great shiner. "Good evening, Adams," she greeted him. "You waited up for me—I thought I told you there was no need for that."

"So you did," Adams said diplomatically, wondering how the lady could utter such a bold-faced untruth. Calling upon his professionalism, he replied, "I am sorry, miss, I fear it is a habit I am accustomed to."

"I see." Mary frowned in drugged disapproval. "Well, since you are here, please be so good as to inform Lord Ravenstoke that he may set me down. He does not seem to want to listen to me."

"But, my dear," the duke protested, "I fear I am just like poor Adams on this head—it is a habit I am accustomed to."

"I could walk by myself," Mary said, looking away from both men. "There is no need for all this."

"Ah, it is clear the lady chooses to malign us both,

Adams." Ravenstoke sighed. "Alas, she is too capable for our useless ministrations." A silent, indulgent look—and a sense of agreement—passed between the two men.

"Indeed, my lord, so it would appear," Adams murmured.

"Does her maid wait up for her?"

"No, my lord. As Miss Castleton said, she does not encourage it."

"Excellent, then we may scrape through without the servants gossiping."

"Certainly, my lord. I will ensure that."

"Very well, I'll take her to her room, then. See to it that she is not disturbed in the morning."

"If you have finished discussing what she needs, she would like to reach her bed sometime before dawn," Mary murmured. "Lay on, Macduff . . . and good night, Adams."

"Good night, miss," Adams called softly as Ravenstoke carried Mary towards the stairs. He stood just a moment before shutting and locking the door, deep in conjecture.

Mary sighed ever so softly as Ravenstoke carried her into her room. She looked around at the familiar surroundings and felt safe again, truly safe. Ravenstoke lowered her to her feet; after the briefest of moments, Mary resolutely pushed herself away from the warmth and strength of his body.

"I am . . . fine, thank you," she said. For no sensible reason, she started to tremble. I must be belatedly reacting, she thought, foggily, and she realized she was swaying slightly, too.

Straightening herself with determination, she walked slowly across the room to the window, where moonlight streamed inwards. She leaned her head against the cool pane and stared out into the night, a feeling of desolation engulfing her.

"Are you sure you are all right?" Ravenstoke asked quietly.

"I'm sure, my lord," Mary lied, as sudden tears slid down her cheeks. "Thank you for rescuing me. I . . . I would never have been able to . . . to stop him."

"Don't think about it. I would have come for you no matter what," Ravenstoke said roughly.

"But if you had not come just then, he would have—"

"Don't say it. I would have come. Now try to rest. Everything will be all right."

"Will it?" Mary asked bitterly, helpless to stem the maelstrom of emotion that swirled within her. She stared desperately up at the stars. "Will it ever be all right?"

"It will," Ravenstoke said, his voice sounding oddly agonized. "I will make it so."

"You will make it so?" Mary chuckled hollowly. She knew it must be the laudanum making her feel as she did, but she nevertheless turned upon him. "And how will you do that, my lord? How will you possibly do that?"

"For God's sake, only tell me what it is you want, Mary, and I'll get it for you."

"You wouldn't be able to."

"Tell me, Mary, only tell me."

"I want . . . I want to be left alone. By everyone. I want to live far away from men—all men."

There was a deep silence in the room as the two figures faced each other, her words echoing between them, the ghostly moonlight giving only hints of their expressions.

"I can't do that," Ravenstoke said, finally.

Mary's chin lifted. "Why not? It is what I want."

"You only say that now because of your fear and hurt. But you could not live that way. You would never be happy."

"Are you so sure, my lord?"

"Yes. Ask anything but that."

"Ah, yes. Here comes the conditions, always my lord's eternal conditions!" Something snapped within her; reckless anger pushed to the forefront of her conflicting emotions. "So you say you will get me anything I want—as long as I marry? Is that so?"

"Yes."

"Does that mean you will get me any man I choose?"

Ravenstoke's tension was a palpable thing. "Yes. I said I would."

"Very well, my lord," Mary purred, stepping within an inch of his unbending figure. "If it is a man I must have—then the man I will have is you."

"What?"

Mary heard the inrush of his breath. A prevailing calm came over her. "I said I will have you, my lord."

"No!" The word rasped in the duke's throat.

"Yes." Even though her anger had led her to say it, she realized that it was her deepest wish. Steadying herself with a deep breath, she raised trembling hands to his shoulders, the cloak sliding from her bared ones. "You did say you would get me whoever it is I want."

"But not me!"

"Why not you?" She moved closer, her body relaxing against his. Ravenstoke groaned and drew her fully into his arms. They clung to each other in the darkened room, their kiss one of open, passionate need. Lips and bodies melted into one desire, one thought. Mary arched back, drawing Ravenstoke down to her in a timeless demand. Yet as his lips brushed the hollow of her breasts he drew back, setting her quickly away. "No. Don't do this, Mary."

It took her a moment to orient herself. "Why not? You said I should marry someone—why shouldn't you?"

"Why shouldn't I? Because I'm not cut out to be a husband!"

"And I? I would make a good, obedient wife?"

"You deserve someone better than me, Mary. Someone younger, someone not so old in the ways of the world."

"But I would not want a man like that. I am not so good or kind myself."

"No, Mary. I would make a hell of a husband."

"I am not so sure of that. And at least I could be myself around you. Only think on it, my lord."

"My God, do you think I haven't?" he said harshly. "I've thought it out over and over again!"

"And?" Mary's breath froze within her lungs.

"And it would not do," Ravenstoke concluded in a defeated voice.

Mary stood, paralyzed, as if lightning had struck her on the spot. In one breath he had offered the world by saying he cared; in the next he had ripped it from her. "You . . . you wish me to marry someone else?"

"Yes. Yes, I do!"

"Very well," Mary said, shaking. "Whom should it be?"

"Anyone you wish, for God's sake!" He added, more slowly. "Anyone who is your equal, who can give you the respectability and steadfastness you deserve."

"I . . . see."

"You—you've said things tonight that were caused by the laudanum, but in the morning you will think better of it. You will be grateful—someday—you never had me for a husband."

"Perhaps," Mary replied, struggling to regain her dignity.

"I only hope that when you find your husband and settle down, you will not banish Grandmother or me entirely from your life."

"No—of course not." Mary swallowed hard. "Why, you can be . . . godparent to my future brood of children. I can just envision it. Disreputable Uncle Alastair coming to visit on the holidays—and at Christmas you can bring gifts, and dangle another man's children upon your knee."

"Stop it!" Ravenstoke spun away from her. Regretting her cutting words, Mary reached out apologetically to the broad back that now faced her. She shivered as she felt the whole frame of the man tremble at her touch; then she knew, knew instinctively that she could cause this man to take her to himself and his bed that night. The urge to damn his wishes—and her beliefs—gripped her.

She could bring him to love her, if only for a night. But what of the morning? She shook her head and withdrew her hand, sadly. She could not do it to the man she loved, entangling and entrapping him against his will. And, more than anything, she could not make him think worse of himself than he already did. "Please . . . don't be noble," she pleaded softly, almost to herself.

"I will do the right thing by you, for once." Ravenstoke had heard her.

"I can do no differently, then." Mary said it with regret, knowing that she had lost, bested by his honor and hers. "I will do what you wish; find me a

171

respectable man, and I will wed."

"Who . . . who do you wish?"

"It doesn't matter."

"Very well. . . . Good night, Mary." Ravenstoke walked towards the door.

Mary watched in silence as he started to leave, but then the fears and injuries of the night closed in upon her again. "Ravenstoke, stop!"

"Yes?"

"Don't leave me. I . . . Not tonight."

"My god, Mary, I can't stay. Don't ask it."

"No. Not for anything but company. I know it was foolish of me to try to seduce a seducer. I remember what you said."

"I said that? That was before I knew any better. I —"

"We . . . we could play cards! Or chess!"

"Chess? With your eyelids already drooping?"

"Yes," Mary said desperately. "I just can't face — I don't want to be alone tonight."

"My poor Mary . . . you could tempt a saint, let alone an imperfect mortal like myself. Very well, I will stay — but no cards. I'd only fleece you. Come here, little one. If I am to dangle your children upon my knee, I might as well dangle their mother."

Mary nodded numbly as he walked over and took her hand. He led her to the large winged chair before the fireplace and sat, pulling her down upon his lap. Mary, needing the strength of this one man, burrowed close.

She smiled sleepily as he stroked her hair. "I'd never have thought to be dangled so paternally upon Rake Ravenstoke's knee."

He chuckled slightly. "And I never thought to be holding you so innocuously."

"But surely you did? I am not your type. You said

yourself I did not attract you, that day at the inn."

"Must you remember every idiotic thing I said. Besides, I said that in order to set your mind at rest."

"You did?" Mary yawned. "That is at least a comfort. I thought you totally unattracted to me."

"Yes, I know," he said wryly. "You've well nigh stretched my resistance to the breaking point at times."

"But never far enough." Mary sighed. Her eyes were closing; the laudanum was reclaiming her.

"No. I am not that far past redemption." The duke received no reply. He sighed himself. He should put her to bed, now, while she slept, but he could not bring himself to do so. Tomorrow he would find her a husband. Tomorrow she would probably not even remember what she had offered him — but tonight he would hold her as his own and imagine how things could have been if he had lived his life differently . . . and she were not the woman she was.

Chapter Nine

LORD RAVENSTOKE IS AN INDUSTRIOUS MAN

Lady Sophia, her face set and stern, cracked open the door to Mary's chamber, a meager sliver of morning light sneaking past her into the room. With great trepidation, she forced herself to look to the bed.

A flicker of surprise crossed her face. It turned rapidly into outright disbelief as her eyes scanned the room and found two somnolent people both residing in one chair. She walked silently up to the sleeping, entwined couple; just as silently, she studied the wearied, bruised faces and torn clothing. Her lips pursed. Reaching out, she brushed a fallen lock from her grandson's forehead.

His eyes opened at her touch, but he did not move.

"Good morning, Alastair," Lady Sophia whispered. "Mind telling me what you are doing in Mary's bedchamber? I own I was pleasantly surprised to discover the bed itself empty, though somewhat confused. Could this be a latent vein of chivalry surfacing? Or are you just losing your touch?"

This won a smile from Ravenstoke. "How'd you know I was here, Grandmother dear?"

"How could I not, with Adams acting as peculiar and fidgety as an old maid with a suitor. When one's butler takes to officiously standing guard over a particular lady's boudouir, and flushes red when asked simple questions regarding other people's whereabouts, one knows something is afoot."

"Poor Adams. You must have made short shrift of him."

"Nonsense, though I left him my smelling salts. Why isn't Mary waking up?"

"She . . . had an exhausting night."

Lady Sophia's eyes narrowed. "Did she? Well, then, let us get her properly to bed and remove you hence before her maid stumbles upon you. No one, but no one, would believe that you, a libertine of the first water, merely slept in a chair with Mary. I can hardly credit it myself," she added under her breath. "Now do hurry."

Ravenstoke obliged, gently lifting Mary and carrying her over to the bed. Lady Sophia flung back the covers, and the duke laid Mary down, tenderly removing her arms from about his shoulders, where they had crept sometime during the night. With weary unawareness, he reached to remove her torn dress.

"What do you think you are doing, young man?" Lady Sophia asked. "No, don't say it. Just leave this room, and I will see to the child."

Ravenstoke gazed at Mary a moment, and then at Lady Sophia, his eyes shadowed and unexpectedly vulnerable. Her expression softened, and she raised a kind hand to his cheek. "My poor boy, you must go tend to yourself. I will see to Mary. There is nothing else you can do at present, so go. We will talk later."

Ravenstoke nodded wearily, and, with one last look at Mary that wrenched Lady Sophia's heart, left the room.

A half-hour later, Lady Sophia covertly studied her grandson as he brooded before the fireplace in the sitting room. Gone was the dishevelled and vulnerable man in Mary's room; in his stead stood the cool, elegant, Rake Ravenstoke. Drat, Lady Sophia thought to herself, she should have talked to him before he'd had time to raise his infernal guard.

"Would you care to tell me what transpired last evening?" she asked, sipping a ratafia, thinking it unfortunate that ladies were not allowed brandy. A presentiment told her that she might just require some.

Ravenstoke's gaze remained fixed upon the fire as he answered softly, "Jameson abducted Mary last night."

"My God!" As Ravenstoke remained silent, she forced herself to ask, "Did he . . . did he—"

"No, I arrived in time. Just in time, from what I saw."

"I see. How did he manage to get at her?"

"He drugged her at the ball."

"At the ball? But how? Mary knows better than to go near him."

"He didn't do it. Lady Jane did it for him."

"My God!" Lady Sophia sat a moment, a stiff, regal picture. "You killed him, I hope?"

"No. I would not have the scandal that would be attached to it. Not for Mary."

"A pity."

"Yes, but it might cheer you to know we will not be seeing him again."

"Indeed?" Lady Sophia brightened.

"It seems the good squire, filled with remorse, no doubt, set sail on a transport ship to Australia. Certain circumstances, of course, will not allow his return."

"Why, how very obliging of the squire," Lady Sophia murmured. "I wager he was surprised by his change of heart?"

"Appreciatively so, I should think."

"Excellent. And Jane Pelham?"

"Her parents have decided to take her on an extended trip to the continent."

"I see. Well, I suppose that will be adequate — though Jane would have thrived in Australia, I dare say."

Ravenstoke smiled. "I see I should have left it to you."

"In the matter of that woman, yes. Well, it is settled. Now, what happened after you rescued Mary?"

Ravenstoke's expression became shuttered. "What do you mean? I brought her home, of course. That was all."

"I gathered that. I'm sure of it, in fact, for I give you credit to have used the bed rather than the chair, if anything had transpired."

"Mary was unwilling to be alone last night."

"So you stayed on and told her bedtime stories? Of course, you always comfort women in that fashion."

"What would you have had me do?"

"I would have had you — Oh, never mind. Far be it from me to shock one of our nation's leading libertines with my immoral suggestions!" Studying his stony expression, the duchess decided on a new tack. "Well, then, after last night, what are we going to do? It is apparent to the slightest intelligence that Mary needs the protection only matrimony offers. Though it pains me to say it, there is something about that girl that positively attracts trouble."

"I quite agree—and Mary finally realizes it as well. Therefore, she has consented to wed."

"Has she? And who has she decided to wed?"

"Who? Why, any one of the worthy suitors that flock about her, I should imagine. She has her choice."

"Does she?"

Ravenstoke did not answer.

"What are you doing, Alastair? Surely you do not mean to have her marry some other man?"

"What would you have me do? I love her, Grandmother."

"I see. You are so much in love with her that you encourage her to marry another man."

"Yes!"

"I don't wish to appear behindhand, but why not marry her yourself?"

"Need you ask that?"

"I'm sorry," Lady Sophia said mildly, "but I do."

"You ask a man of my ilk why I should not marry a woman like Mary? Lord, and I always thought you sane and reasonable!"

Lady Sophia pursed her lips in consideration. "I see. You would find it impossible to be faithful to Mary, is that it?"

Ravenstoke's sharp laugh cracked through the room. "Not be faithful to her? That's rich. I'm already faithful to her, whether I like it or not. I find I don't even care to look at another woman—a sad case for a man like myself, wouldn't you say?"

"No, I wouldn't. And I already knew that. Oh, don't look so stunned, my dear. I've always kept myself abreast of your latest flirts and ladybirds, very much as I do the latest fashions. Though I haven't quite decided which changes more, your mistresses or women's necklines. However, your name has not been linked to any other of late—not since you brought Mary to me. So if you are already this besotted, why not wed her and have done with it?"

"Because of the very past you so aptly described. Mary doesn't need a man whose past history will always haunt her. She suffered enough from that kind of life with her stepfather. She says she cares nothing for reputation, when she has every right to do so. Do you know that when I pulled her from that damn tree and she faced being alone with me, she had no fear of the kind of man I was? And she should have. It was her right. She's far more a lady than any of those blushing, simpering misses that fall into hysterics if a man but looks wrong at them, and who'd rather throw themselves from a cliff than possibly be alone with a libertine.

"Mary's a true lady and deserves a true gentleman for a husband. One that can offer her an untarnished name, not sniggers and sly comments, or questions of what her rake of a husband is up to and does she really think she can keep him happy? I know the *ton* and the gossip and the backbiting, and I would never submit Mary to its viciousness. No, she deserves a man who, by his very past, promises her a life of fidelity and respect. Maybe then she will be able to learn to trust a man again, and to regain what men like her stepfather and I have destroyed for her."

"But will she ever learn to love gain?"

"I have no doubt," Ravenstoke said bleakly. "Love could grow with a man like that. Rather than possibly die with—"

"Her dark angel?"

Ravenstoke spun around, struck.

"Laudanum seems to make Mary loquacious in her sleep," his grandmother said. "She kept calling for her dark angel, which made me fear that she was suffering from fever or, worse, derangement. I feel so much better knowing that it was only you she wanted."

"It is the drug that makes her say those things."

"Oh, very well, be stubborn. So Mary has finally agreed to wed one of the suitors she's attracted."

"Yes . . . last night impressed upon her the dangers of her position."

"Last night, you say?" Lady Sophia quizzed. "Well, if there is to be a wedding of any sort, I'd best be about my affairs. There is much more to be done than you would know," she added in an odd tone. "What are your plans for the day?"

"As you say, if there is to be a wedding, I must be about my affairs." Grandmother and grandson offered each other a challenging look, then departed with similarly determined expressions upon their faces.

"Alastair, old man, how do you fare?" Tyndale inquired as he lowered his well-dressed body into the chair beside Ravenstoke in White's lounging room.

"I fare, Jason, I fare."

"My, my, is that a bruise I see over your eye?"

"Why, yes. It is of no significance."

"I see." Tyndale nodded, then paused. "By the bye, did you ever find out what that bedlamite Castleton was raving over last night? A shame to see a man that high in his altitudes, what?"

"Castleton never could hold his drink. It seems that his rantings were over some fair tavern wench who had the fine good sense to bolt with another gallant rather than him."

"Is that so?" Tyndale asked, looking directly at Ravenstoke.

"That is the story, I believe," the duke answered, responding with a steady gaze.

Tyndale smiled. "Then that is the story—after all, you ought to know. Should I, perhaps, apprise the others of this tale? Just to assuage their curiosity, mind you?"

"I would greatly appreciate it. Feel free to tell anyone you choose."

"It will be my pleasure," Tyndale grinned. "After all, no one managed to extract anything but screams and curses from Castleton last night." Ravenstoke raised an inquiring brow. "It seems the old reprobate fractured his leg when tossed out of the club. By the time he found his way home, he'd succeeded in making a clean break of it."

"Serves him right." Ravenstoke's attention turned to the sober individual walking into the room, a man of medium height, medium color, and medium dress. "I hope you will excuse me, Tyndale." The duke arose. "I would have a word with Brestfort."

"Brestfort? You are just full of surprises today, my dear Alastair?"

"Am I?" Ravenstoke smiled. "Why is that?"

"Well, I could not help but notice that you have also spoken to Townsend and Clive as well, this morning. Together with Brestfort, they represent the three dullest sticks ever to grace society. I do hope you are not intending to reform on us and forsake your poor old rackety friends."

Ravenstoke's smile grew broader. "No, of course

not. It is quite past my capabilities to reform. No, this is merely a favor for a lady."

"Involving Townsend, Clive, and Brestfort? 'Gad, what lady of your acquaintance would ever wish to make their acquaintance?"

"That, I am not at liberty to say."

"Of course not. Well, hope to see you later at my little card party."

"That you shall. Good day, Tyndale—I am much obliged to you. Do remind me that I owe you one."

"Think nothing of it. Though I'd give anything to hear the truth of the matter."

"Perhaps someday . . . when we are old and grey."

Tyndale laughed appreciatively. "I have a feeling it is well worth the wait. Hi-ho, do not let me detain you from the exhilarating conversation I daresay you shall hold with the witty Brestfort. Ah, I think I see Mosely over there—such a sad rattle, you know. His tongue runs on hinges. But then, he is such fun when one has a good tale to set about."

"What, pray tell, is going on here?" Lady Sophia stormed into the drawing room, her cane snapping hard against any pieces of furniture unfortunate enough to fall in her path.

"What do you mean?" Mary asked quietly, looking up from the sewing she leaned over. Her face was paler than usual, a heavy dusting of powder masking her bruises.

"Don't play the meek innocent with me, my girl! It doesn't become you; neither does that tatting. Now what is this I have heard about you receiving two gentlemen this afternoon? I step out for a mere hour, only to return to the shocking news that you have received a visit in private from not one, but two gentlemen. Whatever has come over Adams to allow them in at all? I declare, he has gone totally daft."

"Don't be displeased with him, he found it excessively difficult to turn the gentlemen away since it was the duke himself who informed them that I was at home and eager to receive them."

"What? Alastair said—" Lady Sophia choked back the words, but her eyes narrowed dangerously as she sat down upon a nearby chair.

"It seems that both men were adamant that they be permitted to see me, since Ravenstoke assured them of my desire to receive them."

"But whatever for? Adams said it was Clive and Townsend who visited. Two highly estimable gentlemen, I am sure, but neither is a crony, or even an acquaintance, of Alastair. So why would he send them around?"

"To propose to me of course," Mary said. She clipped a thread while Lady Sophie stared at her in flabbergasted astonishment; then she smiled and laughed.

"Surely you jest," Lady Sophia said, still bemused.

Mary laughed all the more. "Oh, my dear lady, if only you could see your face. Forgive my laughter, but that is exactly what I needed. I assure you it is no jest; both Townsend and Clive saw fit to lay their hearts and hands before me this day."

"My God! What did you do?"

"I refused them, of course."

"Good girl. Why, I've never heard of anything so outrageous."

"Indeed. After all, everyone knows that Clive lives under the cat's paw with his Mama; any woman would have to be a noddy to accept his suit. And as for poor Townsend . . . well, I own it is not his fault, but I cannot quite like his nasal voice. Only consider those tones over the coffee cups every morning—"

"Mary, what are you rambling about? Surely you would not have entertained the thought of accepting them under any conditions, nasal tones or not."

"My dear Lady Sophia, since Lord Ravenstoke has been so kind as to 'land' these gentlemen for me, it only behooves me to make a push to choose one of them," Mary said with control. "And rather soon, I would dare say, if poor Adams is not to succumb to the strain of turning the rejected suitors away. Neither gentleman took kindly to my refusal after receiving the duke's blessing."

"Now, Mary, I mislike that tone in your voice very much. I can well understand your anger, but don't let Alastair goad you into something rash."

"I am not angry."

"I see that I should have talked to you immediately this morning rather than making my calls, but I had no notion that my tottyheaded grandson would work so fast or that you would allow him to bullock you into wedlock— Oh, do come in!" her ladyship snapped in response to a quiet, repeated scratching at the door.

A stiffer-than-usual Adams entered. "My lady, Viscount Brestfort is here and begs an audience with Miss Castleton."

"So it's Brestfort now?" Lady Sophia sputtered. "Well, I won't have it! Send him on his way. I'm going to kill Alastair!"

"Very good, my lady." Adams spun with amazing alacrity to do her bidding.

Mary's voice, however, stopped him at the door. "No. Do allow him in, Adams."

Adams turned slowly and reluctantly. "Miss?"

"Please do allow him in," Mary repeated, smiling. "Now this is better—finally Ravenstoke has sent someone acceptable. I will be pleased to see him."

Adam's eyes swivelled towards Lady Sophia, pleading for reinforcement. That lady looked at Mary's set face and shrugged. "Oh, very well. I wash my hands of it. Let the dolt in."

"Very well, my lady," Adams said, but he did not move.

An amused—even warm—smile lighted Mary's face. "Don't fret so, Adams. Remember, what I do is for your sake as well as mine."

Adams cast a confused look at Lady Sophia before murmuring "Yes, miss" and exiting.

Adams reentered with Viscount Brestfort on his heels, a pretentious smile on the viscount's lips. The smile slid a tad upon finding Lady Sophia present as well—a frigid Lady Sophia, at that.

"Dear Miss Castleton, I appreciate this audience you've allowed me," Brestfort said, bowing formally. "And Lady Sophia," he added, though his voice weakened perceptibly as she pinned him with an icy stare.

"Viscount Brestfort, what a pleasant *surprise,*" Mary said. Her stress on the last word caused the duchess to sniff disdainfully. "Do come in and sit down. Lady Sophia, I am sure you have urgent business to attend—please, do not let us detain you."

"But no, my dear. I cannot possibly leave you alone with the viscount. Why, how improper that would be. Whatever would he think?"

"Very true, my lady," Brestfort nodded solemnly. "Under normal circumstances, it would be terribly improper, and I am sure Miss Castleton would never have suggested it, save for the occasion. Lord Ravenstoke assures me that you would fully understand my visit."

"I told you," Mary murmured quietly to Lady

Sophia.

"Did he?" Lady Sophia smiled through clenched teeth. "But then, what would a rake such as my grandson know about propriety?"

"Indeed, my lady, I admit I harbored apprehensions myself on this hand. However, if I am not alone with Miss Castleton above ten minutes, I am sure it would not be improper."

"You would only need ten minutes," her ladyship replied sweetly. Mary's eyes widened, but Brestfort seemed to take no offense.

"Madam, I would never go beyond what is pleasing—"

"If that far," the duchess murmured.

"Lady Sophia, I am sure you could leave us for a moment," Mary said quickly, lest her companion's comments finally penetrate the viscount's thick consciousness. She cast Lady Sophia a compelling glance.

"Oh, very well," Lady Sophia said ungraciously, rising. "But don't, darling Mary, do anything that I wouldn't approve of."

"I am sure Miss Castleton could never do anything that was not totally acceptable," Brestfort said, directing a condoning smile toward his lady love.

"Oh, lud!" Muttering under her breath, Lady Sophia left the room.

"Now, sir," Mary smiled as kindly as she could, for Lady Sophia's comments had at least created some sympathy within her for her suitor. "Perhaps now we can discuss whatever brought you here."

Brestfort smiled with an air of importance. "I am sure it comes as no surprise to you, Miss Castleton, that I hold you in the highest esteem. Though I must say that I was unaccountably surprised and pleased when Lord Ravenstoke was kind enough to divulge

186

that you, my dear lady, would not be indifferent to my suit."

"Yes—how kind of him."

"Therefore, Miss Castleton," the viscount said, walking over and—after selecting the perfect spot—kneeling down before her with conscientious precision, "I would be greatly honored if you would—"

"Excuse me, miss," a voice called from across the room. "My lady thought you might wish for tea."

Stiff with embarrassment, Brestfort sprung up and turned to discover Adams standing in the doorway, a tea service in hand.

"Did she?" Mary bit back a smile at Lady Sophia's obvious maneuver. She smiled reassuringly at Brestfort. "Very well, Adams, do set the service down."

"Yes, miss." Adams walked over with a painstaking formality that far outshone the viscount's efforts, and set the tray down upon the table, before Mary. He immediately busied himself pouring tea, a service Mary never required him to perform. "Do you take lemon, sir?" His manner suggested there was nothing amiss in the viscount's standing at attention like a sentry.

"Thank you, Adams," Mary said quickly. "I will serve the tea. Do tell Lady Sophia that we have all we need." Adams bowed and, with stately measure, trod from the room. "Please," Mary went on, "do continue, my lord."

The viscount breathed a sigh and, after locating the very spot he had chosen before, knelt down again with awesome precision. The fact that it was his second time did not dilute his attitude one wit. "Miss Castleton, I hold you in the highest esteem. It would do me the greatest honor if you would—"

"Excuse me, miss." At the sound of Adams's voice, Brestfort popped up again, reminding Mary of a wooden puppet whose strings had been abruptly jerked. "The lemons, miss. I forgot them."

"How unusual. Do bring them in."

With even slower measure than before, Adams trod the length of the room and placed a single dish upon the service tray with calculated deliberation.

"*Et tu,* Adams," Mary murmured. The butler was turning the dish every which way, as if unable to decide how to place it. His response to her words was a bland look; finally he bowed and, as the couple watched him in obvious impatience, promenaded from the room.

"Please excuse the interruption," Mary said, smiling as charmingly as she could. "Both Adams and the duchess are overzealous in their concern for their guests' welfare."

"It is to be . . . applauded . . . I am sure." Brestfort eyed the door with wary suspicion before once again venturing to take up his kneeling position before Mary. No matter the obstacles, the Viscount Brestfort was a man who performed things according to Hoyle. Mary sighed sadly, telling herself she should respect that in a man.

Brestfort cleared his throat and, after one harried look about, began to recite his litany. "My dear Miss Castleton, I hold you in the highest esteem. I would be greatly honored if you would—"

"Excuse me, miss."

Mary let out an exclamation, and a hand shot out to restrain the viscount before he could rebound to his feet. "Yes, Adams?" She refused even to look up.

"The sugar, miss."

"Of course. I should have known. Do bring it in." Then, feeling her determination wane, she realized that Lady Sophia's delaying tactics might well succeed if she did not take matters into her own hands.

"And yes, Lord Brestfort, I would be pleased to accept your offer of matrimony."

A surprised gasp echoed through the room, and the sound of china hitting the Aubusson carpet was heard. Mary smiled in satisfaction. "The sugar, Adams?"

"I fear so, miss."

"Excellent. I am sure the viscount and I did not wish for it anyway."

"Yes, miss," A trace of reproach threaded Adams's voice; neither Brestfort nor Mary spoke as he cleaned the broken china away.

Mary waited for the closing of the door. "I'm sorry, my lord. I do hope you will forgive my brashness, but . . . I thought it for the best," she added meekly. Brestfort neither rose nor spoke; it was as if he had taken root. "My lord, I hope you do not take it as an impropriety, but we do only have ten minutes."

"Er . . . uh . . . no. Then you will marry me?"

"But of course. Did not Lord Ravenstoke suggest that I would?"

"Yes, he did, but—"

"Well, children, how are we doing in here?" Lady Sophia practically carolled. For the third time in eight brief minutes, Brestfort bolted to his feet. He whirled around and hastily settled his jacket as the dowager duchess walked into the room and sat down in the chair opposite them. "Ah, I see I have arrived in time for tea."

"Yes, but I do hope you can do without sugar." Mary smiled in amusement; Adams must not have steeled himself to inform Lady Sophia of the news, for the dowager duchess was enjoying herself far too much. "And you must congratulate me, for the viscount and I are to be wed—"

189

"What?" The satisfaction slipped from her ladyship's face. "But how?"

"He just swept me off my feet," Mary said, smiling up at Brestfort, whose chest seemed to be increasing in inches by the second.

"Of course. He didn't even need ten minutes," Lady Sophia murmured in disgust.

"Yes, he's made me the happiest woman in the world," Mary said quickly, to cover the duchess's disapproval.

Lady Sophia seemed to pull herself together, for she nodded stiffly and said, "My congratulations, Brestfort, you are marrying a fine woman."

"Thank you, Lady Sophia. I believe she is an exceptional choice myself. Well, I must take my leave of you, for I must inform my family of the momentous occasion. Strange . . . this morning I'd no notion that I would become an engaged man, but as Lord Ravenstoke reminded me, there are times when one must be a man of action."

"Ah, yes — my grandson has always been a believer in action. Unfortunately. I have no doubt you will wish to visit her stepfather soon to arrange the settlements."

"But that has all been seen to." Brestfort looked aghast. "Please forgive me, Lady Sophia, if, due to my overenthusiastic speech, I gave the impression that I am the type of here-and-thereian that would so cavalierly ignore convention as to propose to a lady before the necessary arrangements between her father and I had been made. I assure you, you may always count upon me to behave in the most honorable manner. With this point clearly made, Brestfort took Mary's hand and bowed over it. "My dear, you have made me the happiest man! Shall I have the pleasure of seeing you at the Honeywitt ball tonight?"

"Yes, certainly," Mary said. "Now, do not let me detain you, for I am sure your family will be as anxious to know what has been arranged as we have been."

The viscount, smiling happily, missed the point. "That is so like you, Miss Castleton, always kind and thoughtful. Until tonight, then."

There was a moment's silence in the room as both ladies stared after the departing viscount. "Poor man," Mary said sadly. "I wonder if he even knows what has happened to him."

"Hah! Don't waste your sympathy on that jumped-up whopstraw! As bloodless as the rest of his family. Well, Mary, you've certainly landed yourself in the basket this time—with the help of my want-witted grandson, I grant, but whatever possessed you to such a mad start?"

"I don't see it as mad. After all, Bresfort seems all that is amiable and well situated. As a whole, he should not render me one moment of difficulty."

"Stuff and nonsense. The man will drive you to insanity. He's a pompous prig, puffed up with his own consequence."

"He is no worse than any of the others." A weary tone seeped into Mary's calm voice. "I shall marry him and have done with this all, so do not think to deter me. Indeed, you should be happy, for I have found a suitable match, the very thing we set out to accomplish. And I understand your concern—I truly do—but Ravenstoke is correct. It is time I accept my life for what it is, and settle."

"Poppycock! Ravenstoke is an interfering, wooden-headed male who doesn't know any better. But you! You should! You don't love Brestfort."

"No, I don't. But perhaps our life will be far

better for it. I will make him an acceptable wife—and you know I have always said I would not be comfortable in the sway of powerful emotions. It is best for me to avoid such love."

"I'd say it is slightly too late for that."

Mary did not try to deny it. "Yes, you are right. It is far too late. But there is nothing else that can be done."

"Good God, girl, what is this namby-pamby attitude?" Lady Sophia exclaimed. "I fear you have let Ravenstoke sway your reasoning. He's had his way for far too long, and I don't mind telling you, I had counted upon you to set him straight. If only you had . . . had . . ."

"Had what?"

The duchess caught herself up sharply. "I'm sorry, my dear. I should not even suggest such a thing to you. But if you'd only make a push to . . . to . . ."

"To what?" Mary gentled as she saw the duchess to be truly upset. "I did make a 'push,' you know—if attempting a seduction is what you were suggesting. But I failed. It is extremely mortifying when one can't even seduce a man well known for . . . that propensity."

"My God, the chivalrous fool!" Lady Sophia's face was a study in outrage. "He didn't tell me that."

"I should hope not. And I would not have told you, except that I wished you to understand why I did what I did. I never want to lose your regard."

"You could not, my dear. But it is a mistake. Don't let my fool boy destroy both his and your life."

"Destroy his life? No, I would never. That is why marrying Brestfort is best for all concerned. I could not force Ravenstoke to change his life when he does not wish it. Just as I can no longer live here, taking advantage of your kindness."

"But I love your presence here—as does Alastair. If you wed Brestfort, you will cause my grandson great pain, as well as yourself, though he will not admit that to you. I know in the beginning I warned you away from him, but I have changed my mind. I have never seen him care the way he does about you. For all the many women he's had in his life—which I cannot claim to have been few—none has truly understood him, or cared to, for that matter.

"But you do understand him, and you do care. Don't, don't leave him to himself. Don't condemn him to his past life."

"If I thought that . . . No, Ravenstoke has decided, and I believe he is right. Now, if you don't mind," Mary said quietly, rising, "I believe I am tired and would like to rest."

"Yes, of course." Lady Sophia's heart went out to the girl. "But I still think you are making a grave mistake. Even in that you are a perfect couple—both of you are far too proud, with too little knowledge of yourselves."

Chapter Ten

LADY SOPHIA'S MACHINATIONS

Mary stood in front of Lady Sophia's mirror, arms slightly outstretched, patiently awaiting her ladyship's return. A radiant white satin wedding gown, encrusted with myriad seed pearls, enshrined her person. It seemed to Mary that just as many pins equally entrapped her, insidiously hiding in the tucks and seams, just waiting to prick her.

She studied the perfect bride reflected in the mirror and wondered how she had ever come to be in this particular place, what exact turn had set her upon this path. Whose pride had brought her to this—Ravenstoke's or her own? Unwilling to contemplate the matter as she had, time after time, she made to swing away from her image when a sharp pinprick in the seam along her back stayed her.

Footsteps and breathing sounded near her, and she sighed in relief. "Thank heaven you have returned, my lady. How odious of you to leave me waiting here, while all the time these bloodthirsty pins you've placed everywhere rave for my blood. There is a particularly offensive one right now, in my back. Can you help me, since I dare not move?"

"Exactly where is this vampiric pin?"

Mary breathed in sharply, and her eyes flew to the mirror where she saw Ravenstoke moving close to her reflection. She studied his image, aware that her eyes were devouring him, but she was unable to stop herself. She had not seen him since her engagement a month ago. Oh, a few times she had, but there was always a crowded room securely placed between them, or the distance of the park, or they met in passing and were just close enough to wave hello. She took note of every line and shadow of his face. Did he look tired, or was it her own weariness that caused her to imagine it?

"Did you need that 'bloodthirsty' pin plucked out or not?"

"Indeed. It is the one there." Mary attempted to bring her arm down to point, gasped, and decided against such an unwise move. "It . . . it is the one in my lower back."

"Perhaps this one." Ravenstoke bent down, studied her back and plucked at a pin. She could feel his breath upon her neck.

"I'm . . . not sure." Mary moved cautiously and gasped again. "No, that was not the one."

"How about this one?" He held it up to the mirror as if Mary could identify the culprit.

She smiled, despite the tension growing in her at his nearness. "No, not that one. It is lower in my back—and to the right."

She flushed as his hand ran along her back, gently pressing on the small of it. "In this area?"

"Yes," she answered quickly.

"Good God, Grandmother has you hedged in— there must be twelve pins in this one seam alone. Is it this one?"

"Ye— No, unfortunately not. It must be more to

195

the right." Mary bit her lip as Ravenstoke's hand ran along her back once again. She realized now that she should not have asked for his aid. His closeness was both a pleasure and a torment.

"My dear, if we continue in this manner, the dress itself will fall off you long before I discover the offending pin." Ravenstoke's voice was oddly exasperated.

Mary chuckled, an action she regretted as another pin slid into her side. "Please don't make me laugh, my lord, for now we have a second offender. But that one I most definitely will not ask you to find."

"Is that so?" Ravenstoke's tone lightened. "Damn, now I've pricked myself. The devil! I'm sorry, my dear, but I just got blood upon your gown."

"Then both our blood is upon this wedding dress, for I—" Mary stopped as she suddenly saw Ravenstoke's face darken in the mirror. The import of what she'd said struck her then, as it evidently had him. She lowered her eyes, trying to mask her feelings. A warmth circulated through her as Ravenstoke's hand slid to the back of her neck.

"You will be happy."

Mary looked up at this. The duke's face was set and determined. Keep telling yourself that, my lord, she thought sadly.

Yet what was done was done, and there was no turning back. She smiled reassuringly at him and lied for both of their sakes. "Certainly, my lord, I will be happy. Now . . . could you please find that odious pin?"

Ravenstoke smiled at her; it was almost a look of gratitude. "I will try my level best." He bowed his head once again over her back. "Here, we must be more organized in this attack."

He began pulling out pins willy-nilly, flinging

them in any direction, the sound of them dropping easily heard in the silent room. Mary wondered what Lady Sophia would say when she came back to find all her handiwork strewn over the carpet.

"Any luck yet?" Ravenstoke asked.

Mary, her attention called back, shrugged cautiously. "Yes, you must have found it. Thank—"

"What in heaven's name is going on in here?" an astonished voice asked. With most of the irritating pins gone, Mary found she could turn; Ravenstoke had already done so.

Lady Sophia stood before them, fingers tapping on her cane.

"Why, I was merely rescuing Mary from distress."

"Is that so? And why, pray tell, is she distressed?"

"Some mean ogress left her defenseless against a surfeit of pins—"

"Alastair, you dratted boy," the duchess said, as her eyes focused upon a betraying pin in his hand. "Don't dare tell me you've pulled them all out when I took such pains to fit the dress."

"My dear, I believe the pains were all Mary's."

"Wretched boy, I haven't seen you for nigh on a month! And when I do, you've ruined a considerable amount of hard work. Now I must do it again— which I wouldn't have to do if Mary would oblige me by ceasing to drop weight every time I turn around."

"What is the matter?" Ravenstoke asked quickly. "Are you not feeling well? You can ill afford to become thinner."

Mary flushed slightly, thinking that even the dangerous Duke of Denfield could possess the irritating obtuseness so common to the male gender. "I am perfectly fine, my lord. 'Tis merely all this racketing about. It is called bridal nerves, which Lady Sophia will assure you afflict all brides."

"I will?" that lady asked, brows rising in disbelief. When she saw her grandson's face tighten with concern, however, she relented. "Oh, do not let that concern you, my boy, for we have a far more serious situation on our plate."

"What is it?"

"Castleton."

"What has he done now?"

"It is not what he has done, but what he will be unable to do. He will not be able to walk Mary down the aisle."

"Why not? He is on crutches now," Ravenstoke objected.

"Precisely. Now, Alastair, do not say you think that appropriate. I refuse, after all my preparations, to have Castleton ruin them by clomping down the aisle for all the *ton* to watch. I daresay he'll manage to trip up Mary, and then where will we be? With her on crutches as well? Good lord, man, look at her dress — he'll never negotiate around it. Though it is very lovely, don't you think?"

"Yes . . . very lovely," Ravenstoke said after a pause.

"Now, if we were to postpone the wedding another month . . ."

Ravenstoke and Mary stared at each other. As one, they exclaimed, "No!"

"Very well," Lady Sophia said sweetly. "If you refuse to postpone the wedding — though what this indecent haste is, I don't know — then we must resort to my second plan. Ravenstoke, you will give Mary away and walk her down the aisle."

"What? Impossible!"

"Oh, no. Really, dear, it is perfectly suitable and will answer nicely. All the world and its brother knows that I sponsored Mary. It is only proper that the head of the Denfield family be represented in this marriage."

"Grandmother, don't even think it!"

"Now, Alastair, don't attempt your dangerous look with me, for it won't fadge. You don't scare me. And after you've been so beneficial in this union, I think it quite appropriate. Furthermore"—she raised her hand before the duke could speak—"I have already asked Brestfort. He thinks it a marvelous idea. And we all know how nice he is in his notions. We both think you will add prominence to the ceremony."

"But not respectability," Ravenstoke gritted out.

"If that is what worries you, only consider; you will still lend more style than that reprobate Castleton. At least we can depend on you not to arrive castaway."

"Do not count upon it!"

"I have also asked Lady Jersey for her opinion and she can find no fault. Indeed, she was delighted with the plum."

"You told Silence! Oh my God!"

Mary chuckled, and both grandson and grandmother turned to her. "Lady Sophia, how could you? Only imagine Lady Jersey's transports over such a delicious morsel of gossip."

"Vixen," Ravenstoke said softly, the anger fading from his face. "Do tell her it will not serve."

Mary caught Lady Sophia's mischievous pleasure in the situation, and she smiled. She was not that far gone in spirit that she could not enjoy the poetic justice of it all. "Why, my lord, I think it an extremely reasonable notion."

"Very appropriate." Lady Sophia chuckled.

"Mary!" Ravenstoke's voice was threatening.

"Come, my lord, in truth, I would far prefer you

walking me down the aisle than . . . than my stepfather."

Ravenstoke, in a manner most unlike himself, took a quick turn about the room and then stepped before Mary. "You would have me do this?"

"It is only fitting." She swallowed hard.

"You will exact your pound of flesh will you, infant?"

"A pound for a pound, my lord."

Ravenstoke sighed. "Very well. If you both are set upon it—whoever said women were the gentler sex did not know what he spoke of."

" 'Tis only because we've been so long around you, Alastair," Lady Sophia replied. "Now, come with me, for I have certain questions to ask. Typical of your species, you have made yourself scarce this past month while the wedding preparations were being made, but I will not accept that any longer. Tomorrow is Mary's engagement ball, and I have things for you to do." She marshalled him from the room. "I expect to see more of you, if you please."

Mary smiled wryly as Lady Sophia's voice drifted away. The dowager duchess's hopes would most likely be dashed on that score if she planned on Ravenstoke being available. No, he'd played his part in bringing her to the altar, but now he would bow out. A pin pricked her shoulder then, and she realized she was still entrapped within her wedding dress. Appropriate too, she thought. Gingerly lifting the folds of the dress, she went in search of a maid to help her.

"My dear, are you sure you will not allow me to mount you more appropriately?" Brestfort asked as he and Mary rode in the park the next morning. "I cannot think that mount suitable for you."

"Firefly?" Mary asked, surprised. "Why, she is the sweetest creature. Faith, she is a bit playful and high spirited, but there is no malice in her whatsoever. She and I were fast friends the minute Lord Ravenstoke brought her to me."

"That is something else I cannot fathom. How Lord Ravenstoke could have been so careless as to mount you on such a horse! Though, perhaps it is understandable, for—no disrespect intended—Ravenstoke is not precisely the man to know the kind of mount a *lady* would require. Why, the beast is far too large for your size."

"That is because I was accustomed to Satana before this."

"That great brute of Ravenstoke's? No, now you jest—I must accustom myself to your levity, I see." The viscount wagged a finger at her. "No, my dear Miss Castleton, you must allow me to be the judge in this matter. Only think what would happen if the beast were to run away with you. It would be impossible for you to control her—even to expect you to would be preposterous. No, I will find you something far more suitable, some horse like my Bucko."

Mary shuddered as her discerning eye gazed upon Brestfort's mount. Bucko was as slow and sedate as a horse could be, but he also possessed lazy and rather malicious streaks, if one cared but to look into his eyes. "Truly, my lord, that won't be necessary."

"No, no, my dear. You must allow me to be the judge of this." Brestfort smiled as warmly as his nature permitted. "It would be my pleasure, for I could not rest thinking of my sweet dear riding such a dangerous creature. Oh, look, there is Lady Sophia in that carriage—and Lord Ravenstoke riding beside her as well. One does not see him here often."

Or anyone else, for that matter, Mary thought wryly, since the rest of the *ton* wisely chose to remain in their warm cozy beds so early in the morning. Brestfort, however, was one of those who firmly believed in the health of early rising, taking his mount out well before the park grew even slightly populated. Which was a lucky thing; the viscount could not lay claim to the term "bruising rider" in any sense or form.

"You know, my dear, I must confess," Brestfort was saying, "that at first I feared her ladyship did not fully approve of me, so formal and brisk was she. But now I see it was all of my imagining. It is merely her fine sense of reserve and decorum that creates such an impression, which I quite understand. She must maintain the highest standards possible, I make no doubt, with Ravenstoke being so . . . so uncaring as to the family's good name."

"No disrespect intended, of course?" Mary asked with a twist to her lips.

"Of course not. Far be it from me to cast aspersions on the family that has been so good as to sponsor you. Why, as it stands, it is almost as if I were aligning myself with the Denfields."

"Are you sure that is something the Brestfort name can support, considering the duke's . . . blatant disregard for family honor?"

"That is something I have contemplated deeply, but do not let it trouble you. I have come to the conclusion that the power of the Denfield name can not truly be mired by Ravenstoke's behaviour. And, as for the Brestfort name, well, it has been unmarked for generations. Surely it will only add to the Denfields' consequence to be connected with our respectability and rank."

"Which I am sure the duke and dowager duchess are duly grateful to you for," Mary said dryly. "And think, if your name is so beneficial to the Denfields, only imagine what wonders it can do for the Castleton line. It is a great comfort to me to know that if I am ever unfortunate enough to sink below reproach, your good name shall well protect me."

Brestfort frowned a moment; then his brow cleared. "You are making another sally, I see. What a playful nature you possess—something I am sure I will grow accustomed to, in time."

"Yes, I am sure," Mary said with an effort at control. Unconsciously, she increased her pace; Brestfort, not responding, allowed his Bucko to fall directly behind Firefly, an unfelicitous move. Bucko, viewing Firefly's rump so opportunely set before him, decided to enliven his dull existence. Reaching ahead, he sunk his yellow molars smartly into Firefly's rear.

Firefly whinnied in surprised pain. Bucko succeeded in another vicious nip before his victim, taking true exception, hied herself off at a gallop. Brestfort, exclaiming in shock, spurred Bucko after them in an attempt to catch up with Mary. Feeling the chase and unwilling to suffer another assault, Firefly wheeled on the oncoming pair and reared.

Mary, riding proper sidesaddle, flew from the horse. Both Firefly and Bucko, absent of restraint, indulged in a fine display of equine histrionics, snorting and stomping. Brestfort's fearful cries could barely be heard above the din, but the sound of hooves could be, as Ravenstoke rode into the confusion.

"Good God! Get your horse out of there, Brestfort! He'll trample her!"

"But I—"

"Get your damn horse away!" Ravenstoke swung down from Satana. Hearing the dangerous note in the duke's voice, Brestfort sawed to no good purpose on his reins.

Ravenstoke swore, strode forward, and laid his crop across Bucko's rump. The horse snorted in surprise; deeming it time to depart, he pelted away, carrying his shouting, jostling master off with him.

Ravenstoke grasped the frightened Firefly's reins and pulled her away from Mary, who had huddled over, covering her head. A safe distance away, Ravenstoke dropped the mare's reins, then strode back to Mary.

"It's over, my dear," he said as he knelt beside her and enfolded her in his arms.

"Thank God," she replied shakily, her hands sliding from over her head to Ravenstoke's broad shoulders. She could feel his heart beating in time with her own and clutched him all the closer. Breathing in a deep gulp of air, Mary gasped, "For a woman who prides herself upon her horsemanship, I do land myself in scrapes."

"Only when you are around ham-fisted clunches," Ravenstoke murmured, brushing her hair back from her face.

"Beware, sir, you speak of my future husband." Mary grimaced as she shifted.

"Where are you hurt this time?" The duke ran testing hands along her arms.

"I am fine, I believe—"

"My Lord Ravenstoke, unhand my fiancé!" Brestfort, dishevelled, his cravat flapping about his ears, limped up, evidently having abandoned his trusty steed.

"Good lord, I'm merely checking her for injury. I find that ravishing a lady immediately after she has taken a spill does not fare well for the venture."

"Ravish . . . My lord, please refrain from such reprehensible language when around my fiancée. I merely meant that this should be done in private."

"Ah, that's what I would consider improper," Ravenstoke replied. He continued to run his hands around Mary's neck as she chuckled.

"My lord, this is not seemly!"

"Mary should not be moved until it is ascertained that no bones are fractured. And I'll be damned if, for propriety's sake, we move her before we are positive. Ergo, she will be checked here. How decadent of you to have fallen off your horse in public, infant," he murmured in Mary's ear. "Could you not have waited until you were private in your bedchambers?"

"But then Brestfort must needs be there," Mary whispered back. "Improper again, my lord, very improper."

"Well, then, let me do it!" Brestfort exclaimed, approaching. "It will be more seemly for me, as her fiancé. You are, you must admit, the last man that should be doing . . . doing *that* to her!"

"Do you know what you are looking for?"

"Well, no—"

"Then I am the first man who should be doing *that* to her. Now do stop being a nuisance, Brestfort."

Brestfort's retort was stymied by the arrival of Lady Sophia in her carriage. "Mary, my dear child, are you all right?"

"Perfectly so," Mary said, quirking an inquiring brow at Ravenstoke.

"In excellent health." He nodded. "Though too thin, by far. You were lucky this time."

"That is what I've been telling her," Brestfort

cried. "That horse of hers is far too dangerous an animal for a lady's mount. Why, she could have been killed!"

"The only uncontrolled and dangerous horse was yours, Brestfort," Ravenstoke said, his green eyes frosting. " 'Gads, man, if you knew the horse was a biter, why did you allow him to get so close to Firefly?"

"He . . . he has not been a biter before," Brestfort said, unable to meet Ravenstoke's eyes. "And you are mistaken—Firefly sidled in front of him. You could not have understood the matter from the distance you were at."

"My grandson has an extremely observant eye," Lady Sophia drawled. "Especially when it pertains to certain matters—or people."

"Yes, he has very fine eyes," Mary could not resist saying. "He always spies one when one does not wish him to."

"You were lucky I did, this time."

"But I wasn't lucky the first time."

The duke's face darkened. "Mary—"

"Do bring Mary up to me in the carriage," Lady Sophia said quickly, fearing the looks in both Mary's and Ravenstoke's eyes. She was amazed that Brestfort was so dense as to miss the strong undercurrents swirling about him. "You will need to rest this afternoon, my child. How dreadful to have taken a spill the very day of your engagement ball. Indeed, I am surprised that you ride so early this morning."

"But you know we always ride at this time," Brestfort said, confused. "We were surprised to see you here this morning."

She glared daggers at him. "I did not think you would ride today, considering the momentous evening ahead. As for my grandson and I, we were here to discuss details of the ball tonight."

"And you requested I be here," Ravenstoke murmured suspiciously.

"There never seems to be any other time that I can commandeer your company," the dowager duchess said with feigned innocence. "Besides, you know I'm too too nervous over today's preparations. I thought the morning ride might calm me."

"And here it has been anything but calming. How very upsetting for you," Ravenstoke said with a touch of irony. "Very well, let us not keep Mary waiting. You take her up, and I will attend Firefly." With very little conscious thought, he cradled Mary within his arms and lifted her into the carriage.

"Here now!" the viscount objected. "Unhand the lady. I shall carry her!"

"Oh, for God's sake!" Ravenstoke said, his eyes flashing dangerously. "I begin to find your overly conscientious manner fatiguing, Brestfort, very fatiguing."

"Overly conscientious?" Brestfort flushed. "It is only proper that I carry my fiancée."

"He has you there," Lady Sophia said with amusement. "Do hand her over to him, Alastair."

"I am perfectly fine," Mary objected, wriggling in Ravenstoke's stiffening arms as the men glared at each other. "Set me down, and I can manage for myself."

"No," Ravenstoke said tightly. After a tense pause, he transferred Mary into Brestfort's waiting arms.

"I am fine," Mary said angrily. "I feel like a sack of grain; now set me down!"

"Ravenstoke has the right of it, my dear," Brestfort said with a grunt as he took her squirming body in his arms, he being far shorter and lighter than Ravenstoke. "I'm sure you are putting a brave front on it, but your delicate sensibilities must be totally overset. Say what you like, Miss Castleton, but we will acquire a much gentler mount for you on the morrow."

"Silly twit," Lady Sophia murmured under her breath as the viscount delivered this pompous pronouncement while lurching unevenly as he carried Mary to the carriage. She smiled, however, as she saw the stiff, stunned expression upon Ravenstoke's face; casting her eyes upward, her ladyship sent a silent prayer of thanksgiving to heaven. She couldn't have arranged things better if she had tried. Faith, she doubted that anything could be better than this!

"My dear Lady Sophia, everything has been simply perfect tonight, and the future couple is so distinguished. I am sure this is the engagement of the season," a matron in purple gushed to the dowager duchess, who had gained a moment's respite.

"Why thank you, Matilda, it does appear we've had quite a turnout."

"Oh, Sophia, you are far too modest." The matron tittered, the purple feathers on her turban bobbing and wobbling. "It is an absolute squeeze, my dear. It's such a pity, though, that your grandson could not be here as well. It was a matter of urgent business, was it not, that kept him away?"

"Yes, of course it was, Matilda dear," Lady Sophia said, her smile stiffening.

"Alas, is that not how it always goes?" Matilda's smile widened maliciously. "Men always must attend to their . . . business . . . at the most inopportune times. Oh, there is my Brian waiting for me — such a dear, sweet boy to escort his mother to a ball. You will excuse me?"

"Cat," Lady Sophia muttered quietly as the matron sailed away. "I could kill Alastair tonight."

"Damn fine party you've got, Duchess," Castleton boomed as he clumped up, employing but one crutch; the other hand was occupied in holding a sloshing drink. "And damn fine champagne," he added, plunking himself down on the seat next to her. "Stap me if I can believe it; we did it! We got the chit shot off—and to the Brestfort family, no less! 'Pon rep, it is wondrous. My little Mary to marry a Brestfort. Always thought they were too damned starchy and high in the instep for my liking.

"But they should suit Mary fine. How did you like my engagement announcement?"

Lady Sophia shuddered delicately. "It was . . . wondrous, Castleton. Especially when you ended with the 'Drink one, drink all' line."

"Knew you'd like it." Castleton nodded, pleased. "Figured it'd impress the Brestforts. Eh, Brestfort, my fine buck," Castleton called as that young man approached them. "How are you enjoying yourself?"

"Excuse me, Mr. Castleton. My Lady Sophia, have you seen my dear fiancée?" the viscount asked with a deep bow.

"Why no, not lately."

"I can't find her, and the Duke of Enden wishes to speak to her," Brestfort said, his chest swelling with pride. "It has been an excellent party, my lady. But you say you have not seen dear Miss Castleton?"

"No, I haven't." A sinking feeling entered the duchess's chest. "But I did see her near the balcony doors. Perhaps she stepped out for a breath of fresh air."

"Unaccompanied, madam?" Brestfort's brows rose. "No, no. Miss Castleton would never do such a thing."

"But, my lord, I am sure it is such an overwhelming night for Mary that she might have needed time to compose herself."

"Er, yes, my boy," Castleton agreed nervously, sharing an apprehensive look with Lady Sophia. "Probably didn't want everyone to see her cry—females do that sort of thing at these affairs. You just go look, cheer her up, romance her a bit, what?"

"Yes . . . perhaps," Brestfort said, nodding solemnly. "The dear thing is probably hoping I will come and comfort her. We are engaged, after all."

"That's the ticket!" Castleton said. "Best you go find her!"

"Castleton, perhaps you would care to help the viscount?" Lady Sophia suggested.

"No, blast it. That's Brestfort's job, not mine anymore. It's his problem; she's his now!"

"That's right. She's mine now," Brestfort said with surprise. His eyes took on a new light. "I will find her and . . . comfort her."

"I mislike the look in that boy's eyes," Lady Sophia said as he strode away.

"I mislike the words 'balcony' and 'fresh air,'" Castleton grumbled.

"I never thought I'd say this, but I agree with you. I mislike those words very much."

Ravenstoke walked quietly through the gardens, intent upon slipping into the ballroom through the side doors; he did not wish for an announcement or grand entrance. He had stayed away from Mary's engagement party as long as he could, but he knew he would finally attend it. He could not have it whispered that he had insulted both his grandmother and Mary with his absence, but by now the announcement that Mary was to wed Brestfort would have been made. That was what he had wished to avoid, after all.

"No, my lord, I think we ought to go inside now," he heard a voice say in the darkness. "Please, release me and let us return."

Ravenstoke cursed softly. He knew that voice. Rounding the corner, he cursed again; he knew the scene just as well. In the dim shadows, he could see the back of a man bent over Mary's slight form. Mary seemed to be pushing him away and the man was clumsily grasping her, still attempting to claim a kiss. 'Gads, did she never find men who knew how to hold her properly?

Rage filled him. Would he never be free from this scene? Here he had Mary prepared to be safely wed and protected only to discover her suffering importunities from incompetent clods once more. Without further consideration, Ravenstoke stalked up to the couple, spun the man around roughly, and landed him a stunning facer. The man yelped in pain, reeled back with his hand to his face, and, stumbling, crashed against the balcony doors and slid down them in a heap.

Ravenstoke followed after him, but Mary grabbed his arm urgently. "Ravenstoke, no!"

Still in the grip of rage, Ravenstoke shook her hand free and lifted his fist. Mary seized it again, making his blow go wild, so that it smashed harmlessly but loudly into the balcony door. "It's Brestfort, Alastair! It's Brestfort!"

"What?" Ravenstoke's fist froze in midair and he stared at her, nonplussed. "My God, why didn't I think of that?"

Before either of them could move, the door, barricaded by the vanquished Brestfort, rattled and trembled. "Mary? You out there? What the hell is going on?"

"Oh, lord, Stepfather!" Mary muttered as Ravenstoke rushed to help her haul Brestfort's unconscious form away from the door. The door exploded open a moment later.

"I'll save you girl, I'll save youuu!" Castleton crashed through, pitched forward, and slid, rattled, and bumped across the hard stone of the balcony floor. "Blast it!" He pulled himself up to a sitting position. "What the deuce is this?"

He received no reply, as Mary and Ravenstoke were intent on dragging the now-moaning viscount to his feet.

"Would you care to tell him, my lord?" Mary asked curtly as she brushed at Brestfort's clothes.

"Just rushing to the rescue again," Ravenstoke said as he held the unconscious Brestfort up. "Forgive me, but it was an all-too-familiar scene. I reacted precipitously."

"That you did!" Mary declared. "And to hit the man was totally unnecessary. Remember in the future that you no longer need to rescue me. That onerous task now belongs to Brestfort."

"Onerous is correct."

"As if this morning wasn't bad enough, you had to do this!"

"Mary, you here?" Castleton was finally able to focus on something other than his pain. "Good. Thought someone had hauled you off again."

"No, though I wish to God they would!"

"She is fine," Ravenstoke said loudly, as the three coherent participants realized they were no longer alone. Half the crowded ballroom was gaping at them, while the other half pushed up eagerly from behind. "There is nothing wrong," Ravenstoke repeated. "Everything is all right."

At that inopportune moment, the Viscount Brestfort chose to return to the conscious world. Propped between Mary and Ravenstoke, he groaned, rolled his head drunkenly, and opened one eye. The other was purpled and swollen shut. "Ravenstoke. You hit me."

"So I did. My apologies. I mistook you for another."

"Another what?"

"Why, another man."

"Another man? What do you mean?"

"I mean, I did not recognize you and thought it was another kissing Mary."

"Well, I never!" Suddenly, Brestfort noticed the crowd and reddened. Puffing up considerably, he jerked away from Ravenstoke so rudely that he jabbed the duke in the stomach. The crowd gasped. "Explain yourself Ravenstoke! Why should you think Mary would kiss any other man than me?"

"You have it the wrong way around, I fear. I thought you were kissing her—there is a difference, *n'est-ce pas?*" The crowd tittered appreciatively. "Which is only proper upon your engagement, Brestfort, I am sure. I had not intended any insult—it is merely that I thought a different man kissed her, which, you must admit, would have been an importunity. The light was dim, and I did not recognize you, you see."

"Another man? I take exception to that. My fiancée is not the type of woman to attract such attentions."

"I will assume you do not mean that as an insult to Miss Castleton," Ravenstoke inquired dangerously. "For certainly she is charming enough to draw the attention of many admirers."

The men were amazed at Ravenstoke's fortitude, while the ladies condemned Brestfort as an ill-mannered boor and found Ravenstoke a dashing cavalier they would die to have. Brestfort became slightly nervous as he not only noticed the crowd's disfavor but Ravenstoke's tense jawline. "Well . . . well . . . not exactly."

"I am glad to hear it, for I would be forced to take exception to that. But I knew you could not mean it, for, after all, Miss Castleton is your fiancée and deserves your highest respect."

"Yes, yes—but you hit me!" Brestfort reminded him stubbornly, causing the crowd to mutter and lay bets on his fate.

"Brestfort's a dead man for sure," one overly loud voice whispered.

"Ooh, yes, it does serve him right," a female voice replied.

"I believe I have apologized," Ravenstoke said with frigid politeness. "However, if you wish to call me out, I will be only too happy to oblige you."

"My lord, no!" Mary's hand went out to him.

The duke looked down at her a moment, his eyes hooded and his posture rigid. "But as it was only in concern for Miss Castleton's welfare," he continued in a controlled voice, "I should think a duel unnecessary. I should very much mislike to wound Miss Castleton's future husband—but that is up to you. What is it to be, Brestfort?"

"I . . . I could not meet you," Brestfort said, turning pale. He had not realized his extreme danger until that moment. "I . . . I mean, I would not wish to cause my beloved any distress. It would cut up all her peace."

"Yes, yes, it would," Mary said at once, just as

214

pale.

"And Miss Castleton's welfare is all that matters," Ravenstoke said. "Is that not so, Brestfort?"

"Yes, it is," Brestfort said, his lips twitching into a nervous smile.

"Well, there now, that is enough," Lady Sophia stated firmly as she forged her way to the front of the crowd. "Gracious, Alastair, you've managed to draw such a crowd that I found it impossible to make my way through." The elite bystanders had the grace to laugh in embarrassment and some, who had complained bitterly when stabbed with the duchess's cane only a moment ago, now fell back even further for that grand dame. "When I told you to try and make it to my ball if you could, I did not mean you had to create such a stir."

"A thousand apologies, Grandmother," Ravenstoke said with an excellent leg. "I only sought to do your bidding."

"Well, the one thing I can't deny"—his grandmother chuckled—"is that you do add dash to a party." The crowd laughed. "Now, let us adjourn to the ball. I fear the musicians are falling into a severe melancholy with no one to listen to them. Brestfort, do come with me, so that we may attend that eye of yours. And someone be so kind as to assist Mr. Castleton from the floor and discover his crutches. They must be about somewhere."

The crowd was sluggish to react, reluctant to leave the small drama, but Lady Sophia's voice brooked no refusal. They evaporated slowly through the doors, snatches of conversation swirling about: ". . . can't believe Ravenstoke backed down" . . . "lucky Brestfort to have Miss Castleton's skirts to hide behind" . . . "fortunate lady, to have Ravenstoke to champion her so . . ."

The crowd finally dispersed under Lady Sophia's watchful eye; indeed, so expert was her direction that no one noticed the two people who still stood upon the balcony.

"I'm sorry, little one," Ravenstoke said, quietly. "I did not mean to ruin your party."

"Or my fiancé? No, do not apologize again," Mary said softly. Amazing herself, she lifted a hand and brushed a fallen lock from Ravenstoke's forehead.

"You'd best wed him soon, Mary. Or I will kill him."

"Don't," she said sharply. "I could not go through another engagement like this."

Ravenstoke clasped her hand as she pulled it away from him and raised it to his lips. "Never, my dear. Do not worry — I only jested."

"But I did not. Do let us go in now, my lord. My fiancé will be wondering where I am."

"Yes, he will, which is only right. And you have my word on it, infant, I promise not to interfere anymore."

Mary nodded mutely. It was the way things should be, but she felt as if an iron hand clamped her heart, squeezing the life from it and leaving her bereft.

Chapter Eleven

OH, JOYOUS OCCASION

"To pro-os-per-ity and a loooong life to-oo-gether," Castleton slurred, lifting a weaving wine glass.

"A toast!" A very solemn Brestfort burped, shying his glass against Castleton's. "To my lovely, lovely bride."

It was clear to the plainest eye that Castleton was tap-hacket, while Viscount Brestfort was merely a bit on the go.

"Come on, R-R-Ravenstoke, it's your turn. A toast, the boy's gettin' r-r-riveted on the morrow, b'gad!" Castleton, red and shiny faced, beamed at his companions.

"To the most fortunate of men," Ravenstoke murmured, raising the only steady glass at the table.

"Yes, that's me," Brestfort nodded, stabbing a finger into his chest. He might already have been slightly in his altitudes, but it said much about the man that he sat erect within his chair, no relaxing of his correct style noticeable, except for the vacuous expression upon his face.

Castleton, however, sprawled more on the table

than in his chair, his cravat a mangled, damp affair. "We-ell, my buck, ready to be shackled for life?"

"Is a man ever?" Brestfort asked with a giggle. A glance in Ravenstoke's direction caused him to take another swig from his glass. But . . . but I am ready, of course. No doubt about that. I'll wed my Miss Castleton with pleasure. Everyone thinks—knows—I'm a lucky dog. Stole a march on everyone else, didn't I?"

"That you did," Ravenstoke said with subtle irony.

"I swept Miss Castleton off her feet. She said so herself." Brestfort brightened once again. "Fine girl. Will make an excellent wife. Unexceptional. Knows everybody."

"Noooo, didn't know that," Castleton said in amazement. "Everybody?"

"Everybody that is anybody." Brestfort nodded. "Knows how to behave, but got a strange sense of levity. Doesn't seem to put people off, mind you."

"Queer sort of chit," Castleton agreed. "Queeer sort, never could un-un-understand her. . . ."

"But I . . . I will become accustomed to that. I mean no one takes exception, why should I? She's a pretty little thing, no hurly-burly miss. Knows what's due her."

"We talkin' about the s-same gal?" Castleton asked in drunken confusion. "No, c-can't see that, she's always in trouble—why . . ."

"Would you like another drink, Castleton?" Ravenstoke interrupted, raising the bottle temptingly before the man's face.

Castleton's bleary eyes focussed with single-minded desire upon the bottle. "Would I!"

He reached out his shaky glass and Ravenstoke filled it to the brim. Castleton grinned in sheer ecstasy and drained the half-glass that remained by the time the wobbling vessel reached his lips. He sat up straight and gasped, "B'gad, that's good!" Burping loudly, he promptly toppled from his chair.

Brestfort blinked and leaned slightly forward, the better to view Castleton's empty chair. "Why, he's fallen to the ground," he observed, his tone disapproving.

"Yes, so he has," Ravenstoke remarked. "Do not let it trouble you—he is accustomed to sleeping on the floor."

"Very well," the viscount said after a moment. "I can't say I approve, though—terribly irregular."

"Yes, but there is no one left in the club to notice," Ravenstoke observed. "No reason to let it worry you. After all, a man has only one night before his wedding. Do you look forward to your marriage?"

"Indeed." Brestfort nodded dutifully. "And of course, I know I can say this to a man like you—to my wedding night as well."

"Why?" Ravenstoke asked baldly.

"Why?" Brestfort repeated, nonplussed. "Well . . . surely you must know what I mean. Ah, I see. Forgive me if I was indiscreet. True, true, but the prospect of the wedding night carried me away. Indeed, we will not say another word on that head."

"No, I meant why are you looking forward to the wedding night?" Ravenstoke explained patiently.

"Well . . . well . . . because . . ." Brestfort was at a loss. "Surely I need not explain to you, of all men—no disrespect intended—why I look forward to that night. I am sure I could not tell you anything new on that score."

"You are too kind," Ravenstoke murmured. "But

that is my very point, dear Brestfort. Do you know everything you should for your wedding night?"

"Do I? Why, of course I do," Brestfort sputtered. "Perhaps not as much as you, but certainly enough to get me through . . . through tomorrow night," he said, lowering his voice and looking about.

"I am glad to hear that. But how do you know?"

"Ah, I see." The viscount tried desperately to make sense of Ravenstoke's question, unwilling, ever since the contretemps of the engagement party, to displease the duke. "You wonder, since I hold such an excellent reputation, if I have had any experience in that quarter? Indeed, my lord, I am a man about town, after all. I have had my *affaires de coeur,* and my mistresses. I am no different from any other man, I assure you."

"And do you plan to take mistresses after you wed Mary?"

"I had not considered that yet, but I would imagine that naturally I—"

"Would not," Ravenstoke purred.

"W-would not?"

"Of course not."

"Not even a discreet one? Even my father, who is the highest stickler, considers it acceptable—as long as one is discreet."

"A common enough belief, but a fallacy. Take it from a man who knows these things, there can never be a discreet affair. The wife will always know, even if she pretends otherwise. Furthermore, I am not sure that your judgement in that department can be trusted."

"I beg your pardon?"

"I worry about your taste in mistresses, Brestfort," Ravenstoke said kindly. "That last little straw damsel of yours could not be considered either

220

discreet or discriminating in her clientele. Did not your father stress upon you the importance of a clean and healthy mistress? It would not do for you to catch anything unfortunate that you might impart to Mary."

The viscount goggled a moment before he managed to say, "You knew about Felicity?"

"As I said, she is not the most discreet. Though I own, I only cared to look into the matter a week ago. Your style the night of the engagement party had me a trifle concerned. I was not quite pleased to discover Felicity was your chosen paramour."

"But . . . but a man must have his fancy pieces!" Brestfort exclaimed, unable to believe it was Ravenstoke uttering such strictures. "Would you have me totally inexperienced?"

"No, indeed. Just more discriminating in your choice of instructress. I would not have you taught the wrong things, my dear Brestfort. Which leads me to my next concern."

"And what is that?" Brestfort took a quick swallow from his glass.

"How do you intend to treat Mary tomorrow?"

"What! That is none of your business, sirrah!"

"No, but I am making it my business. I fear that Castleton, the one who should be offering you such advice upon this special night, is slightly discommoded. Therefore, I will stand in his stead for the traditional paternal talk. Look upon me as a proxy father."

The viscount downed an entire glass at a swallow, unable to imagine Ravenstoke as anything close to fatherly.

"Now, how do you intend to deal with Mary on your wedding night?"

"Why, I . . . I shall do my manly duty by her, of

course. I mean, the union must be consummated. You . . . you have no objection to that, do you?"

"Why, of course not, I only inquire upon the hows of it. Do you perhaps intend to treat Mary as you do your ladybirds — or I should say your ex-ladybirds?"

"My God, I cannot credit this conversation." Brestfort stared wildly about; alas, not a soul except the snoring Castleton was nearby to aid him. Even the waiters were elsewhere. He swallowed. "Naturally, I would never think of treating my lady wife as I do women of the other sort. Not in any moment would I so far forget myself. Miss Castleton is a lady, after all."

"Which means?"

"For God's sake, Ravenstoke, must I be plainer?" The viscount choked, beginning to perspire.

"Yes, I fear you must."

"I mean, I know full well that ladies have no . . . no fondness for such baseness, and that I need be quick and clean about it."

"Quick and clean about it? My dear man, she is an innocent, and you intend to be quick about it?"

"Well . . . well . . . yes," Brestfort said before he could stop himself. "Is that wrong?"

"Yes, my dear man. Mary is an innocent and cannot be treated like Felicity."

"But . . . but what must I do differently?"

"Listen, for that is what I intend to tell you. I misliked the way you handled Mary the night of your engagement party — "

"Is that why you struck me?"

"No, no, I truly thought you someone else. Good God, man, if I struck every man inexperienced in the art of love, I'd be taking on half the world. Even my famous luck couldn't keep me from dying

222

on the field of honor, then. However, you are different. You must learn to be more accomplished, for I would not suffer Mary to have an ineffectual lover."

"Well, indeed! I have never had any complaints!"

"Of course you wouldn't, not from women like Felicity whom you've paid. Don't be a block!"

"My God, Ravenstoke, you go too far!"

"Now don't fly up in the boughs, Brestfort." Ravenstoke poured the shaking man another drink. "Do but consider what I am to tell you in the light of free and expert advice, advice that many take a lifetime to acquire. Now, despite the prevalent notions, all women are the same. The, as you say, quick way is not the best, and for a woman to receive the slightest pleasure from the experience—"

Brestfort's eyes bulged. "Pleasure? But a lady does not look for—"

"Don't be a sapskull. Why should a base-born woman enjoy the experience while a lady is not allowed to? Good gracious, man, the inordinate amount of married women taking cicisbeos should tell you something. They take them because their husbands ignore the simple fact that women, too, desire the pleasure of love. But you will not give Mary cause to look elsewhere, do I make myself clear?"

The viscount stared into the duke's stern eyes and nodded. A serious doubt as to whether he would even survive till the wedding night seized him, so cold and dangerous did the duke appear. Marriage to the much-feted Miss Castleton, Brestfort realized, might not be the triumph he had considered it. "Perfectly clear," he gulped.

"Excellent, now listen carefully." Ravenstoke proceeded to enlighten a flushing viscount upon the facts of the male and female as the viscount had never been enlightened before, or, in truth, cared to be ever again. In one short hour, he was told more than all his respected years on the face of the earth had taught him—indeed, even more than his father, friends, and lovers all together had told him. Perspiration wilted his cravat and he choked as he understood that the stern oracle before him fully expected him not only to remember everything said, but to employ those very same teachings within the short span of twenty-four hours. It was enough to unman a fellow!

"Now, do you have any questions?" Ravenstoke asked dispassionately, as if he were a tutor addressing a slow-witted child.

"No . . . no. You have covered more than enough," Brestford said thickly. "My God, Ravenstoke, you truly are a libertine. The things you not only know but can even say . . ."

"Do stop acting like an old maid, Brestfort," Ravenstoke commanded. "You did say you were a man about town, didn't you? It is a subject, I assure you, that I do not often choose to discourse on, especially with another man. But in this one instant, I deemed it necessary. It was clear that you did not possess such information, and I would not have Mary face any more discomfort or distress than necessary."

"Regardless of mine," Brestfort replied, shaken totally out of his composure.

"A home truth, my dear Brestfort. And may I say, once again standing for Castleton—"

"No. No. No more," Brestfort pleaded. "I promise I will remember everything you said."

"Excellent. Then we should have no difficulty. Only remember," the duke said softly, "that if you

224

ever choose to cause Mary the slightest heartache — nay, the slightest displeasure — I will not hesitate to run you through. Better she be a grieving widow than a discontented wife, do you not think? Well then, drink now, for tomorrow you become the luckiest of men."

Brestfort had not the look of the luckiest of men but rather that of one hearing the doors of Newgate slam shut securely upon him. He smiled weakly and raised his glass, much as a gladiator saluting his Caesar before death.

"Well, my dear, let us drink to your forthcoming marriage tomorrow," Lady Sophia said, as she and Mary sat quietly in the drawing room. "I cannot imagine why you do not choose to do something tonight — this sitting alone at home and doing nothing is giving me a headache."

"I merely did not wish to deal with the crowd of well-wishers that I attract," Mary said quietly.

"Now that I can very well understand. If I face one more smiling matron, I swear I will be forced to commit mayhem." Rather than ringing for Adams, Lady Sophia walked over to the sideboard and lifted the duke's favorite brandy.

"Lady Sophia, what do you think you are doing?"

"I am having a drink," the older woman snapped. "I am fully old enough to have something a little stronger than wine, don't you agree? Do you join me?"

"Er, no, I do not think I am old enough."

"Tish, don't be impertinent," Lady Sophia shot back. "I have never required this before, but I think I do now."

"Do you think that wise if you have never experienced any before?"

"Look who talks of wisdom! If we are considering what is wise, I will refrain from this drink if you will but refrain from your marriage to that popinjay Brestfort."

"Then have your drink, my lady. Though I do not think you will receive pleasure in it."

"Pooh, it must be beneficial or else the men would not imbibe so regularly of it."

"Oh? Since when do you consider men to be the most intelligent on that head?"

"You have me there, my dear." Her ladyship smiled as she poured herself a glass of the amber liquid. "But if they are allowed to drink tonight — and don't mistake the matter, that is exactly what they are doing this very minute — then I am allowed to as well. Do not expect me to face this debacle tomorrow without sustenance. Are you sure you will not join me?"

"No, please. I prefer to face the morrow with a clear head."

"If only you were facing it with a clear head . . . You would be giving that odious toady his comeuppance rather than driving a poor old lady to drink." The duchess took an experimental sip from her glass. Her face twisted. "My God, is this the stuff that the men rave over and cherish? You are right; they must be all about in their heads. Please, Mary, call the wedding off and do not force me to take another taste of this vile drink."

"I am not forcing you to do anything. I refuse to be blackmailed, so do not think it."

"No, you only allow my foolish grandson that privilege. Imagine, letting him lead you by the nose right into matrimony — and with an impossible prig at that!"

Mary sighed. "We've been over all this before. Please, let us not discuss it once again. I have had my choices in the matter—although not many—and I have made them. I would not jilt the viscount this close to the wedding, anyway. Do allow me some honour."

"There you go again—honour! Honour is for men; they are generally the only ones foolish enough to tout it."

"Then let us not call it honour but . . . kindness. No matter what you say, it is the viscount who has been treated unfairly in this whole affair."

"Ha, then rectify that and leave him at the altar. Get him out of this before it is too late." The duchess took another distasteful sip. "I can tell by your expression that you will not listen and I but waste my breath. Very well, then, come sit beside me, my dear child, and tell me how you may be happy."

Mary fought back the sting of tears as the duchess's tone softened with concern. She rose and went to sit beside the older woman who drank her brandy with resolution. "I shall make myself happy. I am determined. It is not as if the viscount will be a demanding husband or purposefully unkind. And he would never, like my stepfather, drink and gamble everything away or keep low company. For that I must be grateful."

"That may be well and good, but only consider your children, my dear. Can you really tolerate all those little Brestforts strutting about, all stuffed shirts like their papa?"

Mary laughed. "You do paint a lowering picture, but they will be my children too, so perhaps there will be hope for them yet."

"Very well . . . but can you truly learn to live without love?"

Mary stared off into space, a sad smile touching her face. "Funny, that has been my ambition for as long as I can remember—to live without love. Oh, I don't mean simple human affection or company, I mean the burning passion and all-consuming love."

"Why?"

"Because I fear to become like my mother."

"How so?"

"She was so full of life itself with father. He was her whole world. And when he died, she had nothing left of herself—she was just a shell."

"Oh, my dear . . . I know you've talked on this before, but I thought it merely a comment in passing. I did not know it ran so deep within you. My dear child, do you not realize that you are not your mother, you are a totally different person. I knew her. I thought her charming. But she did not possess the sense of self or strength of will that you have. The life and love you would have would be different than your mother's, or anyone else's for that matter, because you are you. Can you not see that?"

"Are you so sure I am that strong? I do not feel strong anymore." Mary smiled bitterly.

"But you are. Your life is up to you—you need not live your mother's life over again. Indeed, you sound like Alastair, allowing the troubles of his parents to haunt his life. It does not have to be that way. Love does not always make you weak. I tell you, I loved my Robert with a great passion, and no one ever considered me weak."

"No, I would say not."

"If you had seen me directly after his death, you would not have recognized me. Yet, given a year or two, I finally found life important again. And I do not consider that time of grief, or the remaining sorrow of missing him, as too great a price to pay for the years I loved him. Who knows, your mother might have found herself again if she had had more time."

"I . . . I had never thought of that." Suddenly Mary wearily laid her head upon the duchess's shoulder, letting her tears silently fall. "I had never thought of that . . . thank you."

The duchess put her arm around Mary's shoulder and patted her comfortingly, silence falling in the room.

"Oh dear, what have I done?" Mary said abruptly, still sniffling.

"Landed yourself squarely in the briars," the duchess said, patting her head. "Now, if you choose to, you can remove yourself from this coil."

Mary pulled herself up, dashing away her tears. "You mean jilt poor Brestfort."

"That ninnyhammer is not poor anything. And I have more in mind than just jilting him," the duchess went on, smiling mischievously. "Do you wish to hear my plan? I have had everything set in readiness in the hope you would come to your senses and wish to escape this imbroglio. But, alas, you never came to me."

"Tell me what you mean," Mary said quietly. The duchess, after exclaiming in excitement, began talking. Mary listened intently.

The duchess finally stopped. "Well, dear, what do you think? Is it not a wonderful plan?"

"Indeed. It is what I wished for in the beginning. And you would promise not to tell Ravenstoke my whereabouts?"

"My dear, I set it up that way, did I not?"

Mary looked carefully at her companion. "That would be imperative, for I could not bear his coming after me and we going through all this again."

"No, of course not."

Mary considered a moment, then shook her head regretfully. "No, I could not bring myself to do it. I could not leave the viscount at the altar."

"But why not?"

"Because I am still not sure that I am not running away from life, as your grandson has always maintained."

"But surely, my dear, if you—"

"No, I've allowed the wedding to go this far—I will marry the viscount tomorrow. I thank you for your consideration and kindness in trying to help me escape, but I am tired of running. Now," Mary said quietly, "I think I would like to go to bed. It will prove a long day tomorrow."

"Make that a long lifetime. Oh, very well, go ahead, then."

"Are you coming up?"

"No, indeed not." The duchess raised the glass of brandy. "This vile drink is tasting better by the minute—and there are far too few of those before I must watch you ruin your life."

All the *ton* could be found under the roof of St. Matthew's the next noontide. There was not one who wished to miss the famous union of Viscount Brestfort and Miss Mary Castleton, especially when the infamous Duke of Denfield was to walk the bride down the aisle.

However, the respectful whispers in the sainted church were slowly increasing to flagrant chatter as the clock struck fifteen minutes past the appointed hour.

An usher could be observed walking down the aisle to where the dowager duchess sat. He bent and whispered something that caused her ladyship to glare at him, then rise and proceed back down the aisle with precarious precision. It could also be seen that the bride's father—stepfather, rather—twisted in his seat to watch her retreat, a slightly worried expression on his ruddy, hung-over face.

The duchess, however, did not maintain her silence once she reached her grandson in the antechamber. "Well, Alastair, what is this all about?"

"Mary has not yet arrived."

"What of it? That is not so uncommon. It is but fifteen minutes past the time. I myself was twenty minutes late to my wedding. If a girl cannot be allowed some small leeway on her wedding day, it is a shame. Faith, Alastair, do stop acting like an expectant father or you'll send me into hysterics soon."

Ravenstoke bowed sardonically. "A thousand apologies, Grandmother. I can see that you do not feel quite the thing. You look a trifle pale."

"I'm fine!" Lady Sophia snapped quickly. "I merely have a slight . . . headache. I do wish everyone would stop inquiring about my health today—now, where is Brestfort?"

"I . . . I am here," a weak voice said from over in a corner. A slightly yellow viscount stepped out from the shadows. Though his raiment was everything a well-heeled bridegroom's should be, his eyes were glazed and his breathing shallow.

"My God, you look burnt to the socket," the duchess exclaimed. "No doubt dipping too deeply last night."

"Er, yes, that is all," the viscount said quickly, flushing deeply and unable to look the lady in the eye. After last night's discussion, he was sure he could not even look his own mother in the eye.

"Yes, well, that was to be expected," the duchess said with surprising leniency, her own eyes turning away. "I suggest we proceed."

"But, Grandmother, Mary has not arrived yet."

"I know that! I know that! But she will."

"You are positive?" Ravenstoke asked, his tone sharpening.

"So that is it." Lady Sophia eyed the duke with displeasure. "You thought she might yet slip her leash. Well, it is a pity, but she intends to go through with this ceremony."

"But why wouldn't she?" Brestfort asked, bewildered.

"No reason at all," Ravenstoke said, casting his grandmother a quelling stare.

"No, none at all," the duchess said irately. "For she is a woman of honor who would not back away—no matter what the ones who love her say! I left her only this morning, donning her gown."

"Very well," Ravenstoke said, his eyes lidded. "I was merely a trifle concerned at the delay."

"I only wish it was with good reason," the duchess said darkly. "Now that that is settled, you'd best send Brestfort up the aisle with his groomsmen."

"Now?" Brestfort yelped, all show of dignity forgotten.

"Yes, now," Lady Sophia said. "It will give the guests something to watch until Mary's arrival."

"As you say." Ravenstoke nodded, adding quietly, "Later on, my dear, do allow me to mix a concoction that I know will remedy your . . . headache."

The duchess stiffened, her brow rising. "Why you

impertinent puppy! How did you guess?"

"It's in your eyes," Ravenstoke said with a gentle smile. "Now return to your seat; I'm sorry I bothered you."

"Thank you," the duchess said, and turned. "You'd better offer young Brestfort some of that concoction as well. He looks downpinned."

Brestfort jumped as if from a trance. "Er . . . what did you say?"

"Come on, Brestfort," Ravenstoke commanded sternly. "It is time for you to walk down the aisle."

"But . . . but Miss Castleton isn't here yet. Shouldn't we wait?"

"You heard Grandmother—Mary will arrive," Ravenstoke said. "In fact, I will go myself and see what is detaining her."

"How very kind," Brestfort said mechanically. "Well then, this is it."

"Yes," Ravenstoke replied, his tone flat. "This is it."

Ravenstoke found Mary's maid in the hall outside her room. "Martha, what is keeping your mistress?"

Martha stopped, looking perplexed. "My lord?"

"What keeps your mistress? Where is she?"

"Is she not at the wedding?"

"No, of course not," Ravenstoke said impatiently. "I would not be here otherwise."

"But I left her fully prepared some thirty minutes ago. She said she needed but a few moments to compose herself."

"Yes, most likely." Ravenstoke smiled. "She has probably forgotten the time, worrying over the placement of some curl or another."

"Yes, my lord," Martha said dubiously, for Miss

Castleton rarely dallied over her toilet.

"I'll just go and remind her." The duke continued down the hall to Mary's door. He rapped firmly upon it and called, "Mary, are you ready?"

He received no answer and rapped again. "Mary, what is keeping you?"

He turned the doorknob and found the room locked. "Mary, let me in." Still there was no answer. "Mary, open the door or I will break it down."

Silence met his ears. He stood for a moment in contemplation and then leaning his broad shoulders against the door, heaved, splintering the wood and bursting the door open.

"Mary, what is all this . . . ?" His eyes scanned the room and his voice stilled as he saw the open window, curtains fluttering in the breeze. He walked over to it and cursed. A knotted rope of bedsheets trailed to the ground below it. He peered about; but saw only a quiet, silent landscape, devoid of runaway brides.

Pulling his head in from the window, his face thunderous, he spun around to study the room again. Mary's wedding gown lay in a shimmer of satin across the sheetless bed. He walked over to it, reaching out to touch the cool fabric. A white envelope, nearly invisible, lay against the white of the gown. Only the bold lettering on the paper stood out: My Lord Ravenstoke.

The Duke of Denfield picked up the missive and, after the slightest hesitation, pulled the letter from its wrapper and began to read.

"My dear Lord Ravenstoke,

I beg pardon for the inconvenience I am about to cause you, but I cannot find it within myself to wed the Viscount Brestfort. I have tried my very best to do so, but for me it is impossible. Therefore, I have decided to make my escape—an escape, you must admit, that is long overdue.

I can only hope I have performed it in a manner that would do Master Marcus justice. I have finally claimed my future as my own responsibility, my lord, as I should have done well before this time. I ask you not to be troubled. I have found a safe and settled position that pleases me well; do not imagine I am lost on the streets of London, in dire need of your rescue. You have my word that you will not find me in a bawdy house six months from now. Nor will you find me anywhere else, so please do not attempt the search.

I thank you and the duchess for all that you have tried to do for me; I shall miss you both, and wish you all the happiness in the world. Indeed, I am sure that your life cannot help but be happier without me to either rescue or settle. I am sure, when you talked me down from that tree so long ago, you never imagined what a difficulty I would become. I am sorry to leave you to apologize to the viscount, but he will find this is for the best. I could never have been the wife he thought I would be.

Your most unobedient servant,

Mary

Ravenstoke stared at the note in his hand, his face grim. Yet as he slowly folded the paper and placed it securely within his waistcoat, a strange, almost relieved smile, lightened his features.

"I should strangle you, infant," he murmured gently, yet he strode from the room with a much easier tread than he'd demonstrated upon entering.

Brestfort blanched as the crowd murmured and a forbidding Lord Ravenstoke stalked down the aisle towards him, his green eyes riveted upon the viscount. "M-my lord, what is it?" Brestfort's frazzled mind raced wildly about, searching for any possible insult he might have offered his fiancée, for surely that was what the delay was about, and what displeased the duke. He swallowed painfully; here he was, not even wed to the lady, and Ravenstoke was about to run him through, he just knew it. He cast an appealing eye towards his best man, hoping his friend would stand in as his second.

"Brestfort, I have some disquieting news for you," Ravenstoke said in an ominous tone. "Would you care to step outside, away from all these people?"

Brestfort gasped. Why, the man was going to cut him down without even the benefit of seconds! "No . . . no, I would not!" His voice cracked. "I will stay here with my friends."

"This is news you might wish to hear alone."

"You can't make me do it! Whatever you have to say can be said here."

"You will not like it."

"I will not leave with you. I-I do not know what Miss Castleton said, but I have not done anything to . . . to displease her."

"No, but I am sorry to say that she has run away," the duke replied.

"It's not my fault!"

"No, no. It was Mary's decision alone. She did

not wish to marry you," Ravenstoke said, as kindly as possible.

The viscount's face twisted with emotion, and he slumped back, leaning against the altar rail for support. A moment he stood so, then he exclaimed to the hushed crowd, "She doesn't want to marry me! Thank God! She's run away! It's not my fault!"

The crowd roared in shock, but one voice surmounted the others. "Run away? Not again, dammit!" Castleton tottered to his feet, his crutches prodding hard against his neighbours' toes. "Ravenstoke, dammit, say it isn't so!"

Ravenstoke raised his hand for silence; no matter the high excitement snapping through the crowd, it calmed at his command. "I am sorry to say that Miss Castleton has decided she and the viscount will not suit."

"Not suit! Not suit!" Castleton howled, hopping up and down upon his one good leg. "Blast it, he's a viscount, for God's sake! What do you mean, not suit! She's run away—always running away! The chit's a raving luna— Oof!" The duchess's cane stabbed him fiercely between his shoulderblades. Caught off guard, he toppled over, falling atop the nearest seated bodies. Crutches and curses flew up into the air.

"Do be quiet, you toad." Only those nearest the duchess heard the words. She rose with awesome dignity and turned to face the congregation. "Of course, the dear man is overset, as is the Viscount Brestfort."

The crowd rustled at this, for it could not be denied. The viscount sat before them upon the floor of the nave, shaking his head dazedly and repeating, "Not my fault . . . thank God, not my fault . . ."

"Therefore, let us adjourn," the dowager duchess continued. "And leave the viscount to his . . . disappointment. Yet, since you have all been so kind as to attend today, let us meet in the reception room. There is food and champagne aplenty; it would be a shame to let it go to waste."

A strong ripple of approval radiated from the crowd, giving the dowager duchess her due for offering a party when her protégé had, just minutes ago, sunk below reproach and jilted her fiancé in such a tardy and public manner. They rose with pleasure from their pews.

Ravenstoke watched as the groomsmen lifted the viscount and carted him, still muttering, from the altar. The duke went to his grandmother, who stood talking with those reluctant to leave. "I would speak with you, madam." His steely eye effectively terrorized the well-wishers into retreat. "Did you know anything of this?"

"No, but thank God she did it. I could simply hug the child."

"Then you know where she went?"

"Where she went?"

"Yes, went! She truly ran away."

The duchess's face fell. "I . . . I had not considered that aspect. I don't know." She said it in all sincerity. The evening before was a blur, and she did not remember one jot of the conversation she had held with Mary. "But surely we will find her. I have complete faith in your ability. Gracious, she cannot have gotten far.

"Now, my dear Alastair, I plan to drink as much champagne as I can possibly hold. Don't bother to provide your concoction, for I feel infinitely better. Why . . . I feel wonderful! Mary did it! She ran away!" The duchess beamed, despite her grandson's dour face, and she patted his arm. "She's fooled you this time, my dear, truly fooled you. Mary ran away!" Chuckling, she departed.

"Mary ran away!" a morose and disembodied voice repeated. Ravenstoke looked about and walked over to the front pew, from where the murmur had arisen. He discovered Castleton sprawled out flat on the floor, caught between the pews where he had fallen.

"Mary ran away!" The man struck his fist against the floor, tears in his eyes. "Blast it, so close to the Brestfort money and she bolts! Now I'll never get her shot off, never!"

"Yes you will," Ravenstoke said. "Only let me find the woman, and you will."

Chapter Twelve

LOST . . . AND FOUND

"My God! It has been three months and still no trace of her! Why? How is it possible?" Raven-stoke's voice rang with frustration.

The duchess looked up from the book she had been reading before he had erupted into her chamber, quite uninvited. She studied her grandson with a dispassionate eye. He still possessed his rakish charm, but deep lines were etched around his eyes and his broad shoulders held a defeated weariness. In a more natural grandmother, such signs of stress would have caused pain, but the duchess merely smiled complacently. "Come now, Alastair, you will find her. I have no doubt."

"It is as if she dropped off the face of the earth. I have hunted everywhere! God, I even find myself accosting urchins on the street in the hopes one might be Mary. What could have happened to her?"

"My dear, calm yourself. She did write that she was safe; do credit her with some common sense."

"Even the Runners cannot find her trail. Where could she have found shelter in such haste?"

"Oh, I don't know. But remember, her stepfather, too, once thought Mary had dropped from the face of the earth, when she was safe with you."

The duke's eyes darkened. "Thank you, dear. If I have not already imagined the worst possible fates for her, you must mention that."

"I only meant that if Mary said she was safe, you should take her word for it."

"Where could she possibly have gone?" Ravenstoke growled, stalking about the room. "If I ever get my hands on the woman again, I'll strangle her."

"So that is why you continue to scour the country? So you may kill her?"

"No, no it isn't." He stopped his pacing and sank down onto a chair, his hands running through his raven hair. "I . . . I only desire to ensure her safety, that is all."

"I see. Once you have determined that she is well, you will leave her be? Allow her to live her own life as she sees fit?"

A moment passed while the duke sat silently. The duchess held her breath, awaiting his answer. "No . . . I could not do that."

"What do you intend, then? To drag her back, kicking and screaming? To try to coerce her into marriage again? I mislike telling you this, and I hope you do not take it as an insult to your persuasive powers, but you'll have a difficult time bringing another suitor up to scratch. Not after the way she jilted Brestfort at the eleventh hour. You must admit, she did do it up in rather complete style."

"Yes, she did," Ravenstoke said, his lips curving in a tender smile. Then he sighed. "No, I would not compel her to marry. Oh, dammit!" He rose and walked to the fireplace. "Who am I fooling? Perhaps it is best that I don't find her, for if I did, I would force her into marriage. If I was a better man, I wouldn't, but—"

"I see." The duchess's eyes filled with disappointment.

"—she'd marry me whether she said yea or nay!" Ravenstoke concluded softly.

"Well, it's about time!" Lady Sophia's voice rang out clearly.

"What?" Ravenstoke turned in shock.

"I said it's about time, you stubborn, obtuse, odious boy," Lady Sophia said, smiling. "I have been waiting forever for you to say that."

Ravenstoke stiffened and his expression sharpened. "Why?"

"Why? Because, my dear boy, if you promise not to offer your aged grandmother harm, she will disclose your Mary's whereabouts."

"Mary's . . . Grandmother, if you knew—"

"I didn't, at first. It took the first month for me to realize what Mary had done. For her to have escaped so completely, she had to have had everything planned carefully, which started me to thinking. You see, Alastair, I had, myself, devised what I considered a brilliant plan of escape for Mary before the wedding."

"What? But why?"

"Because she was wasting away, nigh killing herself to wed Brestfort—in order to please you."

"But . . . she never said that to me."

"Did you really think she would?"

Ravenstoke looked stricken. "No. No, she wouldn't. But I thought it was the best life for her."

"I know, son, and she began to think it was, too—as well as being the best for you."

"My God!"

"Yes, that is what I said many times, watching you two moonlings make a mull of everything. Therefore, I had hunted down a faraway post I knew to be available, and set everything up in readiness, in the hope Mary would come to me and admit she could not wed Brestfort."

"And?"

"She never came—at least, not that I can remember."

"Then how could she . . . ?"

"I said that I could not remember. I don't remember the night before the wedding."

"Why, the little devil—"

"And she showed every intention of going through with the ceremony the next morning. But I have checked my sources, and she is exactly where I would have sent her."

"Where is she?"

"You promise you will marry her?"

"Nothing could stop me."

"Not even Mary? If she chooses to be difficult?"

Ravenstoke's lips twitched. "Grandmother, you are absolutely ruthless. But no—not even Mary."

"Then bring her home, son. For I miss her dearly."

The Honorable Teddy Scuffington looked up from his morning paper and his pretty wife Clarissa looked up from the half a muffin she was painting with butter as their butler announced that the Duke of Denfield desired to speak with them immediately.

243

"The Duke of Denfield? Lord Ravenstoke?" Teddy stared at his manservant in bewilderment. "But I don't know the man—not personally," he added. Although he lived far in the country and only once or twice had he and Clarissa toddled up to town, he had heard of the infamous Rake Ravenstoke.

"I do not know him either—do I, Teddy?" Clarissa asked.

"Ah, no, dumpling. He's not—"

"I do hope you will forgive the intrusion, Scuffington." A tall saturnine gentleman stood in the doorway. "I have a question for you."

"A question?" Teddy swallowed as he took in the man's impressive height and demeanor.

"Yes. You employ a governess, do you not?"

"Oh, yes. Indeed we do." Clarissa was happy to answer. "She's an excellent creature, don't you agree, Teddy?"

"Yes, excellent." Teddy's mind floundered, trying to fathom why the duke would inquire after their governess. The woman was excellent with their children, but she had nothing in the looks department. A brown, thin little squab with spectacles as thick as bottle-bottoms and hair so skinned back as to make a man wince. "Why do you ask?"

"Is her name, perchance, Mary Castleton?"

"Now isn't that funny?" Clarissa said. "Her first name is Mary, but her last name is Smith. You must have the wrong governess."

"Yes, sure to have the wrong governess," Teddy agreed quickly.

"Smith? How unoriginal. I would not have thought it of her. And where would she be at present?"

"Oh, I don't know," Clarissa said sunnily. "In

244

the nursery, I imagine, with my little darlings."

"And where might that be?"

"Why, on the second floor, of course."

"Er, yes," Teddy said. "The second floor and—"

"Don't bother. I am sure your butler will be glad to inform me." There was muffled sound from outside the door. "My gratitude to both of you." Ravenstoke bowed and departed.

"Well, what a strange man," Clarissa observed, picking up the other half of her muffin. "He did not look the type to be interested in children and education."

"Nor governesses." Teddy shook his head. That was why he lived in the country; town folk were such a confusing lot.

"I won't, I won't! I don't like porridge!" Master Johnny shouted.

"Nurse has made it for you," Mary said, controlling her temper. Johnny could not help being spoilt, the way he had been raised. "Now, I—"

"I tell you I won't!" Johnny shrieked and flung his spoon on the floor.

"That, sir, is enough." A stern voice rang out from the door, and Mary whirled, aghast. Johnny turned too.

"Ravenstoke." Mary's voice was choked with mingled joy and fear.

"Cor!" was all Sally, the nursemaid, could choke out.

"Hello," Little Samantha was the only one to greet the duke. She stuck her fingers in her mouth, in obvious enchantment.

"It seems, my dear, every time I find you, you're being attacked by men. Though this one is rather young, I'd say."

"I am not young! I'm—"

"Young and very rude." Ravenstoke walked over to Mary, forcing the obstreperous Johnny to step back.

Mary's heart pounded as he came closer. She was half-tempted to step back as well. "How . . . how did you find me?"

"With great difficulty. You and Grandmother were very clever. But you should have known I'd find you eventually."

"I had hoped not."

"Mary . . ." The green in Ravenstoke's eyes intensified.

"I want muffins!" Johnny piped up.

Ravenstoke stared down at him. "Excuse me, but I was talking." He bent down until he and Master Johnny were eye-to-eye. "One gentleman does not interrupt another, is that clear?"

"But—"

"There are no buts. Nor does a gentleman ever raise his voice to a lady or throw spoons at her. And if he has been so unobliging as to do so, he apologizes. Do you understand?"

Johnny nodded.

"What do you say, Master Johnny?"

"I'm sorry, Miss Smith."

"Excellent." Ravenstoke stood up and looked at Mary. "And when a gentleman apologizes profusely, a lady forgives him."

Mary tore her eyes away. "I forgive you, Master Johnny."

"I'm sorry, Miss Smith," Ravenstoke repeated softly. Mary didn't answer.

"Now you forgive him," Samantha chirped brightly, clapping her hands in delight.

"There is . . . nothing to forgive," Mary said as calmly as possible.

"Then you will come home with me?"

"This is my home now."

"I'm sorry, my dear, but it is not." The duke stepped closer, much closer. "The duchess has sent orders for your return." With lightning speed, he picked her up in his arms.

"Gawd!" Sally made the sign of the cross; she had not overlooked the fact that Mary had called this wickedly handsome man Ravenstoke. Sally's cousin worked in London and knew all the gossip.

"You let Miss Smith down!" Johnny screeched, ineffectually kicking at Ravenstoke's shins. Samantha merely stuck her fingers back into her mouth.

"Be quiet. Miss Smith is leaving. Be a gentleman and make your goodbye."

Johnny stopped in midkick. No one had ever expected him to act in a certain manner, and no one had ever given him the dignity of being a gentleman. He pulled in his last howl and hiccupped, "I'm sorry. Goodbye, Miss Smith."

"Goodbye, Johnny. I'm proud of you." It was all she could think of to say while being carried off, out of the room. "Goodbye, Samantha . . . Sally." She waved before she was completely gone.

"I suppose it would be of no use to ask you to set me down so that we may discuss this?" Mary asked as Ravenstoke carried her along the hallway.

"Of no use."

"Even if I wish to remain here?"

"But you could not possibly wish to remain here," the duke said reasonably as he carried her down the stairs. "Master Johnny is insufferable and past redemption."

"True, but he only throws spoons at me. He

247

never tries to force me to marry other people."

"Give him time and he will. I know the type well." Ravenstoke tuned right at the bottom of the stairs. "And if you wish me to throw spoons at you every morning and not eat my porridge, I promise I will."

Mary flushed. "Where are you taking me?"

"Why, you must serve your notice, my dear. How ragmannered of you if you did not."

"Ravenstoke! Don't you dare carry me in front of . . ." It was too late. He had taken her into the breakfast room. Teddy glanced up from his coffee only to spew it over *The Times* as he discovered his governess clutched in Rake Ravenstoke's arms. Clarissa merely put her muffin down and observed, "So, you found her, did you?"

"Yes, I did, and I thank you. However, it pains Miss Cast—Miss Smith—to inform you that she must quit your employ."

"Quit my employ?" Clarissa's face took on a pout similar to her son's. "But I don't wish her to."

"Ah, but she must. She has other spoilt children that require saving."

"Teddy, do stop him!" Clarissa cried, as Ravenstoke performed a graceful bow and Mary murmured a goodbye as he walked from the room. "Stop him!"

"Now, sweetcakes, don't take on so. I'll get you a new governess. Can't stop him—the duke's not a good man to disagree with, you know. Though I'll be demmed if I know what he wants with our governess. Must be mad."

Ravenstoke chuckled as the words floated out to him in the hall. "I knew the fellow was a pea-brain."

Mary could only laugh. "And his wife's no better. She'll cry the whole day through now. My God! A closed carriage, my lord? And outpost riders?"

"Indeed. I am improving in my style of abduction, don't you agree?"

"Yes, yes, you are," Mary replied. The duke opened the door and settled her inside; after signalling to the driver to depart, he climbed in opposite her and closed the door.

Mary looked at him and felt not fear or anger, as she should have, but an absurd shyness.

It turned to indignation as Ravenstoke spoke. "You look a fright." He reached over and briskly took the colored spectacles from her face, throwing them to the carriage floor. "Better! You will never dress this way again!" His hands quickly undid her hair, pulling the pins out with an expertise she did not care to think about.

"My lord . . . Ravenstoke . . ." Her hand clamped abruptly over his wrist as he ruthlessly reached for the top button of her high-necked brown serge. "Stop that!"

"No." His hand stayed where it was. "How could you do this to yourself?"

"I am dressed as a governess." Her eyes were steadily fixed on his. "An employment I prefer to wedlock. Do not think you can take me back and coerce me into another marriage. I don't care how elevated the gentleman; I will merely escape, and none of your schemes or contrivances will stop me."

"None?" the duke quizzed gently. "Then you don't mean to play cards, or chess, or anything else with me? A pity."

"No. I won't be fooled into marriage."

249

"But this time I have the perfect mate for you." Ravenstoke slowly tugged on her collar until she was forced to lean over to him. His other arm swiftly wrapped about her waist, and he hauled her onto his lap. "The man I have in mind has a far more open view of the world than Brestfort. And finds your levity invigorating." He nuzzled her ear as he spoke.

"Y-yes," Mary asked, too lost in the pleasure of his arms to contemplate what he said.

"And he likes a woman with intelligence who can discuss politics and culture and . . . other matters." His lips came down gently, but when they met hers an overriding intensity flared between the pair and Mary clasped him all the tighter as his hands caressed her.

After a few dizzying moments, she drew away. "My lord, what are you doing?"

His smile was winsome. "I'm seducing you, my dear. I admit that a travelling carriage is not the most romantic of settings, but I thought I'd best work quickly before we reached the next posting house and you decided to escape as a scullery maid or some such." He kissed her once more with intoxicating passion.

"But . . . but why?" she asked as soon as she could pull herself away from his warm, wandering lips.

"Why? Because I cannot trust anyone else to do it." His hands ran down her back, sending a shiver through her.

"But you said I must not show this side to anyone but my husband."

"I know." He smiled and kissed her deeply.

As his words penetrated Mary's passion-filled mind, she stiffened and pushed him back. He studied her with serious eyes, waiting. "Who is this man you would have me marry?" she asked, her heart pounding in anticipation and fear of his answer.

"He is not very respectable. And has an infamous reputation."

"Still you would have me marry him?" Mary was afraid she was drawing the wrong conclusion.

"Yes, for he is changed and finds that he has interest only in one woman—something you must believe. And I have come to doubt that any man, no matter how respectable or noble, could ever love you as desperately as this rake does."

"Or I he," Mary said softly, drawing his face to hers, "or I he." She kissed him as she had dreamed of doing for so very long.

This time he was the one to draw back. "Then you will marry me?"

"Yes. But what would you have done if I had said no?"

"I would have made you."

Mary laughed, delightedly. "No chivalry this time, my lord?"

"Chivalry be damned, I cannot live without you. I almost went insane these past few months without you, though I'm not sure that watching you with that fool Brestfort wasn't worse. And the thought of walking you down the aisle to that clod almost sent me raving mad."

"And I thought I'd go crazy. I've missed you so very much." She kissed him, not on the lips but on the lines that radiated from his eyes, as if she could kiss away the pain that had caused them. "I fear we belong together, my lord."

"Yes, sweet Mary, we belong together." He laughed happily. "No wonder I've stooped to every conniving trick to keep you from escaping me. I was rescuing you so you could rescue me."

Mary's eyes fell on a large box on the floor that she had not noticed before. "What's that?"

Smiling mischievously and still holding her tight, Ravenstoke leaned over and lifted the lid from the box. The shimmer of her wedding dress lay within it. Mary's eyes flew to his. "I also have a special license in my pocket."

"Oh, my lord . . . so soon?"

"So soon. I've waited long enough—my whole thirty-five years in fact—and I have very little reserves left, considering all the temptations you've put me through."

"Temptations I've put you through?"

"Yes, indeed. We shall be married within the hour if I have it my way. I will take no more chance on losing you. Be warned, I intend this abduction and seduction to proceed far more differently than the first."

"Ah yes, abduction and seduction," Mary laughed, hugging him close. "Please do continue then, for only you, my dear Rake Ravenstoke, could perform them so well—especially the seduction. Now that I look forward to the most."

REGENCIES BY JANICE BENNETT

TANGLED WEB   (2281, $3.95)

Miss Celia Marcombe's dark eyes flashed with righteous indignation. She was not a commodity to be traded or bartered to a man as insufferably arrogant as Trevor Ryde, despite what her high-handed grandfather decreed! If Lord Ryde thought she would let herself be married for any reason other than true love, he was sadly mistaken. He'd never get his hands on her fortune—let alone her person—no matter how disturbingly handsome he was . . .

MIDNIGHT MASQUE   (2512, $3.95)

It was nothing unusual for Lady Ashton to transport government documents to her father from the Home Office. But on this particular afternoon a gust of wind scattered the papers, and suddenly an important page was lost. A document desperately wanted by more than one determined gentleman—one of whom would murder to get his way . . .

AN INTRIGUING DESIRE   (2579, $3.95)

The British secret agent, Charles Marcombe, had done his bit against that blasted Bonaparte. Now it was time to nurse his wounds and come to terms with the fact that that part of his life was over. He certainly did not need the likes of Mademoiselle Therese de Bourgerre darkening his door, warning of dire emergencies and dread consequences, forcing him to remember things best forgotten. She was a delightful minx, to be sure, but it would take more than a pair of pleading emerald eyes and a woebegone smile to drag him back into the fray!

Available wherever paperbacks are sold, or order direct from the Publisher. Send cover price plus 50¢ per copy for mailing and handling to Zebra Books, Dept. 2931, 475 Park Avenue South, New York, N.Y. 10016. Residents of New York, New Jersey and Pennsylvania must include sales tax. DO NOT SEND CASH.

HISTORICAL ROMANCES BY VICTORIA THOMPSON